**Praise for A
and He**

"Plenty of passion and a story line that will grab your attention from the get-go." —Romance Reviews Today

"Suspicions, lust, loyalty, and love create a heavy mix of emotions." —*Romantic Times*

"Fervently romantic." —Single Titles

"This book sucked me in, and I didn't want to stop reading." —Queue My Review

"Morgan delivers a great read that sparks with humor, action, and . . . great storytelling." —Night Owl Reviews (5 stars, top pick)

"Will keep readers entranced." —Nocturne Romance Reads

A Time *for* Home

A Snowberry Creek Novel

Alexis Morgan

A SIGNET ECLIPSE BOOK

SIGNET ECLIPSE
Published by the Penguin Group
Penguin Group (USA), 375 Hudson Street,
New York, New York 10014, USA

USA | Canada | UK | Ireland | Australia | New Zealand | India | South Africa | China

Penguin Books Ltd., Registered Offices: 80 Strand, London WC2R 0RL, England
For more information about the Penguin Group visit penguin.com.

First published by Signet Eclipse, an imprint of New American Library,
a division of Penguin Group (USA)

First Printing, September 2013

Copyright © Patricia L. Pritchard, 2013
All rights reserved. No part of this book may be reproduced, scanned, or distributed in
any printed or electronic form without permission. Please do not participate in or encourage piracy of copyrighted materials in violation of the author's rights. Purchase
only authorized editions.

SIGNET ECLIPSE and logo are trademarks of Penguin Group (USA).

ISBN 978-0-451-41771-8

Printed in the United States of America
10 9 8 7 6 5 4 3 2 1

PUBLISHER'S NOTE
This is a work of fiction. Names, characters, places, and incidents either are the product
of the author's imagination or are used fictitiously, and any resemblance to actual per-
sons, living or dead, business establishments, events, or locales is entirely coincidental.
     The publisher does not have any control over and does not assume any responsibility
for author or third-party Web sites or their content.

If you purchased this book without a cover you should be aware that this book is stolen
property. It was reported as "unsold and destroyed" to the publisher and neither the
author nor the publisher has received any payment for this "stripped book."

ALWAYS LEARNING   **PEARSON**

ACKNOWLEDGMENTS

Books are never a solo act. It takes a team to nurture a story from that first germ of an idea through the whole long process required to bring it to full bloom. There are so many people to whom I owe a debt of gratitude for making *A Time for Home* the best it could be, far too many to list them all here. However, there are a few I do need to thank specifically:

To my wonderful husband. Thank you for your patience, support, and willingness to share me with the people who live in my head.

To Michelle Grajkowski, my fabulous agent. Here we are in our eleventh year working together, and you're finally getting that soldier book you've always wanted me to write. Sorry it took me so long, and I hope it was worth the wait. As always, it means so much to me to have you in my corner.

To Kerry Donovan, my amazing and supportive editor. Thank you for all of your encouragement and for helping me polish the stories until they are shiny bright! I so appreciate your enthusiasm and hard work to bring Snowberry Creek to life.

To the entire team at NAL for everything you contribute to the process. I know there are a lot of you working behind the scenes to give me great cover art, cover copy, and everything else that goes into bringing the book out. Thank all of you so much!

And finally, a special thank-you to my friends for their support and encouragement. I hope you all know how much it means to me. Hugs to you all!

Alexis

Chapter 1

❧❧

"We're almost there, boy. Then you can stretch your legs."

Nick's canine companion was too busy sniffing the wind to care. Mooch had kept his nose stuck out the window since the minute they'd gotten in the truck. He reached over to pat the dog on the back, still carrying on the one-sided conversation.

"I bet it smells a whole lot different from the streets of Afghanistan, doesn't it?"

Mooch thumped his tail in agreement. In truth, everything here was a whole lot different. Nick scanned the road ahead. So much green that it hurt his eyes. He had to tip his head back to see to the tops of the firs and cedars that crowded close to the two-lane highway. They made him claustrophobic. Too many hiding spots for snipers. Only one way through them, leaving him no avenue of escape.

Nick flexed his hands on the steering wheel and reminded himself that he'd left all that behind weeks ago.

No one here wanted him dead. Not yet, anyway.

"Think she'll forgive me?"

Nick hoped so, because he hadn't been able to forgive himself. Something in his voice finally had Mooch looking at him, the dog's dark eyes filled with sympathy. Of course, maybe Nick was only imagining that the mutt understood every word he said. There was no denying the dog had known his own share of suffering back in his homeland.

His shaggy white fur hid the jagged scar where a bullet had caught him in the shoulder. Mooch had taken one for the team when he barked to warn them about an asshole lying in ambush. The bastard had shot the dog to shut him up, but too late to do himself any good. In retaliation, the squad had made damn sure it was the last time he ever pulled a trigger. Nick's buddy Spence had carried the wounded dog back to camp and conned one of the army vets into stitching him up. After a brief swearing-in ceremony, Mooch had become a full-fledged member of their unit.

In war, some heroes walked on four legs, not two.

Nick spotted a sign up ahead. He slowed to read it, hoping he was about to reach civilization. He'd left I-5 behind some time ago and hadn't expected it to take this long to reach Snowberry Creek. He had mixed feelings about what would happen once he reached the small town, but the two of them had been on the move long enough. Some downtime would feel pretty good.

But instead of announcing the city limits, the sign marked the entrance of a small cemetery. Nick started to drive on past, but a sick feeling in his gut had him slowing down and then backing up.

He put the truck in park and dropped his forehead down onto the top of the steering wheel. In a town the size of Snowberry Creek, how many cemeteries could there be? He reached for the door handle and forced himself to get out of the truck. Sooner or later he was going to have to do this. Nick had never been a coward and wasn't about to start now.

"Come on, Mooch. We've got a stop to make."

The dog hopped down out of the seat. Once on the ground, he gave himself a thorough shake from nose to tail before following Nick up the slope toward the rows of gravestones. Usually Mooch liked to explore new places on his own, but this time he walked alongside Nick, silently offering his support.

It didn't take long to find what they were looking for. There were several granite markers with the last name of Lang. Nick hung a right and followed the row, finally reaching a longer-than-normal stone that held the name of a husband and wife, most likely Spence's parents. Nick had to force himself to take those final few steps to stand in front of the last headstone.

He dropped to his knees on the green grass and wrapped his arms around his stomach. God, it hurt so fucking much to see Spence's name etched there in block letters. His eyes burned with the need to cry, but the tears refused to come. Instead, the pain stayed locked tight inside his chest and in his head, a burden he'd been carrying since he'd held Spence's bloody dog tags in his hand.

As the memories began playing out in Nick's head, Mooch whined and snuggled closer. But even the familiar touch of the dog's soft fur couldn't keep Nick grounded in the present. His guilt and his fear sucked him right back to the last place he wanted to be. Just that quickly, he was in the streets of Afghanistan, riding next to Spence on yet another patrol. Instead of breathing the cool, damp air of Washington, Nick was sucking in hot, dry air and feeling the sun burning down from above as he got caught up in the past and lived through it all over again.

The heat in hell had nothing on Afghanistan in July. Maybe if he could've stripped down to a pair of cargo shorts and a sleeveless T-shirt, it would've been bearable. But only a fool would go on patrol without all his protective gear, and Nick was no fool.

The back of his neck itched. It had nothing to do with the ever-present dust and grit that grated against his skin like sandpaper. No, there were eyes on them. Had been since they'd entered the city. A couple of well-placed shots had cut them off from the rest of the patrol. They were trying to circle around to catch up with the others.

Nick scanned the surrounding area, constantly sweeping the buildings ahead, looking for some sign of who was watching them. In that neighborhood, it could be anyone from a mother worried about her kids to someone with his finger on the trigger.

Leif stirred restlessly. "You feeling it, too?"

"Yeah. Spence, do you see anything?"

Before his friend could answer, a burst of gunfire rained down on them from the roof of a building half a block down on the right. A second shooter opened fire from a doorway on the opposite side of the street, catching them in the cross fire.

Nick returned short bursts of fire while Spence drove like the maniac he was, trying to get them the hell out of Dodge. Leif hopped on the radio, yelling to make himself heard over the racket. After calling in, he'd joined Nick in trying to pick off the shooters.

"Hold on! This ride's about to get interesting."

If more than two wheels were on the ground when Spence took the corner, Nick would happily eat MREs for the rest of his natural life. Not that he was complaining. His friend's extreme driving style had saved their asses far too often. The M-ATV lurched hard as it straightened up coming out of the turn.

"Fuck yeah, that was fun!" Spence's grin was a mile wide as he laughed and flung their ride around another corner.

The crazy bastard was actually enjoying this. Nick shook his head. He loved the guy like a brother, but damn. They made it another two blocks before the shooting began again, this time from behind them.

Leif yelled over the racket, "Ever get the feeling we're being herded?"

Nick nodded. The thought had occurred to him, but what choice did they have but to keep going? The street was too narrow to hang a U-turn, and stopping sure as hell wasn't an option. He continued to scan the area for more shooters and left the driving to Spence, who knew the streets in this area better than anyone. It was like the man had a built-in GPS system. He'd find a way out for them if anyone could.

The gunfire was sporadic now, with longer periods of silence between shots. The streets remained empty, as if the locals had been warned to crawl into the deepest hole they could find and stay there.

"Think we're in the clear?" Leif asked, still studying the rooftops and doorways for new threats.

Before Nick could answer, the whole world exploded in fire and smoke. A sharp pain ripped up the length of his upper arm as their vehicle started rockin' and rollin'. It went airborne and finally bounced to a stop lying on its side up against a building.

With considerable effort, Nick managed to climb out. He retrieved his weapon and shook his head to clear it. The blast had left his ears ringing and, thanks to the cloud of dust and smoke, damn near blind. Nick found Spence more by feel than by sight. He was lying facedown in the dirt with blood trickling from his ears and nose.

Nick checked for a pulse. Thready and weak. Son of a bitch, this was a major cluster fuck. He spotted Leif writhing in pain a few feet away. He crawled over to him.

"Are you hit?"

"My ankle. It's busted up pretty bad."

If the bastards who'd been shooting at them weren't already closing in, they would be soon. Nick needed to get Leif and Spence somewhere safe—and fast.

He got down in Leif's face. "Give it to me straight up. Can you walk?"

After one look at the twisted mess that had been Leif's left ankle, Nick didn't wait for an answer. Neither of his friends could make it back to safety on their own, but which one should he help first? Spence was completely defenseless, while Leif might be able to protect himself for a while.

On the other hand, at the rate Leif was losing blood, he could bleed out before Nick could get back to him; already his coloring was piss-poor. Nick crawled back to the wreck that had been their vehicle and pulled out the first-aid kit. He bandaged Leif's damaged ankle as best he could, but he'd seen enough wounds to know Leif was going to need surgery, and damn quick. His decision made, Nick crawled back to his unconscious buddy.

"Spence, I'm going for help. I'll be back for you ASAP."

Then he muscled Leif up off the ground and half carried, half dragged the poor bastard as fast as they could make it. The rest of their unit would be pouring into the area, looking for them. A minute later, he spotted them two blocks down and waved his rifle over his head to get their attention.

Their medic hit the ground running. "What do we have?"

"His ankle looks bad, but we've got to go back for Spence. I was afraid to move him."

They carried Leif the rest of the way back to one of the vehicles. Nick patted his friend on the shoulder. "They'll get you to the medics. Save a couple of the prettier nurses for Spence."

Leif managed a small smile. "Like hell. Tell him he's on his own."

"Get yourself patched up. We'll be along soon." He stepped back and checked his rifle for ammunition. "Let's move out."

The medic stopped him. "You're bleeding, too. We'll get Spence. You go with the corporal."

No, not happening. He'd return for Spence even if he had to crawl. "I'm all right. Besides, I promised I'd come back for him. Wouldn't want to piss him off. The man's got a temper."

The medic didn't much like it, but he nodded. "Lead the way."

Nick's ears were finally starting to function normally again, and he could hear gunfire in the distance. Son of a bitch! He picked up the pace, doing his best to watch for hostiles as he led the charge back to where he'd left Spence. When they were a block short of their destination, the deafening thunder of another explosion sent all of them diving for cover.

Before the echoes had died away, Nick was up and running, screaming Spence's name. He was dimly aware of the rest of his squad joining him in the mad race to save their friend. Nick's heart pounded loud enough to drown out the agonizing truth that he was too late. The building next to where he'd left Spence was nothing but a smoking pile of rubble.

He coasted to a stop at the corner. The horror of what had happened and what he'd done washed over him in waves. "Spence, where the hell are you? Come on, you dumb son of a bitch, this is no time for hide-and-seek."

Please, God, let him have regained consciousness and crawled to safety.

But he hadn't; Nick knew it in his gut just as he knew it was his fault. There was nothing left of their vehicle now except scrap metal. A huge hole had been ripped in the street right where Spence had been lying, and the building had caved in on itself, leaving the street strewn with rubble. While several of the men stood watch, Nick joined the rest digging in the dirt with their bare fingers, heaving aside rocks and jagged fragments of metal, looking and praying for some sign of Spence.

Finally, the medic froze. He looked across at Nick and slowly lifted his hand. A set of bloody dog tags dangled from his fingers.

"Aw, damn, Spence."

Tears streamed down Nick's cheeks as he reached for the broken chain. He clamped his fingers around the small pieces of bloody metal and held on to the last piece of his friend with an iron grip.

The medic motioned to the rest of the men. When they had formed up, he took Nick by the arm and tugged him back down the street.

"Come on, Sarge, let's go get your arm looked at. We'll get you all fixed up."

Nick let himself be led away, but only because the longer they lingered in the area, the more likely someone else would get hurt—or worse. But they all knew there was no fixing this. Not today. Not ever.

Spence was—

A sharp pain dragged Nick back to the grassy slope of the graveyard. Mooch whined and licked the small mark where he'd just nipped Nick's arm. The poor dog looked worried. How long had Nick been gone this time? Long enough to be damp from the rain that had started falling since he'd knelt in the grass. The dog shoved his head under Nick's hand, demanding a thorough scratching, which felt as good to him as it did to the dog.

"Sorry, Mooch. We'll get going here in a minute."

He pushed himself back up to his feet and dusted off his pants, focusing hard on the moment. It was too easy to get caught up in spinning his wheels in the past. He needed to keep moving forward, if for no other reason than he had to make sure Mooch reached his final destination.

Nick had something to say first. Standing at attention felt odd when he wasn't in uniform, but the moment called for a bit of formality. He cleared his throat and swallowed hard.

"Spence, I miss you so damn much. Wherever you are, I hope they have fast cars and faster women."

Then he saluted his friend and walked away.

Chapter 2

⚘ ⚘

Callie Redding cut through the woods back to her parents' house, where she was staying these days. They had made a suspiciously quick decision to spend the summer in California, saying they wanted more time in the sun. She figured it was an excuse to let her live rent-free in return for watching their house. Their kindness would give her the time she needed to adjust to the change in her circumstances.

Her contract job upgrading computer security for a company down in Oregon had ended weeks ago. She'd sent out a ream of résumés and was waiting to hear back on a couple of promising leads. Temporarily at loose ends, she'd come home for what was supposed to have been a short visit.

Two days after her arrival, word had hit town about Spence's death. The announcement had been closely followed by the second shock: that he'd left everything to her, including his family home.

Weeks later, she was still reeling from the news.

Why hadn't she realized something was wrong when he hadn't answered her e-mails? Granted, sometimes

Spence was out on patrol and didn't have access to the Internet, but she still should've known.

Somehow.

He'd been her best friend, for God's sake. Had been since they were little kids. For years, they had rarely even been in the same hemisphere, but he'd remained a major part of her life. His death had left a gaping hole in her world, not to mention her heart.

The gray, drizzly day fit her mood perfectly. She'd spent the morning going through Spence's house, working on an inventory of its contents. She'd yet to start packing up his personal possessions; that job was more than she could face. It was too soon to remove any sign that Spence had lived next door—that he'd lived at all, which was the main reason she was still staying at her parents' place.

Instead, she'd focused on what could be done to preserve the house itself. Sitting vacant for most of the past nine years while its owner bounced around the world had taken a toll on the old Victorian. However, Callie was sure the house's bones were solid. All the old girl would need was a few cosmetic touches and maybe new plumbing.

Earlier in the week, Callie had been struck with an epiphany. If she were to make the right changes in the house, it would make a great bed-and-breakfast. Recently, there had been several other new businesses opening in Snowberry Creek, all aimed at attracting more tourists to spend time in the town. There was a new bookstore, two coffee shops, and even a small day spa.

Granted, it would take a lot of work to fix the place up. For one thing, there were only hints left of the beautiful garden that Spence's mother had tended with such loving care. Some of the furniture would work; for the rest, she'd have to hunt for the right pieces in antiques stores and at estate sales. It was all a bit overwhelming, but the longer she poked and prodded the idea, the more it felt right.

To honor Spence's memory, she'd bring life back to his home.

Her mind whirled with possibilities as she rounded the side of her parents' house, only to stop short of her goal. Who was that on the porch? The stranger stood leaning forward with his hands cupped on the window beside the front door, shading his eyes to see better as he stared into the house. She couldn't see his face, but he didn't look familiar.

She hesitated, taking the few seconds while he was still unaware of her presence to study her unexpected visitor. He was dressed in civilian clothes, but she was willing to bet he was military. All doubt was removed when he straightened up. That short blond hair and shoulders-back stance were unmistakable.

A medium-sized white dog with brown spots moved into sight. It stared at her and whined to draw his owner's attention to her. As soon as the man looked in her direction, she recognized him. His name was Nick Jenkins, one of the close-knit bunch who had served with Spence.

He started down the porch steps, the dog trailing after him. "Callie Redding? Sorry to drop in without calling ahead, but I'm—"

She smiled and started forward, finishing his introduction for him: "Nick Jenkins, Spence's friend."

His smile faded as he shook her hand. "Yes, I was."

When the dog whined again, Nick reached down to pat him on the head. "And this is Mooch. He served with Spence, too."

Callie knelt down and held her hand out for the dog

to sniff. When he took a tentative step forward to bump her hand, she gave him a good scratch under his chin. "Hey there, boy. Aren't you a handsome fellow?"

She glanced back up at Nick. "I should've recognized both of you immediately. We met when Spence and I were Skyping, not to mention he sent me tons of pictures from Afghanistan. I'm making a scrapbook to give him when he—"

A razor-sharp pain cut right through Callie's heart as she stopped midsentence. It wasn't the first time the realization Spence wouldn't be coming home had blindsided her. She pushed herself back up to her feet.

"God, it just hits me hard sometimes." She hated the quiver in her voice. "I still have trouble believing he won't be coming home."

"It sucks, doesn't it?"

As he spoke, Nick stared past her toward the trees. Callie bet he wasn't even seeing them at all and could only imagine what dark thoughts had him looking so grim. Had he been there when Spence had died? She didn't ask and didn't want to know.

The rain started up again, giving her the impetus to get all three of them moving again. "Look, why don't we get in out of the rain? I was about to eat lunch. It'll just be sandwiches, but you and Mooch are welcome to join me."

When he didn't immediately answer, she touched his arm. "Nick? Let's go inside."

This time he blinked and shook his head. His expression looked a bit ragged, but at least he was seeing her now. "Sorry, Callie. Guess I got lost there for a minute."

"Not a problem."

The rain was coming down harder now. "Let's go in the house before we get drenched."

She started up the steps, waiting until she reached

the porch to make sure her two guests were following her. Satisfied that they would join her shortly, she unlocked the door and stepped inside. After kicking off her shoes, she headed for the kitchen.

"Make yourself comfortable in the living room while I get everything ready."

Right now she needed a few minutes alone to collect herself. Damn, why did this have to be so hard? She'd always wanted to meet Spence's friends in person, not just online. He'd talked about them so much that she felt as if she already knew them. But that was before. Meeting Nick with Spence gone felt odd, although not exactly wrong. Regardless, she owed it to Spence to make his friend feel welcome.

She set out plates and silverware. By the time she'd gathered the sandwich makings and made a tossed salad, her pulse had slowed to somewhere close to normal.

She peeked into the living room. "Nick, if you'd like to wash up, we can—"

Oh, my. Just that quickly, he'd dozed off in her father's chair with Mooch curled up at his feet. Should she wake him up? No, if the man was that tired, better to let him sleep.

She whispered, "Mooch."

The dog looked up at the mention of his name. She patted her leg and said, "Come on, boy. Let's let Nick rest while you and I have lunch. He can eat whenever he wakes up."

Mooch stared at his sleeping friend for several seconds before finally following her into the kitchen. She led him straight to where she'd left him some food and water. He looked at the bowls and then back up at her, as if asking permission.

"Go ahead and eat, Mooch. My mom's dog won't

mind me giving you some of his food. I'll sit over here and keep you company."

While the dog gulped down the canned dog food, Callie sat down at the table and made herself a sandwich. The soft sound of snoring wafting in from the other room made her smile. The poor man must have been exhausted to fall asleep in a stranger's house.

As she ate, she made notes about Spence's house, starting with a list of questions about what starting her own business would entail. The biggest one was at the bottom: *Do I even want to do this?*

Yes. Maybe. Probably.

Not that it mattered. Spence's house was now hers, and it needed work done regardless of whether she set up business in it, lived in it, or sold it. She crossed out that last part. No way she'd sell Spence's house. That would be the final step in erasing him from her life completely.

Mooch had finished wolfing down his food and was sniffing his way around the kitchen. When he reached the back door, he whined and gave her a hopeful look.

"Sure thing, fella. Let me get my jacket on."

She was glad to see that the dog wore a collar. He waited patiently while she hunted up a leash. The two of them stepped out in the misting rain and took a leisurely walk around the yard. Mooch stopped at every bush and tree in the place, but Callie didn't mind. It gave her time to think as they made the complete circle back to the door.

Once they were inside, Mooch allowed her to rub him down with an old towel that her mom kept by the door for just that purpose. After she had him dried off, they checked on Nick. Still asleep. Mooch immediately curled up at his master's feet and closed his eyes.

All right, so she had two tired males camping out in

the living room. Maybe it should worry her to have a man she barely knew making himself at home, but she couldn't find it in her to boot him out. Spence had trusted Nick with his life; that was good enough for her.

She poured herself a cup of coffee and settled back in at the table with the phone book to make a list of people she needed to call. Once she had more information about what all was involved in starting a business, she'd have a better idea where to start. Happy with her plan, she put on her headphones, turned on her MP3 player, and got to work.

"What the hell?"

Nick jerked awake, confused and thickheaded. He looked around the room trying to remember where he was and how he'd gotten there. Meanwhile, Mooch stood up and stretched. He rubbed against Nick's legs on his way out of the room.

Clearly the dog felt at home. Nick replayed the morning's events in his head. He'd driven down from Seattle, stopping at the cemetery on his way to Callie Redding's house. Callie. He remembered talking to her briefly out in front of her house.

Then something she'd said had sent his mind on an instant trip back to Afghanistan. Damn, he hated when that happened. That was twice in one day. Had she noticed? Maybe not, considering she'd invited him and Mooch inside, saying something about lunch.

How long had he been asleep? He checked his watch. Hell, he'd been down and out for at least two hours. He believed it considering how stiff his neck was from sleeping in the chair. He stood up and stretched just like Mooch had.

Where was Callie? He cocked his head to listen but

didn't detect anyone moving around in the house. The only thing he heard was the sound of Mooch slurping water in the next room. At least that was a place to start.

He found her sitting at the kitchen table wearing headphones and tapping her foot in time to music. He stared at her from a short distance away, comparing the reality to the pictures Spence had shared with him. If anything, the photos hadn't done her justice. He liked the way her shoulder-length hair framed her delicate face in soft caramel-colored waves. Nick longed to find out whether it was as soft as it looked, but before he could do something stupid, Mooch walked over to the door to the backyard and wagged his tail in a slow sweep. Before letting him out, Nick thought he'd better check to see if that was all right.

"Callie? I can't believe I fell asleep like that."

When she didn't respond, he reached out to touch her shoulder. "Callie?"

She shrieked and jumped about a foot straight up, knocking over her coffee cup in the process. Luckily for them both, it was empty. He managed to catch the cup before it hit the floor.

"Nick! Don't sneak up on a person like that!"

"Sorry, I didn't mean to scare you." He held out the cup as a peace offering. "In my defense, I did say your name twice before I touched your shoulder."

Then he pointed at her MP3 player. "I don't think you could hear me."

Her shoulders slumped in what looked like relief. "I was busy making notes. Did you have a good nap?"

"Yeah, sorry about that. I'm still adjusting to the time zone change."

It was as good an excuse as any. The truth was most nights he slept only in fits and starts. He couldn't remember the last time he managed to sleep more than three hours at a stretch.

"That's understandable." She set her notepad aside and stood up. "Mooch and I ate without you, but I fixed you a plate. Have a seat and I'll get it for you. Do you want iced tea, pop, or a beer?"

"The tea sounds good." As he pulled out a chair to sit down, Mooch scratched at the door. "Oops, sorry, buddy, I forgot."

She was bent over pulling things out of the fridge. Nick couldn't help admiring the fit of her jeans, but he forced himself to look away. "Callie, is it all right if I turn Mooch loose in your backyard?"

"Sure. I took him out a while ago on a leash because I wasn't sure if he'd run off. I didn't want to risk him getting lost in an unfamiliar town."

"He won't go far, but I'll keep an eye on him."

In fact, a breath of fresh air would feel good about now. As soon as Nick opened the door, Mooch shoved past him to charge down the steps. He took off running across the yard, barking at a squirrel, which took refuge in the nearest tree. Satisfied he'd handled the intruder, Mooch quieted down and made a quick circuit of the yard.

When he finally took care of his business, he came trotting right back. Nick followed him into the kitchen. Clearly the dog was adjusting well to Callie's house and yard. That was a good thing because Nick was really hoping she'd offer the dog a home here with her. He'd miss the furry misfit, but Mooch deserved a permanent home.

And if Nick made up his mind to re-up with the army, he'd have to find the dog a new home anyway. Mooch had been through enough of a change in leaving Afghanistan behind without having to deal with multiple moves.

While they'd been outside, Callie had set out a plate heaped high with food. Nick was sure he couldn't eat it all, but he'd give it his best shot.

He sat down and picked up the first sandwich. Food was another thing that hadn't held much appeal since his return. His mom had pulled out all the stops when he'd gotten back, fixing all of his favorites. She'd said he needed fattening up and teased him that the army hadn't been feeding him right.

Not even her best apple pie had tasted good to him, but he'd gone through the motions and eaten everything she'd put in front of him. In truth, it might have been sawdust as far as he could tell. He was afraid he'd hurt her feelings when he hadn't once asked for seconds like he used to, but sometimes acting normal took more energy than he had.

Nick bit into the thick ham sandwich Callie had fixed for him, expecting to have the same problem. To his surprise, it actually tasted good. He took a second bite. Meanwhile, Callie sat back down and studied a handwritten list. He couldn't read it from where he was sitting, but whatever it was had her full attention. It was a relief not to have to make conversation, another problem he'd had at his parents' house.

He loved them dearly, but their constant questions had about driven him crazy. He didn't want to talk about his experiences in the war with them or anybody else, for that matter. They didn't need to know how bad it had been and wouldn't have understood if he'd actually tried to tell them.

He'd caught them exchanging puzzled looks a few times, as if they were wondering who this taciturn stranger was. He might have looked like their son, but he clearly didn't act like him. Nick had finally given up and announced he needed to deliver Mooch to his new owner. Rather than fly, he'd chosen to drive to the Pacific Northwest from his hometown in Ohio. Nick didn't know how his parents felt about him leaving again so soon, but his own most identifiable emotion had been relief.

Callie finally looked up. "You must have been hungry. Can I get you something else?"

He looked down at his plate to see what she was talking about, only to find it was empty. He'd chowed down on two sandwiches, a healthy helping of salad, and a handful of cookies. Wow.

"No, I'm fine. In fact, I ought to get going." He pushed the plate aside. "I didn't mean to take up so much of your afternoon."

It was too soon to spring the idea of leaving Mooch with her, and it would give him an excuse to come back.

"I didn't have any plans." She frowned. "As I recall, you're from back east somewhere. Are you stationed out here now?"

"No, I'm between assignments."

In fact, he wasn't really living anywhere anymore. He'd given up his apartment when his unit had been deployed. Until he made up his mind what he wanted to do next, he had no reason to put down roots anywhere, not even temporary ones.

"I need to find a motel room for tonight. Are there any here in Snowberry Creek that take pets?"

She bit her lower lip as she thought about it. Finally, she shook her head. "No, but there's no reason you can't stay here. My folks are gone for the summer, so there's plenty of room."

She didn't sound all that enthusiastic, not that he blamed her. A woman alone shouldn't be too quick to trust a man just because they had one friend in common.

Then there was the problem of him wandering around

at night when he couldn't sleep. At his parents' home, he'd slipped out the same way he had as a teenager to walk the streets until he was too exhausted to think.

He carried his plate over to the sink. "I don't want to put you out, Callie. I'll head back toward I-5. There's bound to be some motels along the interstate. Maybe tomorrow I could come back, and the two of us can go out to dinner."

He kept his back to her until she answered. He'd already intruded on her privacy by showing up unannounced. He didn't want her to feel obligated to accept his invitation simply because they'd both known Spence.

Her answer wasn't long in coming. "I'd like that, Nick. But instead of driving all the way back to the highway, I have another suggestion. Spence's house is right next door. Well, actually, it's my house now, I guess. I just can't get used to that idea. He left it to me . . . you know, when he—"

She stopped to clear her throat. When she didn't continue, Nick filled a glass with ice water from the door of the refrigerator and brought it to her. She took a long drink and set the glass down.

"Sorry, it's just that I've been having a hard time getting my mind around the whole idea. You know, of Spence being gone."

"Me, too."

And Nick had actually been there standing on that godforsaken street holding Spence's bloody dog tags in his hand.

There was a world of questions in Callie's eyes as she stared up at him, but thank God she didn't ask them. He didn't want to lie to her about what had happened and couldn't bear to tell her the truth. He sensed a real innocence about Callie, and he didn't want to be the one to destroy it.

"You were saying?"

"Oh, yeah. Spence's house is just on the other side of those trees. You could stay there, if you'd like. I had the power turned back on, so you'd have electricity and hot water. The fridge is empty, but you can either come back over here for breakfast or there's a good café in town."

Could he stand to stay in Spence's home? He guessed he'd find out. "Are you sure? I don't want to be a bother."

"I'm sure. And don't worry, I'd do the same for any of Spence's friends. I'll get you some clean sheets and pack up some food for Mooch. I have enough for tonight and his breakfast in the morning. After that, you'll have to hit the grocery store."

"I've got some kibble out in the truck, too."

Now that they had a plan, Callie turned into a whirlwind. A few minutes later, he was loaded down with sheets and a few cans of dog food. She followed him out to the truck with a sack of groceries intended to get him through the evening and early morning.

Her eyes went wide when she got a look at the clutter and trash scattered in the cab of his truck. For all practical purposes, he and the dog had been living in it for the past week. After he'd quickly tossed most of it into the backseat, Callie handed him the groceries and stepped away. "I'll lock up the house and meet you over there."

Was she afraid to get in the truck with him? That didn't seem likely when she'd already offered to let him spend the night in the same house with her.

"I can wait. There's room in the front seat if you don't mind being a bit crowded. Mooch takes up more space than you'd think."

She bit her lip again, evidently something she did

when she needed to think things through before answering. He found the gesture adorable, but it made him want to be the one doing the nibbling on that full lower lip. He slammed the lid on that thought. Even if he was in any shape to be looking for a relationship, she was off limits. Way off limits.

"Okay, it won't take me long."

As Callie ran back to the house, he couldn't help but stare after her. With some effort, he looked away, turning his attention to Mooch. "Dog, you catch me looking at her like that again, bite me. Hard."

The dog's tail thumped on the ground. His excitement warned Nick that Callie was already on her way back. It was obvious that Nick wasn't the only one who felt the pull of Callie's warm smile.

He opened the passenger door for her and stood back while she and Mooch clambered in. By the time Nick reached the driver's side, the two of them had staked out their territory. She was sitting flush up against the far door with Mooch sprawled half in her lap, half on the seat.

As Nick started the engine, he had to wonder if it was wrong to be jealous of a dog.

Chapter 3

❧ ❧

Callie's parents would have a hissy fit if they ever found out she'd invited a total stranger to spend the night in their house with her. They'd be only marginally happier to learn that Nick was camping out next door. She didn't care. Meeting Nick was like reconnecting with a little piece of Spence, and she wasn't ready to let him drive away. Not yet.

He'd seemed reluctant to take her up on the offer of a free room, and she felt as if she'd bulldozed him into accepting. It was only for a night, maybe two. It hadn't occurred to her to ask whether he had someplace he had to be. He hadn't yet explained why he'd come in the first place.

Yes, they had both been friends with Spence, but it wasn't as if their paths had ever crossed. If Nick had simply wanted to offer his condolences, surely mailing a sympathy card would've been easier than a trip across country. In truth, she should've been the one sending the card. After all, Nick had spent far more time with Spence over the past few years than she had.

"The driveway is just past the trees. It's pretty overgrown, but you won't have any trouble navigating it with this truck."

He turned onto the gravel road, the truck lurching and bouncing along the rutted ground. "The place has been pretty much vacant since Spence enlisted. My dad used to keep the lawn mowed, but it got to be too much for him."

She was babbling, but the silence in the truck was heavy rather than comfortable. The house was set back some distance off the road on an acre lot. The driveway curved around a small island in front that used to be filled with rosebushes. Only a few of the most hardy had survived years of neglect.

"You can park anywhere. There is a garage off to the side, but it's full of stuff."

Nick pulled past the steps and stopped. She opened her own door and climbed down with Mooch right behind her. Nick stood back and studied the house, starting with the front door and then gradually tilting his head back to check out the second and third floors.

"Wow, I knew Spence owned a house, but he never said anything about it being this big."

No surprise there. She also doubted he'd shared how miserable he'd been living there once his parents had been killed. Not only did it contain memories of how happy he'd been when they were alive, but it also reminded him of what a hell his life had become after his mother's brother had moved in to take care of him. His uncle had been a real bastard. Still was.

"There aren't many of these old beauties left in the area, but I've always loved this house."

That was true, but then those bad memories had been Spence's, not hers. "Shall we go in? I'll show you where everything is and then get out of your way."

She headed up the steps to unlock the door. When

Nick caught up with her, Callie held the door open and let him enter first. Once inside, she flipped on the living room light.

"The kitchen is straight back. The appliances are old, but they work. There's a bathroom on this floor and another on the second floor next to the master bedroom."

She led the way upstairs, turning on more lights as she went. With the gray, rainy day, the house needed all the help she could get to banish the shadows. At the top of the steps, Callie opened the first door on the right.

"I'll put you in this room. The bed has the best mattress, and the closet and dresser are empty."

She opened the linen closet in the hallway and pulled out a couple of towels and washcloths and hung them in the bathroom. "These might be a bit musty, but they're clean."

Back in the bedroom, Nick was already making the bed. Between the two of them, they made quick work of it and then headed back down to the truck for another load. She carried in the groceries while he brought in his duffel bag. It was identical to the one that Spence had, another painful reminder that he'd never again show up at her doorstep to dump it behind her couch.

She needed to get home before she gave in to the tears that were burning her eyes. "I'll be around tomorrow morning. Feel free to stop by if you want."

Thinking about Spence's duffel brought another thought to mind. "There's laundry detergent and fabric softener on the shelf over the washer and dryer you can use if you need to do a couple of loads."

Nick gave her a puzzled look. "How did you guess I'm on my last clean shirt?"

She nodded toward the bulging green canvas bag at

his feet. "In all the times Spence came to visit me, he never once showed up with clean clothes. I suspect that it's a survival skill they teach in the military. You know, a special class on how to find a soft touch who'll wash your socks for you."

For the first time Nick really laughed and held up his hands in surrender. "Guilty as charged, although I've only pulled that trick on my mother. I wouldn't think of asking you to do such a thing."

"Well, then, I'll leave so you two can get settled. Oh, and before I go, we should exchange cell phone numbers."

When that little chore was taken care of, she headed back home, still thinking about how much younger Nick looked when he laughed. It was a shame he didn't do it more often.

Mooch followed her through the trees. When they reached the edge of her parents' lawn, she patted him on the head. "Thanks for seeing me home, big guy. I'll be okay from here. You'd better get back to your master."

Because for some reason she couldn't quite put her finger on, she suspected Nick needed looking after far more than she did right now.

"Yeah, Mom, I'm fine. Mooch and I had a nice trip." Nick listened for a while, waiting for her to get to the point. He closed his eyes and gave the only answer he could.

"I'm not sure how long we'll stay here or when I'll be back home."

The silence on the other end of the line was deafening. When his mother finally said good-bye, he could hear the disappointment in her voice, but there wasn't much he could do about it.

Until he found out how the muscle damage in his arm was going to heal, he couldn't make plans. She knew that, but that wasn't the real root of the problem. His folks had made it clear that they were ready for him to leave the army and move back home.

His dad had come right out and said they would like to have some grandkids while they were still young enough to enjoy them. He'd laughed as he said it and punched Nick on his good arm to lighten up the moment. It hadn't worked. They both knew that as their only child, the responsibility to spawn the next generation rested squarely on Nick's shoulders.

He'd had no good answer for them. Yeah, he got that they wanted Nick to live the life they'd always envisioned for him. They'd give anything to see him happily settled with a wife and a couple of rug rats, preferably living within the same zip code as theirs.

That wasn't going to happen anytime soon, if ever. He hadn't had the heart to say so outright, but they'd heard what he wasn't saying anyway. In the end, he'd tossed his duffel in the truck, loaded up on kibble for Mooch, and left. He'd made a habit of calling his folks every couple of days because he knew they worried about him. He didn't do it simply out of a sense of duty. He really did love them, even if he had trouble showing it right now.

As he hung up, he thought about his duffel again and smiled, remembering Callie's teasing on the subject. She was right. If he wanted to have something clean to wear tomorrow, especially if they did go out to dinner, he needed to make use of that washer and dryer she'd mentioned.

"Come on, Mooch. I'll fix you a bowl of water and then start the laundry. After that, maybe you and I ought to do a little recon and scout out the lay of the land around here in case we need to go on a midnight ramble. We don't want to get lost on our first night in town."

And wouldn't that be embarrassing? Normally he had a good sense of direction, but lately his internal compass had been off. He'd hate like hell to wake Callie up in the middle of the night because he couldn't find his way back on his own. That would sure as heck impress her.

When the washer was busy chugging away, he put on his jacket and walked outside. Before pulling the door closed, he patted his pocket to make sure he had his cell phone and the house key Callie had left with him. Mooch had already taken off for the thicket of trees behind the house. At least the dog had found a new purpose in life: chasing every squirrel he spotted.

Mooch stopped at the edge of the woods and waited for Nick to catch up. The dog seemed to enjoy exploring this new world, but he preferred to have Nick along for backup. They both had a lot of adjusting to do to get in sync with living outside of a war zone.

Nick didn't know about Mooch, but he didn't miss the background sounds of gunfire and explosions. On the other hand, it was hard to get used to so much quiet. They'd both been living with the constant adrenaline rush that came from being on high alert twenty-four/seven. At least they were both less jumpy now than when they'd first landed stateside. Nick would take any progress back toward normal that he could get.

The rain had stopped, leaving the air fresh and clean. Mooch ranged ahead, circling back every few minutes to touch base with Nick. They were following what used to be a pretty wide trail. Blackberry brambles and other weeds had encroached on it, but the path was still easy to follow as it wound through the trees.

Had Spence played here when he was little? Probably. Woods like these were the perfect place for a pack of kids to run wild pretending to be cowboys or pirates or soldiers. He could almost hear echoes of a young Spence hollering battle cries at the top of his lungs as he vanquished his imaginary foes.

The image made him smile. Damn, but he missed that guy. Spence had always been the first one to crack a joke and lighten the moment whenever things got tough. The man had taken the business of defending the country damned seriously, but he'd also understood the need to let off a little steam once in a while. Even now, Nick's clearest memory of him was the wicked grin on Spence's face as they ripped through those narrow streets like they were in a Grand Prix race.

He and Mooch had circled around through the woods to a point where they could just catch a glimpse of the house next door. Had Callie ever walked on the wild side with her good friend Spence? That might explain how protective Spence had always acted about her. For sure, he'd always been careful to shield her from the truth of their situation no matter how bad things were. When the two of them had chatted online, he'd kept things light, entertaining Callie with the funny side of war. Now, there was an oxymoron if there ever was one.

He'd left out the blood, pain, and fear they'd all experienced. For Spence, Callie was an escape from the reality of war, a gift to be treasured and protected. At one time, Nick had hoped to have some of that for himself with his ex-girlfriend Valerie.

Yeah, and see how well that had worked out for him. Lost in the past again, he hadn't realized that he'd

left the woods behind. He and Mooch were now standing in the middle of Callie's backyard. Son of a bitch,
they needed to get back to the trees before she spotted
them. The last thing he wanted was for her to think he
was stalking her or something.

"Let's go, boy."

Mooch normally responded immediately, but this
time he plunked his backside down in the grass and
stared at the house.

"Damn it, dog, come on. We need to get out of here."

Mooch favored Nick with a quick glance but then
turned his attention right back to the house. Clearly,
he'd rather be with Callie right now. Big deal. So would
Nick, but that didn't mean it was going to happen.

He stomped back within grabbing range of the dog.
When he tried to snag Mooch's collar, the dog snapped
at him and danced out of reach.

"Fine. Stay there."

Nick walked away, refusing to plead with the un-
grateful mutt. A few seconds later, Mooch came slinking up to him, his whole attitude one of apology. Nick
knelt down to give the dog a careful hug.

"I know, boy, but we've got to give her time to get
used to us."

Mooch, glad to be forgiven, wagged his tail and took
off down the trail, leaving Nick to follow in his tracks.
It was time to change loads in the washer and figure
out what he was going to do for dinner. Tonight he'd
eat alone, but not tomorrow evening. As he let Mooch
back in the house, he realized he had something to look
forward to for the first time in weeks.

It felt surprisingly good.

Nick dialed Leif's number and waited. It took longer
than usual for him to answer, but then his friend wasn't

getting around all that well these days. "Hey, buddy. How are you feeling?"

Leif sounded a little short of breath, but he was definitely stronger than the last time they'd talked. "Better. The physical therapist says I can graduate to walking with a cane with my brace later this week."

"So the exercises are helping?"

Leif sighed. "Yeah, I guess. I haven't been able to pin them down on when I'll be back to a hundred percent."

The frustration in Leif's voice was understandable. All that medical babble would drive anyone crazy, but it was worse when you suspected they were trying not to tell you some hard truths. Leif's ankle had been seriously fucked-up in the same attack that had taken Spence's life.

"Give it some time, Leif. Concentrate on flirting with your therapist or some of those nurses hanging around the place."

His friend snorted in disgust. "My therapist is built like a linebacker and answers to the name of Bubba."

Leif sounded much put-upon, but Nick couldn't help but laugh. "Seriously? Bubba? I'm sure I requested a gorgeous brunette for you."

"Well, he's about as far from that as possible. You must have checked the wrong box on the order form."

"Must have. How are you doing otherwise?"

Leif let out another long breath. "Bored senseless. I've never watched this much television in my whole life. I've tried reading, but nothing holds my attention."

Nick could sympathize. "I've had the same problems."

"Yeah, but at least you're mobile. I'm getting damn sick of looking at these same four walls. Where are you, anyway?"

Should Nick tell him?

"I'm in Washington."

"Then why haven't you been by to see me? I could use an outing. I'm sure a trip to the closest bar to lift a few beers would count as therapy."

"Not D.C., you idiot. The state."

Nick settled back on the couch and waited to see how Leif reacted.

He sounded incredulous. "You actually drove all the way out there to see Callie Redding in person?"

"Yeah. I have to find a permanent home for Mooch. I thought she might like to have him."

"And the same people who shipped the mutt to your folks couldn't have shipped him directly to her?"

Well, yeah, if he was going to get all technical about it. "I thought it would help if she met him first. What if she and Mooch didn't hit it off? Or if she lived in an apartment that didn't take pets?"

All logical reasons for him to deliver Mooch in person; none of them were the real reason he'd driven more than two thousand miles to show up on Callie's doorstep.

Leif wasn't buying it, either. "And so did she agree to adopt the mutt?"

Damn, his friend had him cornered. "I haven't asked her yet, but we only got in town a few hours ago. After traveling for almost a week, neither of us are at our best. I thought it was better to wait until Mooch had a day or two to recover from the trip before bringing up the subject."

Leif knew him too well. "That's bullshit, Sarge, and you know it. We both know why you're there."

Nick's temper, always close to the surface these days, exploded. "I'm here because I got the man she loved killed. Is that what you want to hear, Leif? That it's my fucking fault Spence died?"

He didn't wait for a response. After disconnecting the call, he threw the phone down on the couch. It started to ring within seconds, but he ignored it.

"Mooch, come. We're out of here."

Then he charged out into the night, knowing full well that no matter how fast or far a man walked, he couldn't outdistance his conscience.

Chapter 4

❧ ❧

Nick rolled over and buried his face in the pillow, hoping to fend off another fur-ball attack. Mooch whined louder this time and poked his cold, wet nose in Nick's ear in the process. At least the idiot was smart enough to dive back off the bed when Nick came up swinging. Deprived of a target for his temper, he sat up on the edge of the bed and glared at his tormentor.

"Damn it, dog. Pull that trick again, and I'll ship your ass right back to where it came from."

Mooch knew an empty threat when he heard one. Satisfied his human was now awake, he wagged his tail and trotted right back over to lay his head in Nick's lap. He stroked the dog's head and tried to find the energy to stand up.

Morning had come brutally early, especially considering Nick hadn't staggered upstairs to fall into bed until well after midnight. He'd give anything for a few more hours of sleep, but that wasn't going to happen until after he let Mooch out. He pulled on a T-shirt and headed downstairs in his flannel pajama bottoms to open the front door.

By the time the dog had made a quick circuit of the perimeter and reported back that all was well, Nick was too wide-awake to go back to bed. Still grumbling, he put on a pot of coffee, fed the dog, and parked himself on the steps out front with a bowl of cereal.

Mooch gulped down his own breakfast and went back to exploring the wilds of Spence's front yard. The grass was so high in spots that all Nick could see of the dog was the tip of his tail.

"Careful, dog. I hear they have bears in this part of the country. I bet they'd love a Moochburger for breakfast."

Mooch poked his head up for a brief look in Nick's direction. He yipped his acknowledgment of the warning and went back to sniffing out the local wildlife. A few seconds later, he barked and went bounding across the yard to chase a pair of squirrels up a tree. Looking damn proud of himself for having vanquished the enemy forces, he came trotting back to Nick.

"Yeah, be glad those varmints went up the tree, Mooch. You think you're tough, but I'm betting even money they could take you in a fair fight."

The dog recognized an insult when he heard one and went into immediate play stance, daring Nick to bring it on. It was a game they both enjoyed. They rolled across the porch with first Nick and then Mooch coming out on top. At least Nick managed to fend off his friend's determined efforts to give him a victory face licking.

"Dog, if you behave long enough for me to finish my coffee, we'll go for a run."

Mooch didn't have a huge vocabulary, but then English was his second language. He'd mastered all the important words, though, and knew what "run" meant. Before Nick could stop him, Mooch was heading down the driveway.

Edmonton Public Library
Mill Woods
Express Check #2

Customer ID: **********9854

Items that you checked out

Title: A time for home
ID: 31221109076484
Due: May-31-19

Total items: 1
Account balance: $2.00
May-10-19
Checked out: 3
Overdue: 0
Hold requests: 0
Ready for pickup: 0

Thank you for visiting the Edmonton
Public Library.

www.epl.ca

"Mooch! Let me get my shoes on first!"

He paused to see if the dog had listened to him before ducking back inside long enough to change into running shorts. He waited until he was back outside to put on his shoes to make sure Mooch hadn't gotten tired of waiting and taken off on his own.

He also brought the leash he'd bought for Mooch, another word the dog now knew and hated. Mooch had grown up wandering free on the streets of Afghanistan and had yet to adjust to the trappings of civilization, in particular collars and leashes.

"Come on, boy. You know the rules."

Mooch came slinking over to cower at Nick's feet. "Aw, dog, I'm not mad at you, but rules are rules. When we're here in the yard, you can run loose. Out there on the road, we've got to at least pretend to be like everyone else."

He clipped on the leash. "Let's go."

Resigned to his fate, Mooch charged ahead, pulling the retractable leash out to its limit before slowing to match the pace Nick set for them.

At the end of the driveway, Nick pulled up to decide which way to go. Finally, he turned in the direction of Snowberry Creek. Spence had talked about his hometown a lot, and Nick wanted to see how well his mental image of the place matched up with the real thing.

He'd gone maybe half a mile before he passed another house, but after that it was clear he'd reached the outskirts of town. He reeled Mooch in closer as they turned right at a sign pointing to the business district.

As the two of them pounded down the sidewalk, he made note of the various businesses they passed. Although a bit smaller than his own hometown, Snowberry Creek possessed at least two coffee shops. The closest one, Something's Brewing, promised fresh-baked muffins and pastries. The scent of roasting coffee and cinnamon had him wishing he'd brought his wallet.

"We'll stop there next time, Mooch."

If there was a next time. He'd yet to decide how long he'd be staying in the area. He shouldn't delay asking Callie about Mooch any longer than necessary. She might need to think about it. And if she couldn't take the dog, then Nick would need the time to make other arrangements for him. He had a limited amount of time before he had to let the army know his decision about reenlisting.

A lot also depended on how well his arm healed up. He fought the automatic urge to rub his biceps, knowing the pain was mostly in his head now.

"Time to head back, Mooch."

The dog obligingly turned back at the first tug on his leash. As they started back through town, a car going in the opposite direction slowed down and stopped. Even if he hadn't recognized Callie, Mooch's reaction would have told him who it was.

He checked for traffic and trotted across the road to where she'd stopped her car. Mooch immediately put his paws on the door, wiggling with excitement in hopes of getting petted.

Callie obligingly reached down to scratch his head. The damn mutt acted as if he'd been neglected his whole life until that very moment. Of course, that might just be Nick's jealousy talking. At least she shared her smile with him, too.

"You two are ambitious for your first day in town. Makes me feel guilty for driving such a short distance."

He tugged Mooch back down beside his feet. "It's the first chance we've had for a good run in almost a week. Don't want either of us to get fat and lazy."

Callie gave them both a good looking over. "I don't see that happening anytime soon."

He wasn't sure how to respond to that, so he changed the subject. "There's something I meant to ask you last night. Where's the closest grocery store?"

She pointed behind him. "Mr. Hanson's grocery is a block back that way. If you need more than a few things, there's a bigger store in the next town over. Just follow this road north another five miles."

"Thanks." He shifted from one foot to the other, getting up the courage to ask one last question. "Are we still on for dinner tonight?"

Callie nodded. "Sure thing."

Unfortunately, another car had pulled up behind her, so Nick stepped back. "I'll call you later to get specifics."

She smiled again. "Sounds good. I'm looking forward to it. Enjoy your run, guys."

He led Mooch back to the other side of the road as Callie waved at them one last time before pulling away. She wasn't the only one looking forward to dinner. As he and Mooch resumed their run, he let various scenarios play out in his head. Was she thinking casual and hamburgers? Or steaks and a tie? Not that he had one with him. Should he stop someplace and buy one just in case?

Another sign he still hadn't acclimated to being back stateside. He hadn't been out on a date since before he'd been deployed, not that this was really a date. He wasn't sure what it was, though. They weren't exactly friends, more like two people who'd had one friend in common. Two, if they counted Mooch. He just hoped they'd find something to talk about other than how much they both missed Spence.

Rather than dwell on it, he kicked it into high gear.

"Come on, dog. I'm going to take a shower and then make a quick run into town to pick up some groceries for the two of us."

Even if they left tomorrow, he'd need more kibble for Mooch and a few things for himself. After that, though, the long hours of the afternoon stretched out in front of him with nothing to do.

As they turned back into the driveway, he let Mooch off the leash. He dropped down on the porch step to cool off and catch his breath while the dog made sure the squirrels hadn't returned in their absence. Staring at the overgrown yard, it occurred to Nick that maybe he could make himself useful around the place.

After he got back from town, he'd check out the garage and see what kinds of yard tools he could find. A few hours of manual labor out in the sun would go a long way toward taking the edge off his mood.

"Come on inside, Mooch. I've got places to be and things to do."

Chapter 5

꧁꧂

Callie spent the morning meeting with various people at city hall, talking about permits, building
codes, and zoning. In the end, she'd come back home
more frustrated than informed and not a little discour-
aged. All of her previous experience in dealing with
home repairs was pretty much limited to calling a land-
lord to report a problem. Most of the time, it was fixed
while she was at work, so she didn't have the chance to
see how things were done.

Yeah, her dad had always been pretty handy around
the house, but she'd never done more than hand him
the occasional hammer or screwdriver. She'd preferred
to spend her time at home with her nose in a book or
online playing video games. Looking back, she wished
she'd paid more attention.

As she got out of the car, she heard a noise coming
from next door. What was Nick up to now?

Her mind flashed back to earlier that morning when
she'd seen him running through town. Hot damn, he'd
looked so good, she'd been unable to resist stopping to

watch. Even if he'd been a total stranger, she would've noticed him and the effortless way he moved.

And he'd claimed to be getting fat and lazy. Yeah, right. If anything, Nick looked as if he could stand to put on a few pounds. She hadn't missed that long scar peeking out from the sleeve of his T-shirt. Although it had obviously healed, the wound had left behind a jagged red streak twisting down the side of his upper arm.

It looked recent enough to make her wonder if he'd been injured in the same attack that had taken Spence's life. There was no way she'd ask Nick about it. If he brought it up, she'd listen, but she had no burning desire to learn the details of that awful day.

Perhaps it was cowardly of her, but she preferred to remember her friend as she'd last seen him. She didn't want the image of what had really happened to Spence burned into her memory for all time. It was bad enough to know he'd died on the other side of the world. With some effort, she dragged her mind back to the moment at hand. She paused to listen. Was that the lawn mower running? It sure sounded like it.

She took her purse inside the house and grabbed a couple of bottles of cold water from the fridge before heading next door to investigate. The noise grew louder the closer she got to Spence's place. Sure enough, she spotted Nick muscling the old lawn mower through the knee-high grass in the front yard.

Whoa, mama! If he'd looked good that morning in running shorts and a T-shirt, it was nothing to how the man looked without his shirt on, his tanned skin gleaming in the afternoon sun. Rather than trying to outshout the mower, she'd wait in the shade of the trees until he turned back in her direction before trying to catch his attention.

Mooch, on the other hand, was already heading straight for her at a dead run. She knelt down and braced herself for some serious doggy love. It had been years since she'd had a pet in her life because she moved around too often for it to be practical. Even so, it would take a harder heart than her own to resist a sweetie like Mooch.

After all, the dog was a real-life war hero. Spence had told her all about how the dog had warned his unit about a shooter lying in wait for them. No one knew why a stray would single them out to help, but he had. Not only that, but Mooch had gotten shot in the process. His thick fur covered the resulting scar, but she could still feel it.

"Hi, Mooch. Why don't we go over and sit on the steps while your owner slaves away in the sun?"

Almost as if he'd understood her, the dog immediately bolted for the shade offered by the porch, circling back a few seconds later to make sure Callie knew to follow him. She laughed at his antics. "Go ahead. I'll be along in a second."

Before she'd gone two steps, there was a loud clunking noise from the mower. A second later, the engine died with a loud bang and a huge puff of oily smoke. She watched in horror as Nick screamed, "Fuck no! Incoming! Everybody down!" as he dove for the ground. Mooch charged out into the yard to stand guard over Nick as he lay there covering his head with his arms. The dog's ruff was up as he growled at the poor lawn mower.

Oh, God, the two of them were reacting to the small explosion just as they would have back in Afghanistan. Sensing neither of them would much appreciate having an audience, Callie quickly retreated back down the path toward her parents' house, not sure what to do next. Maybe the smart thing would be to return home and pretend none of this had happened at all.

But was Nick all right? The only way to find out was to check on him. She couldn't very well leave him lying there alone and maybe hurt. Slowly, she inched down the path, listening for any sign that he was back up on his feet. Her patience was rewarded a few seconds later when Nick cut loose with a long string of colorful curse words. Feeling only marginally better about the situation, she counted off a few more seconds, intending to stroll back into the yard as if she'd just then arrived.

"You can come back, Callie. I'm done making a fool of myself. For now, anyway."

So much for her crafty plan. The dark thread of temper in Nick's voice made her even more reluctant to face him right now. She took a quick breath and walked forward, aiming for a calm she certainly wasn't feeling.

There'd been two occasions when Spence had clearly overreacted to a loud sound when he'd been home on leave. The loss of control had both embarrassed and infuriated him. Each time it had happened, he'd stormed off all wild-eyed and angry. He'd stayed gone for hours, until he regained control, leaving Callie alone and worrying about him. She'd hated the whole situation for him, but each time she'd been at a loss as to what she could do to help her friend get past the effects of spending months in combat mode.

When she stepped out of the trees, Nick was standing next to the lawn mower. He avoided looking in her direction until she was within a few feet of him. His attitude wasn't exactly welcoming as he brushed bits of cut grass off his sweaty skin. His expression softened slightly when she held up the bottled water.

"Thought maybe you could use one of these."

At least he accepted the cold drink. Poor Mooch parked himself between the two humans, giving them each worried looks. Nick took a long swig and then dumped some in his hand to splash on his face and neck. Then he poured more in his hand and bent down to offer it to his pal. Mooch dutifully lapped up the cool water and then accepted a second serving.

Nick avoided looking at Callie when he spoke. "Thanks, Callie. That tasted good. It's a lot hotter out here than I realized."

When he straightened up, he gave the lawn mower a nudge with the toe of his shoe. "Sorry, but I think I killed your mower."

Keeping her focus on the machine and not the man, she tried to reassure him. "Don't worry about it, Nick. In fact, as old as that thing is, I'm surprised you could even get it started at all. I know it hasn't been used in years. My father always cut Spence's grass with his own riding mower."

Looking disgusted, Nick glanced around at the yard. He'd cut only a couple of swaths, which just emphasized how overgrown the whole yard was. "Sorry, but it actually looks worse than when I started."

She forced a smile. "I'm not sure that's possible."

Callie wanted to ask if he was all right but knew any questions on the subject wouldn't be welcome. "No one has lived here for years, not even Spence. The whole place needs a lot of work."

Callie tried to see Spence's home through his friend's eyes rather than the filter of her own memories. Yeah, it did look pretty run-down. The paint was peeling, the gutters sagged, and the lawn looked more like a pasture than the front yard of a beautiful old home. Maybe that was all Nick saw, whereas she'd been looking past all of that to the possibilities.

"When I think about everything that it will take to restore the place, it gets a bit overwhelming. I'd planned on finding someone to get the yard back under control first, thinking maybe some high school kid needing a summer job would be interested. Once the worst of it gets cleared out, I should be able to maintain the yard myself."

Nick picked up the T-shirt he'd tossed on a nearby bush and put it on. "Do you think your dad would mind if I borrowed his lawn mower?"

Callie didn't know what to say. While she appreciated the offer, she didn't want him to feel obligated. Not to mention that she'd assumed he and Mooch would be back on the road tomorrow.

"He wouldn't mind, Nick, but surely you can think of something you'd enjoy doing more on a sunny afternoon than mowing my grass."

His eyes flared wide before he quickly looked away. She backed up a step, something about the intensity of his expression leaving her unsettled. What was he thinking about that had him staring off into the distance with his hands curled into white-knuckled fists? Nothing good, she'd bet.

"I scared you screaming like that, didn't I?"

There wasn't any use in lying to him. "A little."

When he finally looked at her again, his dark eyes were stone cold. "Do you want me to pack up now and leave? Just say the word and I'm gone."

She didn't hesitate. "No, Nick, I don't want that at all. To be honest, I was more afraid *for* you than *of* you, if that makes sense."

To support her statement, she took a step closer to him. "Spence had a couple of similar episodes on his last visit home when something startled him. At least you stuck around to talk to me. He just took off. Afterward, I tried telling him I'd rather he not hide from me, but I'm not sure he believed me."

"He probably felt like a fool for jumping at shadows." Nick flexed his hands several times and then rolled his shoulders. "After living on full alert for months on end, it's hard to shut it all off overnight. Most of the time I think I'm handling everything okay, but then I get blindsided by something as stupid as a lawn mower engine backfiring. It makes it hard to be around other people sometimes."

Confessing even that much was obviously difficult for him. Nick swallowed hard before continuing. "Maybe later I'll see what I can do to resurrect this mower. It shouldn't take much to tune it up and sharpen the blade. Even so, grass this high is too much for a regular mower. If you're sure it's okay, I'll use your dad's riding mower to finish the job."

She handed him the second bottle of water. "Why don't I go get it while you drink some more of this? Can I bring you anything else?"

He was already dragging the mower back toward the garage. "No, I'm fine. I made a trip to the store this morning to stock up on a few things."

Callie was about to start back to her parents' house but paused to ask one more question. "One reason I came over was to ask what kind of food you were in the mood for tonight."

Nick stopped midstep but kept his back to her. "Are you sure you still want to go?"

He stood frozen as if bracing himself for a negative response. Did he really think she'd blow him off now? "Yes, I'm sure, if for no other reason than I'm sick of my own cooking."

Her smile felt more genuine this time. "So what sounds good? Seafood, Italian, steaks, barbecue?"

Nick started moving again. "Anything as long as the restaurant is casual. I'm not sure I even own a tie anymore."

She laughed. "I'll keep that in mind. See you in a few minutes."

Chapter 6

Mooch remained close by Nick's side even though he paused several times as if unsure which human deserved his company more at the moment. Nick shot him a disgusted look.

"You'd have to be three kinds of crazy to hang out here with me instead of going with Callie. Besides, you're supposed to be using all of your limited charm on her so she'll offer you a permanent home here."

Mooch evidently decided not to play favorites and took off for the front porch. He flopped down on the rug that served as a doormat, positioning himself where he could keep a wary eye on his surroundings.

"I'll be right back," Nick assured him and continued on toward the garage.

He shoved the mower back where he'd found it. Callie hadn't been exaggerating when she'd said the garage was full of junk. Who had been the pack rat in the Lang family? It didn't seem likely that it had been Spence. At first glance, it appeared that most of the stuff should've been hauled to the dump years ago. After poking around a bit, Nick pulled out a couple of small tables and wiped off the dust and cobwebs to get a better look at them. They could be salvaged with a little work. It wouldn't take much.

Too bad he wouldn't be around long enough to do the job. There was definitely plenty of room in the house for more furniture. He'd explored most of the house last night when he'd had trouble sleeping. Almost every room had empty spots where it looked as if furniture had gone missing.

Maybe Callie had already claimed a few favorite pieces for herself, but somehow that didn't feel right to him. And really, it wasn't any of his business. He stuck the tables back where he'd found them.

The best thing he could do for Callie was take her to dinner as promised, keeping things light and easy. Afterward, he should come back to the house, pack up, and be ready to leave at first light. That was exactly what he would do if he were on his own, but there was still Mooch to deal with. It would be damn hard to leave the dog behind, but it was the kindest thing Nick could do for him.

Somehow he'd have to find a way to broach the subject over dinner. The worst Callie could say was no, and then he'd head back home to Ohio to leave the dog with his parents, at least until Nick got his own life settled. They'd do it if he asked it of them, but it wouldn't be a permanent solution. His dad was planning on retiring soon, and all his folks had talked about was how much traveling they wanted to do. He wouldn't interfere with that if he could help it.

He slammed the garage door closed. "Damn it, Spence, I'm running out of options here, but don't worry. I'll make sure Mooch finds a good home."

It wasn't the first time he'd caught himself talking to Spence, and it wasn't likely to be the last. Maybe it was another sign that he'd yet to accept what had happened back in Afghanistan, but he didn't think so. He knew full well that he'd lost his friend; he had the gaping hole in his life to prove it.

Things just made more sense if he talked them out with a friend. Leif was only a phone call away, but he had his own problems without having to shoulder the weight of Nick's, too. That left Spence.

"By the way, buddy, your lady is every bit as nice as you said she was. She misses you."

They both did. Nick used the hem of his shirt to wipe his face clean of sweat. "I hope you don't mind, but I'm thinking I might have to stick around for a week or so if Callie will let me. It will give her a chance to get to know Mooch better, and she could sure use a hand fixing up this monster of a house you left her. Maybe I can help her get on track with what needs to be done. My dad is a contractor, you know, and I grew up working on one of his crews."

He paused, wishing for an answer he knew full well wouldn't come. Or maybe it had, considering he could hear the distant rumble of an engine heading his way. It had to be Callie bringing him her father's riding mower. He'd use it to cut the grass and then maybe start clearing out the flower beds. Surely she'd understand that he couldn't leave a job half-done.

Only time would tell. But for the moment, he'd get busy and earn his keep.

Nick mowed the entire yard twice, resetting the blade height the second time to get the grass down to the right height. It wasn't perfect, but it definitely looked better than it had. When he had driven the mower back over to Callie's house, he'd decided her yard could stand to be mowed, too.

Callie had stopped by a while ago to say she'd gotten an unexpected phone call and had to leave to meet with her attorney. She hadn't looked happy about whatever it was but hadn't offered any explanations. At least it meant Nick was able to get the mowing done while he had the place to himself. After putting the riding mower back in her dad's shed, Nick walked back over to Spence's place looking forward to a shower and a long nap. He wanted to be well rested for their outing later that evening.

Just as he stepped out of the woods, a patrol car pulled into Spence's driveway. Interesting. What had happened to draw the attention of the local police?

Mooch wasn't any happier about the uninvited guest than Nick was. The dog remained up on the porch, his head down, a low growl making his opinion of the situation all too clear. For the moment, the man remained inside the car talking on his cell phone, which gave Nick time to reach the porch steps. He sat down close enough to Mooch to be able to grab the dog's collar if the mutt got it into his head that the cop was the enemy.

Pitching his voice low and calm, he tried to reassure his worried companion while they waited to see what was up. "It's okay, boy. Let's assume he's one of the good guys."

At least until he proved otherwise. Too bad Callie wasn't there to run interference. Nick stayed where he was, preferring to let the officer approach him. While he waited, he opened the small cooler he'd left out on the porch and pulled out two soft drinks. He also had a six-pack of beer in there but figured the cop couldn't have one while he was on duty.

The car door finally opened. Nick assessed his visitor, guessing him to be maybe ten years older than his own age of twenty-nine. He'd also bet the man had spent time in the military somewhere along the way. Something about the way he carried himself, or maybe it was that familiar hint of steel in those blue eyes. Nick popped the top on his drink, took a quick sip, and then pasted what he hoped was a friendly smile on his face.

"Good afternoon, Officer. I'm Nick Jenkins, a friend of Callie's. What brings you out this way?"

Calling himself a friend of Callie's wasn't too much of a stretch, even allowing that they'd met only the day before. He was reasonably sure she'd back his play on the matter.

"I'm Gage Logan, the chief of police here in Snowberry Creek. I was driving by and saw the grass had been cut. I try to keep an eye on any vacant houses in the area to make sure we don't get any squatters. We don't get many homeless folks, but there are a few."

Okay, that didn't make any sense. "Do squatters usually mow the lawn?"

That crack obviously didn't win Nick any points with his guest. The man studied Nick for several seconds, maybe hoping he would offer up more information on his own. When he didn't, Chief Logan continued speaking.

"I wasn't aware that Miss Redding had decided to rent out this place."

"That's because she didn't. Rent it, that is." As he spoke, Nick held out the second pop. "Here, you look like you could use one of these."

When the lawman accepted the cold drink, Nick scooted over to make room if the police chief wanted to join him on the steps. "I served with Spence Lang in Afghanistan. I stopped by to pay my respects to Callie."

His explanation evidently satisfied the police chief,

because his stance became more relaxed. "I knew Spence's family. His parents were good people."

But Spence's uncle hadn't been, Nick added to himself. Spence hadn't talked about the man much, but it was obvious there'd been no love lost between the two.

Logan took a long drink. He made solid eye contact with Nick when he spoke again. "I was really sorry to hear about Spence. I know his death hit Callie and her folks really hard. I think it came as even more of a shock to her to find out that he'd left everything to her."

What could Nick say to that? "She meant a lot to Spence. They stayed close even if they didn't get to spend much time together."

Although Spence had hoped to change that when he came home from their deployment.

"How long do you expect to be staying here?" Logan softened the question with a hint of a smile. "I just want to know what to tell my men, so they'll know why there are lights on in the house."

"That will depend on Callie. I'm back in the States on leave and don't have any particular plans. I thought I might stick around long enough to get the yard back in shape for her."

Sensing Nick had relaxed his guard, Mooch lunged down the steps, getting out of reach before Nick could stop him. The cop stood his ground but allowed Mooch to check him out.

"Mooch, come back here. He doesn't need to get covered in dog hair."

"That's okay." Logan held out his hand for Mooch to sniff and then patted the dog on his head, grinning when he noticed he was wearing real dog tags.

"Is he an ex-military dog?"

"No, at least not officially."

The combination of hot sun and bad memories had

images of Afghanistan filling Nick's mind, threatening to take control. He fought hard to keep from getting swept back to the night when Mooch had entered their lives. One of the army docs had told him that if he felt himself slipping back into the past, to concentrate on something physical, something solid. He tightened his grip on the can, focusing on the drops of water trickling down the cool metal. Gradually, his mind cleared.

Hoping he hadn't been silent too long, he finished the story. "He was a stray that took a liking to Spence one night when we were out on patrol. Mooch saved our asses by warning us we were about to walk into an ambush. We made him an official member of the squad after that."

Logan patted Mooch on the head again. "Well, it looks like Callie's place is in good hands, so I'll hit the road."

He looked around one last time. "A word of warning. Spence's uncle wasn't at all happy about him leaving this place to Callie instead of him and his son. He made some noise about contesting the will, but I think he was just rattling cages to see what happened. No one has seen him around lately. It would be nice if that means he's given up and moved on."

"But you're not sure." Nick stood up to face the police chief head-on. "Do you think he poses any kind of threat to Callie?"

Logan set his empty can on the porch railing and took his hat off to run his fingers through his hair. "I'd like to say no, but I can't for sure. When Vince is sober, you can reason with him, but he has a well-deserved reputation of being a mean drunk."

He put his hat back on. "But as I said, no one has seen him in several weeks. Vince disappeared right after the attorney told him the will was airtight. I'm not sure how he'll react if he finds out she's fixing the place up."

"Thanks for the heads-up, Chief. I'll talk to Callie about it when she gets back."

He'd also get his sidearm out of the locked toolbox in his truck and keep it close at hand as long as he was staying at the house. He trailed after the chief, who was heading back to his patrol car.

Chief Logan waved one last time before he pulled out onto the road. The man had given Nick a lot to think about, none of it good.

"Come on inside, Mooch. I'm going to grab a shower and then take a nap. You might want to catch some shut-eye, too. It's going to take all of our energy tonight to convince Ms. Callie Redding that she needs a guard dog around to keep her safe."

And he wasn't just talking about Mooch.

Chapter 7

✲ ✲

Nick's reaction to the rustic restaurant she'd chosen had been an odd mix of good humor and relief. He was the one who suggested they eat outside on the deck, which offered a view of Mount Rainier in the distance. He stared out at the mountain with a small smile softening the harsh lines of his face.

Glancing at her out of the corner of his eye, he said, "Tell me you don't get so used to being surrounded by such beauty that you don't even notice it anymore."

Callie shook her head. "I haven't lived here in years, so it all feels fresh and new to me. But even when I did, I always loved the mountains. Rainier would pose a huge threat to the entire area if it ever acts up like Mount St. Helens did back in 1980, but it's still beautiful."

For the first time since she'd met Nick—was it just yesterday?—he seemed relaxed. She wondered what had happened to put him at ease.

As if sensing her curiosity, he slowly turned to face her directly. "Let me know if the breeze makes it too chilly for you, but I love being outside when the air is this cool. It was hotter than hell when I left Afghanistan, and where my parents live wasn't much cooler, with the added joy of high humidity."

She could have been freezing to death at that moment, and she wouldn't have complained. Not if something so simple chased some of the shadows from Nick's eyes.

Callie was familiar with the menu, so she barely glanced at it. "I'm glad you like this place. It's always been one of my favorites. I love their grilled salmon, and the crab cakes are to die for. They also brew a mean amber ale."

When their waiter returned, Nick looked up from studying the selections. "That does sound good. Want to start off with a couple of the ales and the crab cakes for an appetizer?"

Callie nodded. "Sure, and for dinner I'll have a Caesar salad along with the grilled salmon."

Nick closed his menu and handed it back. "I'll have the same."

The waiter smiled. "Good choices. The crab cakes shouldn't take long."

When they were alone again, Nick went back to staring at the mountain. Normally, the silence that settled between them wouldn't have bothered Callie. However, something about the way Nick was keeping his eyes averted convinced her that it wasn't that he had nothing to say. No, he was just reluctant to share whatever it was that he wanted to tell her.

The suspense was killing her. If he didn't speak up soon, she'd have to find some way to nudge him along. When she was about to do just that, he started talking.

"I have a couple of things to tell you, Callie, and they're sort of intertwined."

She wished he would look at her, but then again

maybe not, considering the expression on his face right then. Even in profile, it was easy to see the growing tension in the clench of his jaw and the way his eyebrows rode down low over his dark eyes. What was he seeing in his mind that had him looking so grim?

"Spence was the one who insisted on adopting Mooch after the dog saved us. It was touch-and-go that first night even after the vet treated Mooch. Although the bullet didn't hit anything vital, the wound bled a lot, especially for a dog his size. Added to that, Mooch was half-starved and filthy, so it was anybody's guess what kind of germs were embedded in the wound."

He lapsed into silence again, his expression bleak as he relived that night. This time she did try to nudge him along.

"Spence told me a lot about what happened on that particular patrol and afterward. He also said that you finally ordered him to get some sleep while you stood watch over Mooch. You have to know that meant a lot to Spence."

Nick shrugged it off. "I owed both him and the dog that much, but back to the story. Once we knew the dog would actually make it, Spence started worrying about what would happen to him when our deployment ended. He called in every favor he could to make the arrangements to ship Mooch back to the States. He wanted to give that idiot fur ball a chance to live a long and lazy life, hopefully here in Snowberry Creek."

Nick finally turned to face her. "When Spence was killed, Leif and I couldn't stand for that dream to die along with him."

Oh, no, she could guess where he was headed with this. It had never occurred to her that along with Spence's house she might inherit his dog, too. What could she say?

"If you're asking me to adopt Mooch, Nick, I can't say yes, not without thinking about it long and hard. I hadn't told you this, but I'm thinking about turning Spence's house into a bed-and-breakfast. It's too soon to know if that's going to work out. If it doesn't, I'll be looking for another contract job, which could be anywhere for any length of time. I often live out of suitcases for weeks at a time."

Their crab cakes and drinks arrived, giving her a few seconds' respite before having to say more. In fact, having Nick dump this on her lap with no warning made her angry, especially because to say no to providing a home for Mooch came with a huge load of guilt.

"For certain, I can't give you a firm answer tonight or even tomorrow, Nick. Not when I don't know where I'll be living in a month's time."

"I'm not really asking you for a commitment one way or another." He was back to staring at the mountain. "I certainly understand what it's like to live in between homes. I'm in the same boat, at least until I decide whether to extend my enlistment. It doesn't help that Leif is trying to come back from an injury that could cost him his career in the army."

He offered her a tired smile. "That one patrol has had a profound effect on all of our lives, I guess."

There wasn't much she could say to that, so she concentrated on enjoying the crab cakes. Unfortunately, they didn't last very long as a diversion.

"You said you wanted to talk to me about a couple of things. What's the other one?"

Nick set down his fork and pushed his plate away. "I was wondering if you'd mind if I stuck around long enough to do the yard work for you."

Now, that she definitely hadn't been expecting. "Really?"

There was a bit of a twinkle in his eyes now. "Yeah, really. I don't have to be anywhere in particular for a while, and I'd like to help."

After poking and prodding the idea, she found she wouldn't mind getting to know Nick better. Smiling so he'd know she was teasing, she said, "So, tell me— do you have any experience as a professional weed puller?"

He responded in kind. "Yes, ma'am, I do, and I can even furnish you with references."

"Seriously?"

Nick laughed. "The truth is my dad's a general contractor who specializes in remodels. I grew up working on his crews summers and during breaks in college. I've mostly done carpentry, but I've done a little bit of everything. That includes a fair amount of landscaping, like the kind you need done—clearing out everything that's become overgrown so you can plant new stuff."

It would be so nice to start crossing a few things off her growing to-do list. "If you're sure, then I'd love to have your help. I can even pay you for your efforts if you don't mind working for minimum wage."

She was afraid he'd refuse that outright, but he surprised her with a counteroffer. "Keep me in groceries and beer, and we'll call it even."

"It's a deal."

The knowledge that Nick would be sticking around for a while pleased her far more than it should have. She figured he was offering only because of some misguided idea that he owed it to Spence to help her out.

And maybe one of the reasons she wanted Nick to stay was that she needed that connection to Spence, too. Their dinners arrived, so they turned their attention to the fresh salmon and the beautiful sunset.

* * *

Nick dropped Callie off in her parents' driveway. He didn't trust himself to walk her to the door without wanting to do more than simply say good night. At least she didn't seem to find it odd that he stayed in the truck watching as she walked up to the porch and let herself in. She waved one last time before turning off the porch light and closing the door.

He drove the short distance back to Spence's house feeling more relaxed than he had been in a long time. Once inside, he grabbed a beer from the fridge and sat out on the porch while Mooch patrolled the yard. But after doing a quick circuit, Mooch made a beeline for the path that led toward Callie's yard.

Nick charged down the steps after him. "Damn it, dog, come back here."

No response. The stubborn beast obviously thought that Callie's place was also part of his territory. Most likely the dog would come back on his own, but then again, maybe not. Muttering a few choice words about Mooch's questionable ancestry, Nick stomped across the yard and took off through the woods after him.

At least the moon was bright enough to make a flash-light unnecessary. The woods were cool and still, but at night the bushes and trees took on strange shapes. Dangerous shapes. Ones that might mean snipers and insurgents could be lurking in the deepest shadows. Nick stuttered to a stop next to a tall Douglas fir, leaning against the rough surface of the trunk, unable to move forward. His pride wouldn't let him retreat.

He was being absurd, and his conscious mind knew it. He'd left that kind of danger behind when the transport plane had gone wheels up, leaving Afghanistan in Nick's rearview mirror. He tried convincing his subconscious of that truth, but it wasn't always willing to listen.

It took everything he had to step forward without

either breaking into a panicky run or bolting back to Spence's house to get his sidearm. But a gun in the hands of a man who couldn't always control his own reactions to the slightest stimulus was never a good idea. He forced his feet to move.

Counting his steps helped, giving himself something to concentrate on besides his racing pulse and how hard it was to breathe. "One, two, three . . ."

It didn't take long before he could see the end of the path where it opened out into Callie's yard. He intended to call Mooch to heel and march right back to where they belonged. But as he drew closer, he knew that wasn't going to happen. Mooch hadn't been patrolling; he'd been hunting for his new best pal. What's more, he'd found her.

Callie's voice carried across the yard. "Yeah, Mooch, I missed you, too, but I'm pretty sure you're not supposed to be over here."

Time to join the discussion. "That's right. He's not."

Nick made his way over to where Callie stood on her back porch. Mooch was too busy worshipping at her feet to even acknowledge Nick's presence.

"Dog, get down here. You shouldn't be bothering Callie." Not that Nick blamed the mutt for preferring her company to his.

No response.

Nick tried again, this time injecting the same authority into his voice that he'd used on raw recruits who weren't performing up to expectations. "Now, Mooch, or the next time I let you out it will be on your leash."

The dog hated the L-word and finally realized he was in big-time trouble. He came slinking down the steps to crouch at Nick's feet. It was hard not to laugh, but the dog had to learn how things were done in his new world.

"Sorry that he dragged you out of the house, Callie."

She walked down the steps. "It's okay, Nick. I was headed out here anyway. I like to sit out here in the dark on my mom's swing by the koi pond and enjoy the night air."

Tilting her head to the side, she wrinkled her nose as she studied Nick. "Want to join me? Or would that only send Mooch the wrong message?"

Yeah, it probably would, but right now Nick didn't care. Hell, he and the dog both ought to do Callie a favor and leave, but right now Nick just didn't have it in him to refuse her invitation. All he had waiting for him back at Spence's place was a six-pack of beer, a book he wasn't all that interested in, and a big lonely bed.

He slammed the door shut on that line of thought. It was time to go.

But when he opened his mouth to say good night, that wasn't what came out. "If you're not tired of my . . . I mean our company."

"Not at all."

Then, to his surprise, Callie took his hand and tugged him along behind her. She led the way to the old-fashioned yard swing near the small pond with a burbling fountain in the middle. Mooch, evidently deciding he'd been forgiven, was already exploring the far end of the yard and slowly making his way back toward his two human companions.

The swing proved to be long enough for Nick and Callie to sit down with plenty of room between them. He dutifully settled on the far end of the seat, but somehow Callie ended up sitting right next to him, thigh to thigh, with her hand still tangled up with his.

Holy crap, Spence would have kicked Nick's ass from one end of Afghanistan to the other for even thinking about touching Callie. Even though Leif was still on crutches, no doubt he would be only too glad to stand in for their fallen comrade. But since neither of them was there to provide a buffer between him and Callie, Nick was on his own.

And right now, under the moonlight with a warm woman sitting by his side, this was simply the best moment he'd enjoyed in far longer than Nick could remember. Come morning, he promised to hate himself for taking advantage of Callie's good nature, but right now he was going stay right where he was.

"Nick, you're thinking way too hard."

Angling his head to look down into Callie's pretty face, he meant to tell her that he shouldn't be there. Or maybe to thank her for making him feel so welcome. Yeah, that would be good. But instead, he did the one thing he shouldn't have.

He kissed her.

Chapter 8

Nick sure knew how to kiss. He tasted like the night: cool and mysterious, his lips surprisingly soft, especially in contrast to the slight rasp of his whiskers against her skin. He probably hadn't shaved since that morning, but she didn't care, and now wasn't the time to be thinking about it anyway.

This was a moment to savor and definitely one for the record books. She sighed and tipped her head back to rest against the strong curve of his shoulder, parting her lips just enough to let Nick know that she'd welcome an even deeper kiss.

The hint worked. He wrapped his arms around her as his tongue swept in and out of her mouth on a quick foray. Murmuring her approval, she raised up to do a little exploring of her own, at the same time tracing the curve of his cheek with her fingertips.

The night air took on a special warmth, surrounded as she was by the strength and heat of Nick's warrior body. At that moment she wanted nothing more than to crawl right up on his lap, to feel the press of her body against his. That would be too much too soon, but if she didn't back away now, she might not be able to resist.

Before she had a chance to retreat, Nick took the initiative and broke off the kiss, jerking back out of reach. He stared down at her, his eyes flared wide and looking a little panicky. His breath came in short gasps, but then her own sounded as if she'd been running sprints, too.

His expression abruptly morphed from confused to absolutely blank, every emotion he'd just been feeling evidently disappearing between one second and the next. Her skin prickled with goose bumps as if the temperature had suddenly dropped ten degrees.

She would have retreated to the far end of the swing if his arm wasn't still holding her prisoner. As if reading her mind, Nick shifted his arm off her shoulders and up onto the back of the swing. Callie inched away, opening up a far larger breach between them than the short distance she'd actually moved.

"Nick?"

His eyes dropped closed and stayed that way for several seconds. When he finally looked at her again, she was looking at a total stranger, so cold and distant.

"Callie, I'm sorry. I can't do this."

Okay, now she was getting mad. "Do what, Nick? It was a kiss. Nothing more."

Evidently he didn't agree. Nick stood up and walked a short distance away, hovering just out of reach. Callie stayed on the swing, not sure what had just happened and not all that anxious to find out.

"I'd better go, Callie. And unless you've changed your mind about me sticking around, I'll get started on the yard tomorrow morning."

He kept his back to her as he spoke. Did he really think she'd send him packing because of one ill-advised kiss? Maybe so, because he sure sounded dead serious. She wasn't even tempted to ask him to leave, if for no other reason than she hadn't had time to decide what to do about Mooch.

Keeping her voice businesslike, she gave him his answer. "I'm not sure what yard tools you'll find over there in the garage, but feel free to borrow anything you need from my dad's toolshed. If there's stuff like fertilizer or weed killer that you need, make a list so I can pick it up for you."

"I'll do that." The rigid set of his shoulders softened a bit. "And, Callie, just so you know, the problem is with me, not you."

She wanted to point out that that was what they all said, but he was already gone. Mooch stopped to get petted one last time and then charged off into the darkness to catch up with his buddy. Callie set the swing in motion, swaying gently as she listened to the soft murmur of the fountain. Gradually, the last bit of her own tension drained away. It was definitely time to go inside.

Tomorrow she'd get back to work on her plans for the bed-and-breakfast. Since Nick would be working outside in the yard, she could work inside on the detailed inventory of the rest of the house. Maybe it was time to start clearing out the garage and attic over there, too.

Hopefully she could keep busy without crowding Nick too much. She paused at the top of the porch steps to listen to the night one last time.

And even knowing he wouldn't hear her, she called softly, "Good night, Nick. You, too, Mooch. I hope you both sleep well."

Then she went inside and locked the rest of the world out.

*   *   *

Nick took sanctuary just inside the tree line. This time the shadows offered him a chance to hide, a place to lick his wounds. God, could that have gone any more wrong? What had he been thinking? That answer was simple. He hadn't been thinking at all. He'd been feeling: the warm press of Callie's body next to his on the swing, the sweet touch of her hand entwined with his, and then her lips against his, their breath intermingling in the cool night air.

How the hell was he supposed to resist all of that?

He stayed at the edge of the woods, watching to make sure Callie was all right. He suspected—no, he *knew*—his reaction had hurt her feelings. Tomorrow he'd find some way to make amends if he could. Maybe some coffee and pastries from that shop he'd spotted in town when he was on his run.

At least he hadn't completely spoiled her time out on the swing. The moon was bright enough for him to see her face clearly. She had the look of a woman finding simple pleasure in the quiet of the night. After a bit, she headed back for the house.

And to his amazement, at the top of the steps she stared back toward the woods right where he stood waiting in the darkness. She said something just before she disappeared back into the house.

Her words had him smiling, some of his fear that he'd ruined things between them floating away on the night breeze.

"Good night to you, too, Callie. I'll see you in the morning."

It wasn't until then that he realized that Mooch had been there with him the whole time. The dog was leaning against Nick's leg as the two of them had silently watched Callie.

He patted Mooch on the head. "Damn, dog, we've got it bad."

His furry companion sighed loudly in agreement. Nick laughed. "We'd better turn in for the night. We've got a lot of work to do around here tomorrow."

As they approached Spence's yard, Mooch froze. He looked up at Nick and then back toward the house, growling low and deep.

"What is it, boy? What are you sensing?"

The dog's agitation left Nick wishing for two things. First, that Mooch could actually answer the question. And second, that he'd brought his gun with him instead of his pocketknife. A four-inch blade wouldn't do squat if whoever was out there was packing.

Mooch finally started forward, his nose to the ground all the way across the yard. By the time they reached the porch, he was back to normal.

"I should kick your furry ass for acting that way over some stupid squirrel or a raccoon, dog."

Nick let them both inside and locked the door.

"You did good." He reassured his buddy with a good scratching. "I said that for their benefit."

After flipping on the light for the upstairs hallway, Nick retrieved his gun from his duffel and positioned himself beside the front window, watching for any sign of movement outside. His gut told him that whatever had upset Mooch was walking around on two legs, not four.

The only question was if the intruder was still out there. A minute later, he heard the sound of an engine starting up and then fading away into the distance. Coincidence? Maybe, but he'd have to wait until morning to look around for any sign that someone had been hanging around the yard while he'd been over at Callie's. If he found anything, he'd be having a talk with the police chief for sure to see if that uncle of Spence's was back in town.

The solid feel of his gun in his hand was a comfort, familiar, although he would have preferred to have his rifle with him. Even without it, though, he'd be fine. It wasn't himself he was worried about. What if it had been Callie coming back through the woods alone in the darkness? The possibilities had him wishing he had a handy target for his anger.

Because no matter what the risk, he'd do whatever it took to make sure Callie was safe. And he wasn't doing it just because he owed that much to Spence. He hadn't risked his own life and seen his friends shot and killed in that hellhole half a world away just to come home and put up with some bastard threatening a woman, and especially Callie.

No way and on no day.

There was nothing more to be done tonight, but tomorrow the hunt would begin.

Chapter 9

🌿🌿

There should be a law against phones ringing before . . . What time was it anyway? Callie raised her head to glare at the clock. Okay, it was almost eight o'clock, but still. It wasn't as if she had to be anywhere by a certain time.

Rolling over onto her back, she grabbed her cell phone off the nightstand. She had a fair idea who it was because none of her friends would ever call her this early. Even if Callie had been up, she had a hard time communicating until after her first cup of coffee. Sometimes it took a second or even third cup before she could function at full speed.

She covered her eyes with her other forearm to block out the bright light. "Hi, Mom. What's up?"

"Oops, sorry. Did I wake you?" Not that she sounded at all apologetic.

"Yeah, but I should probably get moving anyway."

In a couple of hours. "So what's going on? Are you and Dad enjoying your time in the sun?"

"Yes, we are. Your dad is due out on the golf course, but he wouldn't go until I called you."

There was a note in her mom's voice that had Callie sitting up. "Why? Is something wrong?"

"No, well, not exactly." Then she broke off to talk to Callie's father. "I will! Give me a chance."

A sick feeling settled in Callie's stomach as she waited for her mom to get to the point.

"You see, honey, I got an e-mail from Rosalyn McKay this morning. She wanted to know if either of us would be interested in being on a new committee she's putting together to work on bringing new business to town."

All of that came out on one long breath. And none of it had anything to do with Callie. "So why the call, Mom? Surely she wasn't asking if I wanted to be on the committee or anything."

"Not at all." Now her mom was sounding a bit too casual. "It seems she'd been talking to the new police chief. Do you remember Gage Logan? Well, he moved back to Snowberry Creek to take over for Chief Green when he retired."

Again, nothing to do with Callie. "Yes, I knew Gage was back in town. We've talked a couple of times. What does all of this have to do with me?"

"Well, he happened to mention to Mayor McKay that he'd noticed the grass at Spence's house had been recently mowed. She was surprised to find out that you have someone living there now. To be honest, your father and I weren't happy to be the last to know."

Sometimes Callie forgot how fast the grapevine worked in a town the size of Snowberry Creek. "I doubt you're actually the last. There must be someone in town who hasn't heard the news."

Okay, sarcasm wasn't the smartest response, but Nick's presence next door was nobody's business but her own. As tempting as it was to point that out, Callie kept that last part to herself.

"Anyway, your father is worried about you being there all alone with a total stranger living right next door. Do you want us to come back home? Or better yet, you could fly down to stay here with us. A kind of little vacation. It would do you good to get away for a few days."

The fact that Callie had been living on her own in cities far more dangerous than Snowberry Creek seemed to have escaped her parents for the moment. "No, Mom, I don't want you to come back early, and I really don't have time for a visit right now. While I appreciate both offers, I need to make a decision about what to do with Spence's house soon, and I can't do that long-distance."

"But what do you know about this man?"

"Do you remember Spence talking about his two best friends, Nick Jenkins and Leif Brevik? Well, Nick is back from Afghanistan and stopped by to introduce himself. Rather than make him get a motel room, I offered to let him stay over at Spence's house. I thought that would be easier since Nick has that dog with him that saved Spence's squad from an attack. He's hoping I'd like to adopt him. The dog, that is, not Nick."

Although her wayward libido might argue that point. She also didn't mention that her first offer had been to let Nick stay at her parents' house with her. She could just imagine how well that would have gone over right about now.

Evidently the fact that Nick was a friend of Spence's wasn't enough to reassure her mom.

"Besides being a friend of Spence's, what do you really know about this man, Callie? How long does he plan to stay?"

It was time to put an end to this discussion. "I know he was Spence's friend, Mom. That's good enough for me. He offered to stick around a few days longer to finish cleaning up the yard over there as a favor to me. He's on leave and I suspect feeling a little disconnected. Coming back from a long tour in Afghanistan is a big adjustment."

Too wide-awake now to have any hope of going back to sleep, she got out of bed and made her way downstairs to the kitchen. Luckily, she'd set the timer on the coffeemaker last night so the coffee was already made. She filled her favorite mug and added cream and sugar while her mom continued talking.

"How do you know this is even the real Nick?"

Oh, brother. She was really grasping at straws now. "Because I talked to him when Spence and I were Skyping. I'd also seen pictures of him and Mooch, the dog. Believe me, there aren't many dogs that look like him."

She stuck a stale bagel in the toaster. "Tell Dad I appreciate him worrying about me." Not. "But he doesn't need to miss his tee time because of me. I'm fine, and Nick's one of the good guys."

Even if she had a hard time getting a solid read on him sometimes.

"Okay, if you say so, honey. But if you change your mind about wanting to come down for a few days, all you have to do is call."

"Thanks, Mom. Like I said, I appreciate the offer. Now, let Dad get to his golf game, and you go soak up some rays with a good book. And don't worry. I'm fine."

Evidently her mom wasn't quite ready to hang up, because she changed the subject and began talking about some family friends who'd stopped by to see them recently. As she talked on, Callie noticed a movement in the backyard out of the corner of her eye.

Sure enough, Nick was headed this way carrying a

paper bag and two cups in one of those cardboard carriers. He was dressed in a pair of camouflage pants, a sleeveless T-shirt, and heavy boots. He looked as if he'd already worked up a sweat, his tan skin gleaming in the morning sun. Yum.

Which reminded her that she looked as if she'd just rolled out of bed, rumpled and with a bad case of bed head.

"Mom, I hate to cut you off, but there's a contractor coming this morning. I need to get dressed before he gets here, so we can do a walk-through next door."

She disconnected before her mom could do much more than sputter. Although she hated lying to her parents, she wasn't about to tell her mom that she was going to let Nick in the house dressed as she was in flannel shorts and a tank top. No bra, either. Great. Odd how that one little thing made her feel so much more vulnerable.

Nick was already at the door, leaving her no time to do anything but tough it out. She unlocked the dead bolt and opened the door.

"Come on in."

He stepped inside but didn't immediately remove his sunglasses, making it hard to tell what he was thinking. Well, that wasn't true, either, given that his mouth had just curved up in a huge grin.

"I brought breakfast as a peace offering, but I'm guessing I got you out of bed."

Could this get any more embarrassing? "No, my mother had that honor. She was calling to grill me about you staying next door. Seems it was the police chief who told the mayor, who then told my folks. Nothing like a small town for spreading gossip at the speed of light."

His smile faded a bit. "Was she upset?"

"No, just a bit overprotective. Seriously, as long as I'm working in some other city, they don't seem to have problems realizing I'm an adult. But five minutes after I walk back in this house, they want to set a curfew and meet every guy I date or, better yet, his parents. You know, to make sure he comes from good family."

Nick peeled off his sunglasses and hung them on the neckline of his shirt, a bit of devilment twinkling in his eyes. "I've been through my fair share of parental grilling and managed to convince most of them I was harmless.

"However"—he paused to give her a long look from her polished pink toenails back up to her tousled hair— "I suspect right about now your dad would kick me to the curb for what I'm thinking."

Well, then. What could she say to that?

She pointed toward the bag he'd set on the counter. "Can that wait long enough for me to take a quick shower and get dressed?"

"The muffins were still warm when I bought them at Something's Brewing in town. They'll be fine, and it won't matter if the coffee gets cold since you've made a fresh pot."

He glanced out toward the backyard and put his sunglasses back on. "I think I'd better wait outside. You know, to make sure Mooch doesn't get in trouble."

Why did she think that was just an excuse? "It won't take me long."

She watched as he whistled the dog back to his side and then tossed a stick for Mooch to fetch. Watching the man and his buddy engage in some rough-and-tumble play held her riveted. Then, as if sensing her watching them, Nick looked up at her over the top of his sunglasses briefly before throwing the stick again.

Her face flushed hot, hopefully from embarrassment

and not from a little misplaced lust. She stepped away from the door. What was she supposed to be doing? Oh, yeah, a shower, and maybe a cold one would be a real good idea.

Nick chased after Mooch, both man and dog enjoying the game even though they'd already gone on a long run earlier. But after seeing Callie all rumpled and fresh from her bed, Nick had a whole new kind of energy to burn off.

Damn, that woman was temptation personified. Despite his firm resolve to keep things strictly platonic, it had been all he could do to walk back outside without kissing her senseless. Did she have any idea how sexy she was? His mind conjured up the image of her standing in the kitchen, her long legs tanned and bare, the thin cotton of her white tank top doing little to disguise the dusky tips of her breasts.

Nick tossed the stick as far as he could send it. While Mooch chased it down, Nick stared up at the bright blue sky. "Spence, buddy, I could sure use some help here."

No response, but then he wasn't really expecting one. Maybe he'd be better off concentrating on something else. He'd already done a thorough search of Spence's yard with the help of Mooch's nose. If someone had really been prowling the place last night, he hadn't found any sign of it. That didn't necessarily mean no one had been there. The gravel driveway wouldn't show any tracks, and neither would the porch and steps.

The two of them had also skirted the edge of the woods, looking for footprints or broken branches that would indicate someone had been there. No luck there, either.

Despite the lack of hard evidence, Nick wasn't yet ready to write it all off to some stray varmint setting off Mooch's hunting instincts. The one thing they hadn't done was to check Callie's yard, and there was no time like the present. He called Mooch back to his side and did a slow circle along the edge of the woods, studying the ground as they walked.

Again, the only boot prints were his. Feeling marginally better, he sat down on the swing while Mooch did some reconnoitering on his own. A few minutes later, the back door opened and Callie came down the steps carrying the bag of muffins and two steaming mugs of coffee.

He let her come to him but wasn't at all surprised that she sat down on the far end of the swing after handing him his coffee.

She held out the bag of muffins. "You pick first since you bought them."

Rather than argue, he snagged the blueberry. "It was hard to choose. That shop has an amazing selection of pastries. I might go broke sampling them all."

Callie laughed. "I know what you mean. I went to high school with the owner. Bridey worked as a pastry chef in a big restaurant down in California before returning to Snowberry Creek to open her own shop."

Nick bit into the huge muffin, the burst of flavor from the fresh blueberries making him wish he'd bought more. He eyed the bag that still held Callie's muffin.

"You'd better eat that quick because I'm not sure one will be enough for me. Besides, how else am I supposed to find out if I like the blueberry or the peach better?"

Callie immediately pulled her muffin out of the bag and held it out of his reach. "Too late, mister. By and large I'm not a violent person, but I'm not above smacking hands when it comes to defending one of Bridey's pastries."

Then she relented and broke off a piece and held it out to him. It was every bit as good as the blueberry. "Next time I'll know to buy two of each."

"I hate to tell you, but the raspberry and blackberry muffins and scones are every bit as good, so bring plenty of money when you go."

"I'll keep that in mind."

Nick settled back into his corner of the swing, content for the moment to enjoy the rich coffee and the rest of his breakfast. It pleased him that Callie didn't seem to be in a hurry to start her day's chores, either.

He stared up at the tall trees and the puffs of white clouds drifting across the blue sky. It didn't seem quite real to him. He'd been back in the States for weeks, not hours, but some part of him had yet to accept that he didn't need to be wearing body armor all the time.

"How weird is it, Nick? Coming back home after months of living over there, I mean."

Good question, one he had no easy answer for. But for Callie, he'd try. "You don't really live over there. You exist from one minute to the next, doing your best to get through one day after another. I tried not to keep count, but it's hard not to think about how many weeks or months are left until you can come home."

"I bet it's scary."

"Yeah, it is." He washed the memory of all the dust and dirt away with a sip of coffee before working up the courage to look at Callie. "But it's exciting, too. All that adrenaline pumping in your veins, living on the edge all the time. It's addicting."

"That's what Spence said, too." She chuckled softly. "Lucky for him, our old police chief had been in the service, too, because it always took Spence a while to remember he couldn't drive like a madman over here. I learned quickly to do the driving whenever the two of us went anywhere if I wanted to get there in one piece."

It felt good to be talking about his friend with someone else who'd known him so well. "Yeah, well, you haven't seen Spence at his crazy best until you've gone ripping through those narrow streets over there taking the corners like he was a NASCAR driver. The whole time, he'd have this huge grin on his face as he hollered insults at the locals."

Callie laughed, but at the same time her eyes welled up with tears. Nick understood her reaction. A volatile mix of emotions churned in his gut every time he let himself think about his friend. Sharing a funny story with Callie like this allowed the humor to break through, and he could enjoy the memories.

But later he'd feel guilty for being happy when Spence was dead.

Callie's hand settled over Nick's fist. "Spence would never want us to remember him only with grief. It's okay to look back and laugh."

She was right. And maybe someday he'd convince himself that was true. Time to get moving before he did something stupid, like pull Callie into his arms.

He wadded up the paper bag and dumped the rest of his coffee before handing the mug back to Callie. "Well, as my dad always says, those weeds won't pull themselves."

Callie was already on her feet and quickly blocked his escape. Without a word, she slipped her hands around his waist and gave him a quick hug. His own arms were running on autopilot and snapped around her, holding her close. He got lost in the sweet press of her feminine body against his, in the faint scent of vanilla from her shampoo and the flutter of her pulse.

Any words he might have wanted to share stayed tied up in a huge knot in his throat, but he suspected she understood all too well what he couldn't say.

They stood huddled together, taking comfort from each other. The embrace lasted for maybe a minute tops, but just that small contact eased the knot of Nick's pain. He had to let go, had to step back, before she stole yet another piece of his heart. He pressed a soft kiss against her temple.

"Thank you," he whispered and walked away.

Chapter 10

❦❦

Now, this was aggravating.

Callie frowned as she checked her notebook a second time. She had definitely listed a vase when she'd catalogued the stuff on this bookcase. The only note she'd made about the vase was that it had been blue. Closing her eyes, she tried to remember what it had looked like.

An image niggled at the back of her mind. Something about flowers. White maybe. Yeah, that was right. The vase had been about twelve inches tall, medium blue with a vine of white flowers that wound around the vase, starting at the bottom and ending at the top.

"So where is it?"

She looked around the room, but it was nowhere to be seen. There wasn't even a space on the shelf where she remembered seeing it. That spot now held a stack of books that she was almost sure hadn't been there before. A quick glance down her list confirmed that. Nope, no books on that particular shelf.

What was going on? It wasn't the first item that had come up missing since she'd inherited the house. When the attorney had met her at the house to go through it with her, they'd both noticed imprints on the carpet in a couple of places, as if things had been moved around.

Or taken.

As soon as that thought zipped through her mind, Callie quashed it. There was no reason to get paranoid. Another possible explanation would be that Spence had designated a few items to go to other people, and the stuff had been picked up after she and the attorney had gone through the house together. But if that was true, why hadn't he mentioned it? A simple call to check for sure would ease her mind.

Unfortunately, when she'd met with Troy to sign off on more paperwork the other day, he'd mentioned he would be out of town on vacation for a couple of weeks. He'd given her the number of another attorney who was covering any emergencies that came up while he was gone. But a missing blue vase, especially one she couldn't prove had actually been there in the first place, didn't exactly qualify as an emergency. The call could wait until after Troy got back.

At least this time she'd thought to bring her digital camera to add photos to her survey. She stepped back and took a shot of the entire bookcase and then did a close-up of each individual shelf. The front door opened just as she'd moved on to the items on the mantel.

Nick had been clearing out the front flower bed when she'd arrived. He'd had on a sleeveless T-shirt then, but he'd obviously shed it in the interim. Maybe it was wicked of her, but she couldn't resist snapping a quick picture of all that tan skin. One peek at the image on her camera had her giggling. The flash had startled Nick, giving him a slightly demonic look.

Still smoking hot, though. She snapped a second

shot just because. In this one, he looked considerably more disgruntled.

"Okay, let me see them." He closed the gap between them to look at the screen. "Tell me you'll delete those."

"I don't think so. I'm doing a photo survey of everything in the house, which includes you."

He made a quick grab for the camera and jumped back out of her reach. "In that case, we need a couple of shots of you, too."

She could just imagine how those would turn out. Holding her hands in front of her face, she gave in. "Okay, you can delete them. Just give the camera back."

A couple of clicks later, she lowered her hands to take back the camera, only to realize that was exactly what Nick had been waiting for. He snapped several more pictures of her before finally relinquishing the camera, a snotty grin on his face.

One look at the pictures told her why. Not only was her ponytail off center, but she had several smudges of dust on her white T-shirt and a matching one on her cheek. She quickly gave the delete button a good workout. "Okay, so can we agree that we're both a little camera shy?"

Nick reached out to wipe the dust off her cheek. "Agreed."

His touch left her tingling in places that were nowhere near her face. Swallowing hard, she followed him into the kitchen. "Where's Mooch?"

"He's sleeping in the shade out on the porch. I guess he wore himself out watching me work. Want a cold drink?"

"Sure."

Nick handed her a can of pop and then sat down at the kitchen table. "So what's with the camera?"

Callie showed him the list she'd been working on. "I'm doing a room-by-room inventory of all the furnishings, mostly to get some idea of what I have to work with. You know, if I decide to turn the house into a bed-and-breakfast, or even if I don't."

Nick stretched out his legs and leaned back in the chair. "That makes sense. This place is certainly big enough for what you're thinking about."

Sitting so close to him made concentrating on anything else hard, especially when he wasn't wearing a shirt. She forced her attention back to the problem at hand. "I think so, too. Anyway, I'd already started taking notes on things and then transferring the entries to a database on my computer back at the house. I thought I was being careful, but I've already found discrepancies."

"How so?"

She felt foolish for not being able to handle such a simple task. "When I've compared the printout of the database with the actual items, a couple don't match up. Either somehow I've marked them down in the wrong room or I was imagining they existed at all. This time, I'm taking pictures as I check them off the list so I can make sure I've gotten everything right."

Nick sat up straighter. "Are you saying things are missing that were here before?"

What was that odd note in his voice? "Maybe, although that doesn't seem likely. It's just that I could've sworn there was a blue vase on the bookshelf in the living room. It's not there now, but it could be that I marked it down in the wrong room or on the wrong shelf when I entered the data."

"Does anyone else have keys to the house?"

His question startled her. "My folks have a set, and the attorney might have a spare. Why?"

"This place has been vacant for a while. I was wondering if it was possible someone else had gained access somehow. That could explain how a few things might have gone missing. You know, someone taking the opportunity to lift a few things while the house was unoccupied."

One name immediately came to mind. "I suppose it's possible that Spence's uncle, Vince Locke, might still have a key. He hasn't lived in the house since Spence reached the age to take control of his inheritance. They had a huge fight over it, and Spence ended up needing the police to escort Vince and his son, Austin, off the property. They'd moved in with Spence right after his parents were killed in an accident."

She'd been away at college at the time, but her parents had told her all about it. "It was a really ugly situation. From what I heard, Spence offered to let Austin stay on, but he left with his father."

Nick's expression turned stone cold. "Spence didn't talk much about his family situation, but it was clear that there was bad blood. Something to do with Spence being adopted and his uncle calling him a mongrel."

"How awful," she said, flinching at the horrible choice of words. "He never told me that, but considering his uncle, it doesn't surprise me. Spence didn't look at all like his adoptive parents, but there was never any doubt that they loved him unconditionally. You can see it in all the family photos scattered around the place."

She paused to think about how much more to share. "This house had been in his mom's family for a couple of generations. An elderly aunt left it to her several years before she and her husband adopted Spence. When they were killed, Vince evidently thought the house should have gone to him or at the very least to his son, Austin, because they were blood relatives."

The memories of how Vince had treated Spence still had the power to have her seeing red. "That man was the reason Spence spent so much time at my house when we were growing up." Enough about the past. "I'd better get back to work."

Nick finished his drink and stood up. "Let me know if you need any help. Otherwise, I should get back outside before Mooch thinks I've forgotten about him."

Then he winked at her. "Also, I don't want my boss thinking I'm slacking off. She promised to feed me if I do a good job."

"Don't kill yourself out there, Nick. I'm not that good of a cook."

He laughed. "Anything beats a microwave dinner, which is my main dependence when I have to fend for myself."

"I can definitely do better than that."

She reached for the camera and her list, intending to pick up where she'd left off in the living room. Before she'd gone three steps, Nick stopped her.

"As long as I'm staying here, I doubt anyone would be foolish enough to try to sneak into the house, but the locks on these doors are old and easy to jimmy. I'd feel a lot better if I changed them all before I leave. Would that be all right with you? It shouldn't be too expensive to put in dead bolts on the doors, but the locks on the windows could stand to be updated as well."

Troy had suggested that same thing when he'd taken her through the house, and she'd been meaning to call a locksmith. "Are you sure, Nick? Not about the work needing to be done, but about you taking on another big project for me. I'm more than glad to pay for the locks and whatever else that might be needed, but I hate that you're wasting your leave helping me."

"Let me worry about that, Callie. I want to help."

He stared down at his hands as he flexed them. "And maybe I just need a reminder that these are good for something besides pulling a trigger."

Before she could think of what to say, he was gone.

Buying the locks provided a convenient excuse for Nick to make a trip to town without Callie needing to know his real purpose for going. She had offered to let Mooch stay with her, saving Nick from having to ask her if she'd mind keeping an eye on the fur ball. While he had no problem with the dog riding shotgun with him, he didn't like Callie being alone in Spence's house right now. At the very least, Mooch would warn her if anyone came snooping around.

He cruised through town, swinging by the building that housed both the Snowberry Creek City Hall and the police department. The chief of police's parking spot was empty, which was disappointing. He drove on toward the small hardware store a few blocks farther down the street.

The woman at the counter pointed him in the direction of the locks. Callie hadn't said if she was operating on a budget, but it didn't matter. He would pay for the damn things himself if it came to that. It didn't take long to pick out the best locks the store had to offer, and Nick bought out their entire supply of window locks. Hopefully, it would be enough to secure the ground floor. He would order more once he knew how many windows the house had.

Back out in the truck, he considered his options. It didn't take a genius to know that Callie wouldn't appreciate him discussing her business behind her back. That wouldn't stop him, though. He owed it to Spence to make sure his woman was safe.

His woman, not Nick's. It was amazing how much

that truth hurt. He was definitely the understudy in this little play, not the star.

Pulling out of the parking lot, he decided he'd do one last pass by the police department. The parking lot was still empty, but as luck would have it, he spotted the police chief walking into the coffee shop. Should he stop or not? When a parking space opened up across the street, he took it as an omen that he should. More likely it was him grasping at straws for an excuse.

The coffee shop was empty except for Gage Logan and the woman behind the counter. They both glanced in his direction as soon as he stepped through the door.

"Do you have a minute, Chief?"

The lawman studied Nick for a second before nodding. "I need to meet my daughter at school in a few minutes. If you don't mind talking while we walk, I've got time."

"Sounds good, sir."

The police chief smiled. "Call me Gage. We don't stand on much formality around here, and 'sir' brings back too many memories of when I was in the army."

Nick gave him a long look, noting the air of quiet authority the man wore like a second skin. "I'm guessing special forces."

"And you'd be right, even if it seems like it was a lifetime ago. I'm having an iced coffee. What would you like? I'm buying."

"I'll have the same."

They waited in silence until their drinks were ready. Gage dropped a few bills on the counter. "Thanks, Bridey. By the way, this is Nick Jenkins. He's a friend of Callie's and served with Spence."

Bridey's welcoming smile faded a bit at the mention of Spence's name. "Welcome to Snowberry Creek, Nick.

I was sorry to hear about Spence. I went to high school with both him and Callie. Spence was a good man."

Her comment, meant to console, triggered a new stab of grief, but Nick hid it behind a smile. "That he was."

Gage led the way toward the door. "We'd better get going. My daughter nags if I'm late."

Grateful for the change in subjects, Nick asked, "How old is she?"

"Nine going on thirty." Gage shook his head with a rueful smile. "Seriously, I can barely keep up with her now. I can't imagine what it's going to be like when she starts dragging boys home."

Nick laughed. "Maybe some of that combat training you had will come in handy."

"Don't think I haven't considered it. So what's up, Nick? I'm assuming you didn't track me down to discuss the joys of being a single parent."

Nick waited until they were outside to broach the reason he'd sought out Gage in the first place. "I was wondering if you heard any more about Spence's uncle."

The lawman's demeanor changed instantly. "Why? Has there been a problem?"

Nick had to be honest. "Nothing I can prove, but last night my dog acted as if someone had been snooping around the house. I couldn't find any tracks or anything, but Mooch doesn't spook easily."

How much should he share? If he were going to stick around indefinitely, he would've waited until he had proof his suspicions were on target. But he couldn't afford to be that cautious, not when Callie would soon be back on her own. Even if she did adopt Mooch, the dog couldn't keep her safe all the time.

"I've noticed some marks in the carpet that look as

if pieces of furniture have been moved. Today Callie noticed a vase is missing. There's no sign of a break-in, and maybe all of this means nothing at all. I could be jumping at shadows and seeing a threat where one doesn't really exist."

"But maybe it does." Gage tossed the remainder of his drink in a trash can as they walked along. "I'll ask around and let you know what I find out."

They'd reached the school parking lot. A little girl broke away from a group of children waiting in a line by the front door of the building. She headed straight for them.

Gage tracked her progress as he scanned the surrounding area. Nick wondered if it was Gage's police training behind his vigilance or if it was left over from his days in the special forces. It was probably a combination of both with a healthy dose of concerned parent mixed in.

"Thanks for your time, Gage. I didn't tell Callie I was going to talk to you about this. I didn't want to worry her unnecessarily without solid evidence. I'm also going to replace all the old locks on Spence's house with dead bolts before I go."

Gage nodded in approval. "Good thinking. I'll make sure my men know to keep an eye on the place. Any idea how long you'll be staying there?"

"Not yet. I'll give you a call when I know for sure."

"Sounds good."

Gage's daughter had finally reached them. She gave Nick a quick look before staring up at her father. "You're late again, Dad."

The police chief made a show of checking his watch. "Cut me some slack, kid. You only got out of class five minutes ago."

"True, but that means you owe me a treat. That was the deal."

Gage stared down at his daughter. "Fine, Syd, but I think we need to set a time limit on this deal. Nothing under fifteen minutes counts."

She shook her head hard enough to have her braids flying. "Nope. Five minutes."

"Ten."

Gage sighed dramatically, but then he grinned at Nick over his daughter's head when she finally nodded. "She knows how to drive a hard bargain, doesn't she?"

He tugged on Syd's braid. "Okay, kiddo. Ten minutes it is. By the way, Sydney, this is Nick Jenkins. He's doing some work on Callie Redding's house for her."

Syd studied him with the same clear blue eyes that her father had. "Nice to meet you, sir."

"Same here, Syd." Nick chuckled. "Gage, I see what you mean about being called sir. I think I just aged a good ten years."

Gage smiled back at him and held out his hand. "Good talking to you again, Nick. Keep me posted on how things go. We're headed for my folks' place now, which is in the opposite direction from where we started. We'll talk again soon."

Nick nodded his appreciation. "I'll look forward to it. Now I'd better get back to the house. Daylight's burning."

And if he hurried, he might be able to get the rest of that front flower bed weeded and still have time to work on those locks.

Chapter 11

Austin didn't make a habit of stopping by Spence's place too often, so finding out the house was now occupied had come as quite a shock. Who the hell was that guy anyway? Not that it mattered, but Austin was majorly pissed off to learn some stranger had moved into the house. Their house. That was a definite problem, one Austin wasn't sure how to handle. And having that damn mutt sniffing around the place only complicated things.

At least right now the dog was inside with its owner. If either one of them came outside, he would have to make a fast run for his truck. He'd left it parked a short distance away on the dirt road that ran past the trees in back of the property.

For sure, he couldn't risk another near miss like last night; the dog had caught his scent when they'd unexpectedly come strolling back from Callie's place. The last thing he wanted to do was spook them into calling the police.

How was he going to tell his father about all this? The old man was still furious about the terms of Spence's will. Everyone in town acted like Spence was a big deal for getting himself blown up over in Afghanistan. To Austin's way of thinking, a real hero took care of his own. Instead, Spence had left everything to Callie.

Personally, Austin had never figured on seeing one penny of money from his cousin, but Vince Locke sure as hell hadn't seen it that way. As far as the old man was concerned, the two of them should've been the rightful owners all along. Blood meant more than a piece of paper that some fancy-pants lawyer wielded like a magic wand to change Spence from a stray into an official member of their family.

Looking back, Austin realized it had taken balls for Spence to call in the police to toss him and his dad out on the street. Sure, he'd offered to let Austin stay on. It had been damn tempting, but Austin couldn't turn his back on his own father like that.

All water under the bridge now. Now everything belonged to Callie, lock, stock, and barrel. Well, except for a few things Austin figured no one would miss. He'd had his eye on some more, but that plan had just gotten shot all to hell. He couldn't hang out in these woods around the clock waiting for another chance to slip into the old place unseen.

Between his job and checking in on his old man, Austin didn't have a lot of time to spare. With the job market like it was, he barely made enough flipping burgers to keep a roof over his own head, not to mention his father in cigarettes and liquor. Austin had considered cutting him off of both cold turkey, but that would only give the old man something else to bitch about.

It was time to get going. He'd told his boss he wouldn't mind working third shift for a while. The extra money from the shift differential came in handy. As he started to back away, the new tenant stepped out onto the front porch carrying a handful of tools. What was he doing now?

"Oh, hell, I can't believe it."

Dollars to dimes he was changing the locks on the doors. Austin had wondered when Callie would get around to doing that. He'd been surprised she hadn't done so first thing. He certainly would have. Maybe after all these years it wouldn't have occurred to her that he might still have keys to the place.

He stayed long enough to make sure that was what the bastard was doing. Sure enough, he was busy dismantling the old lock on the door. Well, if he thought that would keep Austin out, he was wrong. There were always other ways to break into a house or sneak out of one. He'd learned every square inch of Spence's place. It had been a matter of survival.

There was only a five-year difference in age between Austin and Spence, but Austin had spent his whole life with his old man, while his cousin had had to put up with the man only until Spence got old enough to throw them both out. Lucky bastard.

Austin had learned at an early age how to move quietly to avoid drawing the old man's attention and, worse yet, his temper. Right now, he put that hard-learned skill to work as he slipped back through the trees. On the way to his truck, he wondered about the relationship between the newcomer and Callie. Was that guy simply a tenant? If so, why was he doing all that work on the place? He couldn't have been there long, but already there were some major changes.

Maybe he was trading labor for rent. If so, it was too bad Austin hadn't known Callie was open to such an arrangement. He was good with his hands and would've been glad to fix the house up in exchange for living there. But considering how much time this new guy was spending over at Callie's place, maybe he'd also signed on to give her other, more personal services, too. The kind she wouldn't be interested in receiving from Austin.

Too bad about that. Callie was certainly pretty enough, but she'd always been firmly in the enemy's camp. Maybe that was a good thing, because it kept him from feeling too guilty about liberating a few things from the house. Tomorrow he had an appointment to meet with another antiques dealer to unload the last few items. He'd used several different dealers from all over the area to keep anyone from asking too many questions about how a man like him had come into so many nice things at once.

He'd pocketed the cash, doling out only a few bucks to his father along with a sad story about how little the items brought. The rest of the money would go into Austin's secret stash. Once he had enough, he'd be gone for good. He'd planned to drag this out for a while longer in the hopes Callie wouldn't notice if the odd item went missing now and then.

But now that she'd actually started fixing the house up, time was running out. He'd wait another few days and then make one last shopping trip through the place and call it good.

And if dear old dad didn't like it, too fucking bad.

Changing the lock was trickier than Nick had expected, which was why it took him so long to realize Mooch was growling again. He tightened the last screw and set the drill back down on the porch. Rocking back on his heels to study his work, he moved slowly, trying not to spook whoever was out there.

Damn, if he'd been back in Afghanistan, a mistake

like that could have cost him his life. Reaching into his toolbox, he palmed his sidearm and stood up.

"Get ready, Mooch. Let's nail the bastard this time."

The dog stalked down off the porch, his nose in the air as he tested the breeze. Nick waited until his partner made up his mind which way to go before following. They had a better chance of figuring out where their target was hiding if they kept their search low-key. But hunting alone like this, even with Mooch's help, felt as if he were patrolling the streets back in Afghanistan with a big target pinned to his chest.

Mooch made a sharp right turn toward the woods that ran along the back of the yard. By now, his nose was to the ground as he tracked their prey, while Nick kept his own eyes focused on the trees, looking for some sign of an intruder. Nothing. Evidently Mooch agreed, because he lost all interest in the hunt and wandered back toward the house.

Nick continued to wait and watch. Sure enough, a minute later an engine started with the same ragged sound he'd heard before. It had to be the same guy, making it the second time he'd been caught unawares by him. Well, not again. Tomorrow during the daylight hours, he'd do a little recon now that he knew where the guy had been hiding.

It was tempting to set a trap for him. Nothing fatal, just something that would alert Nick in time to catch the bastard before he had time to escape.

Heading back toward the house, he explained his plans to Mooch.

"Hope you don't mind a late night, dog. I was going to wait until tomorrow to change the lock on the back door, but not now. We'll take care of that chore tonight. I'll sleep a whole lot better knowing it's done."

The dog yipped in agreement. Nick laughed. "Yeah,

easy for you to say. You're not the one who has to do all the work."

Back up on the porch, he gathered up the tools and carried them around to the back door. Hopefully, this one would be easier now that he'd done it once. If not, he had a long night ahead of him.

Callie woke up feeling as tired as when she'd gone to bed, thanks to dark dreams that had left her too frazzled to go back to sleep right away. The details remained murky, but she remembered running through the woods looking for something.

No, not for something, but for someone. Nick.

Great. If that man was going to plague her night thoughts as much as he did her daylight ones, at least the dreams should be steamy and not scary. She wouldn't mind that at all. He'd kissed her only that one time, but it had been enough to whet her appetite for more. Unfortunately, he'd showed no inclination to indulge in a repeat performance.

He'd offered no explanation as to why he'd backed off, but there were times when she picked up a definite vibe of mutual attraction bouncing between them. It could be as simple as him not wanting to get involved because he wouldn't be sticking around for long.

But if that were the case, why didn't he say so? She knew all about the problems involved with short-term dating. Her whole working career had involved a series of moves. It didn't pay to invest a lot of emotional currency in a relationship when she already knew there was a deadline going in.

And it was way too early to be thinking this hard. Maybe a long run would help shake off the weirdness. After a quick shower, she put on track shorts, a tank top, and her running shoes. After stuffing her keys and some money in her fanny pack, she headed out-side.

A few quick stretches later, she set off down the driveway and turned toward town. Her plan was to put in a couple of miles before stopping in Bridey's shop to pick up some muffins for breakfast. A couple for herself and a few more for Nick. Satisfied with her plan, she cranked up her music and settled into a solid rhythm.

She hadn't gone more than a quarter of a mile before she picked up a companion. Mooch did a quick circle around her, his tongue hanging out in doggy laughter.

"Listen, dog, I could run faster, too, if I weighed what you do and had four feet instead of two."

But at the moment, all of Mooch's attention was fo-cused behind her, and his tail action kicked into high gear. Well, rats. She should have known the dog wouldn't be out here by himself. There was no reason to slow down to let Nick catch up with her. With those long legs of his, he'd overtake her soon enough.

Sure enough, a few seconds later he passed her be-fore turning around to jog backward, still keeping pace with her. Show-off. She rolled her eyes and kept run-ning.

"Good morning, Callie."

Not so far. "Good morning, Nick. You're out and about early this morning."

"So are you."

She gave up on listening to her music and pulled off her earbuds and stuffed them in her pack. "I woke up thinking some of Bridey's muffins would taste good for breakfast. I won't feel as guilty about eating them if I exercise first."

He finally turned to run beside her. "That's where I was headed, too. Mind if I keep you company?"

"Not at all, but you'll probably get bored at my pace."

Unless he had a thing for sweaty women. She supposed that was too much to hope for.

"In the army, we learn to adjust our pace to run together no matter what. A squad is only as fast as its slowest man." He gave her a quick grin. "Or woman."

The only saving grace was that Mooch made both of them look bad. He'd take off ahead to go exploring and then would come trotting back to see what was taking his silly humans so long.

When he did it for the third time, she asked, "Does he always go exploring when you're out on a run?"

"Nope, that's new. Back in Afghanistan, he'd stick right beside us every step of the way. Maybe somehow he's realized that it's unlikely that there's a sniper hiding in the bushes around here, not to mention the chance of triggering an IED is pretty minimal."

She nearly tripped. What must it have been like for Spence and his friends to live with that kind of threat hanging over their heads twenty-four/seven? It sure explained why Nick's eyes were never still, always scanning their surroundings for any hint of a threat. That instinct for survival must be nearly impossible to turn off, considering he'd been home for a while now and yet maintained a constant vigil.

At least Nick hadn't had any more flashbacks around her, but that didn't mean much. He'd been so embarrassed by hitting the deck when the lawn mower backfired, it was doubtful he would tell her even if he was having problems.

Before they turned the corner onto the main street through town, she was glad when Nick clipped on Mooch's leash. There wasn't much in the way of traffic, but it was better to be safe. The coffee shop, Something's Brewing, was one of the few businesses open this early. Even so, most of the parking spots were taken, a clear testament to the popularity of Bridey's place.

Nick slowed down to jog in place. "I usually do another two-mile circuit, but we can stop now if you'd rather."

He hardly sounded winded, the rat. Well, she might not be up for another two laps through town, but she could do one.

"I wouldn't want to ruin your routine. But I'm warning you, Nick, if Bridey has run out of the peach muffins when we get back, I won't be happy."

He laughed and resumed running. "Guess we'd better get going, then."

All things considered, Nick was just as glad to cut his run short, not that he'd admit it to Callie. A man had his pride, but he'd been up much of the night. The second lock hadn't taken him all that long to install, but he'd been unable to unwind enough to sleep.

Knowing there had been eyes out there watching the house, watching him, had brought back the familiar burn of adrenaline, ramping up all his predatory instincts. The compulsion to hunt the enemy had kept him and Mooch out prowling the woods until well after midnight. He just wished he knew if the threat was real or if it was all in his head.

Despite hitting the rack so late, he'd been awake since before sunrise. He'd been sitting on the front porch steps with his first cup of coffee when Mooch had sounded the alarm that Callie was on the move. He hadn't planned to run this morning but couldn't deny the dog the chance to spend time with her. After all, the more attached Callie got to Mooch, the better the chance she'd be willing to give the dog a permanent home.

Lucky dog.

But Nick was definitely feeling the lack of sleep. As soon as they finished their outing, he'd take a long shower and then crash for a couple of hours. But tired or not, running with Callie felt damned good. They continued through the town past the school Gage's daughter attended and on out beyond the high school football field. Nick slowed at the corner for a logging truck to rumble by before crossing the street. Mooch sat down and waited patiently for the all clear to cross.

As they turned back toward the business district, Callie nodded toward the dog. "I hadn't thought. We can't take Mooch inside the shop."

"You're right. We could tie him up outside, but he hates that. If you trust me to get the right muffins, I'll go inside and get our stuff to go."

"Sounds like a plan." Then Callie pointed down the street. "There are a couple of picnic tables over by the creek where we can eat unless you're in a hurry to get back to the house."

"No hurry. Let's enjoy the sunshine."

"Great!" She held out her hand for the leash. "Mooch and I will go stake out a spot and wait for you there."

When he handed off the leash, he asked, "One muffin or two? And if there aren't any peach left, what flavor do you want?"

"I'll take two, although I shouldn't. Blueberry or raspberry are my second choices, and I'd like a tall drip, two sugars, light on the cream."

"Got it."

They separated just short of the coffee shop. After she took off with Mooch, Nick slowed to jog in place, unable to resist enjoying the view. Callie ran with a smooth gait, but right now he was more interested in the way those shorts cupped her backside than in how she moved. Hot damn, he'd like to spend hours running his hands along her body.

And he had no right to be thinking that way.

"Sorry, Spence," he murmured. With renewed resolve to behave himself, he stepped into the cool interior of the coffee shop.

Luck was with him. Bridey had just taken a batch of peach muffins out of the oven. He ordered six to go along with his iced coffee and the drip Callie wanted. He'd keep any leftover muffins for breakfast in the morning—if they lasted that long.

"Have a nice day, Nick."

"You, too, Bridey." He picked up his bag of muffins, which smelled heavenly. "I might have to take up running full-time if I keep coming in here."

She laughed and handed him his change. "Try working here. If I had a lick of sense, I'd close up shop and run with you. Unfortunately, I need to make a living and these babies don't bake themselves. Tell Callie hi for me."

"Will do."

He turned in the direction of the small park, walking fast rather than running to avoid spilling the coffee. It didn't take him long to spot Callie, but she wasn't alone. She was talking to a man, and there was no sign of Mooch anywhere.

Didn't that damn mutt know he was supposed to act as chaperone when Nick wasn't there?

As he watched, the man took off his ball cap and used it to wave at someone hidden by a tall stand of bushes. Nick's irritation faded slightly when he realized the intruder was the police chief. Sure enough, a few seconds later, Mooch came bounding into sight with Gage's daughter holding the dog's leash and running hard to keep up.

Mooch was obviously having a great time, too. Come to think of it, this was the probably the first time he'd ever had the chance to play with a child. As Sydney's happy laughter rang out across the park, Nick stopped to enjoy the moment.

"Spence, your dream for Mooch looks like it's playing out just the way you imagined it would."

He realized Callie was watching him with a puzzled look on her face, probably worried that Nick had gotten lost in the past again. As he started forward, it occurred to him that it was Saturday, which probably accounted for the chief of police's casual attire. No doubt it was his day off, and he was out for a morning walk with Syd.

However, that didn't explain why the man was standing so close to Callie. The man had to be a good ten years older than she was. What was he thinking?

Hopefully not about how good she looked in those track shorts and with her hair up in that ponytail, emphasizing the graceful curve of her neck. Holding the bag of muffins and the coffee tray with a white-knuckled death grip, Nick hustled faster. No use in letting the coffee get cold, right?

Mooch finally spotted Nick, barking happily as he charged toward him, dragging Syd along in his wake. She waved as soon as she recognized him.

"Hey, Nick! You didn't tell me you had such a cool dog!"

He wasn't sure about the cool part, but right now the dog was acting like a complete idiot. He'd already circled around Nick twice, effectively tying his legs together with the leash.

"Mooch! Settle down."

The dog ignored him, clearly too caught up in the joy of having a new playmate to behave. If he kept this up, Nick was likely to take a header. Just what he needed with both Callie and Gage watching. At least the lawman wasn't laughing, although Nick suspected it was a struggle. Callie, on the other hand, had a big grin on her face as she waited to see how he'd manage to extricate himself without spilling their breakfast on the ground.

He tried again, this time barking Mooch's name like an order. "Mooch, sit. Now."

The dog belatedly realized that he was in trouble and immediately dropped to the ground. He wasn't completely repentant, because his tail was doing a slow sweep across the grass as if he were plotting his next attack.

"Syd, can you untangle Mooch's leash for me?"

"Sure thing."

As soon as she was done, she and Mooch were off and running again. Such simple pleasures. He envied them.

Chapter 12

❧❧

When everyone was seated at the picnic table, Callie handed out the napkins and then divvied up the peach muffins.

"Are you sure we're not stealing your breakfast?" Gage asked. "Although I'm not sure I care. I love these things."

"I get that," Nick said, smiling. "But I bought extra. If I'd known you were going to join us, I would've bought you one of those iced coffees you like, too."

Gage got busy peeling the paper off his muffin. "I've already had one this morning while I was making rounds."

Their conversation came as a surprise. Callie knew the two men had met the day Gage had stopped by when Nick had been mowing the grass. It seemed unlikely that conversation would have included a discussion about their coffee preferences. If they'd run into each other again, it seemed a bit odd that Nick hadn't mentioned it.

She wasn't a suspicious person by nature, but something was telling her that any other meeting between

Nick and Gage hadn't been by accident. The only question was which one had sought out the other. If she'd had to guess, Nick had gone looking for the lawman at some point in the past few days. If they didn't explain themselves on their own, maybe she'd corner Nick about it later.

"Syd, slow down before you choke yourself. At least pretend you have some manners." Gage tugged on his daughter's braid and softened his comment with a smile.

Gage's daughter had been about to take another bite, but she slowly lowered the muffin back down to the table. Looking genuinely perplexed, she apologized. "Sorry, Dad. You always say that it's rude to keep someone waiting, even if you do it all the time yourself."

Then she pointed at her furry friend. "Mooch is waiting for me."

Nick coughed and covered his mouth, probably trying to disguise his smile. Sipping her coffee served the same purpose. It was amusing to watch the big, tough police officer fumbling for an answer.

Gage shook his head with a sigh. "You're right, of course, Syd. It is rude to keep someone waiting, which is why I apologized for keeping you waiting at school. However, in this instance, I'm sure Mooch won't mind waiting a little longer for you to finish eating."

Then he gave her a hard look. "But before you take off running, you might want to ask Nick if it's okay. He and Callie might have plans that don't include hanging out here watching you play."

Syd's eyes widened in worry as she swallowed her last bite. Until she could talk, her eyes bounced back and forth between the three adults.

"Can I please play with Mooch a little more?"

Nick held up his coffee. "I can't run and drink this at the same time. I'd really appreciate it if you'd give Mooch a good workout while I finish my coffee. That is, if it's all right with your dad."

"Go ahead, Syd, but stay in sight."

The little girl bounced up as if she were spring-loaded. "I will, Dad. Thanks, Nick."

She and Mooch were off and running. The three adults watched them for several seconds. As promised, Syd turned back before they reached the bend in the creek. Evidently satisfied that the pair would follow the rules, Gage picked up his own muffin and peeled away more of the paper.

"I swear I can't remember ever having that much energy, but my mother says I was worse."

Callie watched as the little girl threw a stick for Mooch. When he returned it, she petted him and then threw it again. "Syd is adorable, Gage. You and her mother must be so proud of her."

"I am." As he spoke, Gage stared down at the muffin in his hand. "Her mother is no longer with us."

Nothing like stomping on what was obviously a painful memory. Callie instinctively reached out to put her hand on Gage's wrist. "I'm sorry, Gage."

His eyes were bleak when he met her gaze. "Thanks. At least I have Syd to remind me of her."

Callie didn't know what to say. She happened to glance toward Nick only to realize he was staring at her hand, which still rested on Gage's arm, with the oddest expression on his face. What was he thinking that had him looking so angry? When he realized she was watching him, he got up and walked a short distance away, shifting his focus away from her and Gage over toward where Mooch and Syd were playing.

Moving slowly, she withdrew her hand from Gage's

arm to pick up her drink. She'd only meant to offer Gage a small bit of comfort, nothing more. And what business was it of Nick's anyway? After taking a second sip of her coffee, she set it back down. Right now not even some of Bridey's best tasted good.

Maybe it was time to get back home.

She stood up. "If you'll excuse me, Gage, I should get going."

Nick must have heard her, because he started to turn around. She headed him off at the pass. "Don't cut Syd's time with Mooch short because of me. I'll see you both later."

She dropped her coffee and half-eaten muffin in the trash and jogged off down the path back to the road through town. Maybe later she would be able to figure out what had just happened, but this hot-and-cold crap with Nick was getting old.

When she was out of sight, she paused long enough to turn on her MP3 player before resuming her run. She picked a playlist that featured all of her favorite female singers. Right now, she was in no mood to listen to anything the male half of the species might have to say.

"Don't look at me, dog."

Nick laid on the couch and stared up at the ceiling. "I know I'm an idiot. I don't need you to remind me."

Mooch woofed softly from his position on the back of the couch. He laid his head down on his front paws, his dark eyes watching Nick's every move.

"Callie did nothing wrong. It was all me."

Whoever said confession was good for the soul didn't know what the hell they were talking about. No matter how many times he admitted his actions had driven Callie away that morning, he didn't feel one iota better about it. Of course, maybe she should be the one he apologized to, not the silent emptiness that surrounded him.

After she'd taken off, he'd hung around with Gage for another half hour trying to act as if her desertion hadn't mattered. Unfortunately, Gage had a cop's talent for reading people and saw right through his ruse. He'd waited until Syd had surrendered Mooch's leash to Nick before saying, "I don't know what happened just now with Callie, Nick. And God knows I'm no expert, but I always find groveling works best."

Then with a wave, he and his daughter walked away, the girl babbling happily about what fun she'd had playing with the dog. Mooch had whined as they left, clearly preferring Syd's company to Nick's. But after a couple of tugs on his leash, the dog had given in and joined Nick on the run back to Spence's place. They'd spent the afternoon working in the yard, stopping only when hunger had driven Nick inside.

As tired as he was, he couldn't risk talking to Callie right now. Maybe after that nap he'd been promising himself all day, he'd be in better shape to face her. He could only hope so.

The trouble was he was still too wired to relax, maybe in part because this place held so many reminders of Spence. Sure, Nick got a real kick out of all the pictures of his friend as a kid; on the flipside, he could see the man in the boy, in the kid's wide grin and gleam of devilment in his eyes. God, he missed his friend. He rolled over onto his side, hoping to find a more comfortable position. If that didn't work, he'd try sleeping somewhere else, maybe using a couple of blankets to make a pallet out on the porch.

As soon as he forced his eyes to close, the image of Callie's hand resting on Gage's arm popped into his mind. No doubt that had been her way of apologizing to the man for treading on what obviously had been a sensitive subject. But even if that were true, Nick didn't like it, not one bit. Watching her touch another man had twisted in his gut like a knife.

And how fucked-up was that? He had no claim on her and would be driving away soon, leaving Snowberry Creek and everyone in it in his rearview mirror. Gage might have no interest in Callie, but that wasn't the real issue. What mattered was that he'd still be there when Nick was gone. Who knew what would happen then?

Son of a bitch! Nick sat up, frustrated and angry, mostly with himself but also with the situation. He'd come here to honor his friend and to find a home for Mooch. Two sides of the same coin. A simple enough mission.

So maybe he should start thinking about all of this in terms of an objective to be reached, no different from any other mission he'd been assigned over the years. He needed to assess the situation, look at it from all angles, figure out what needed to be done, and then get busy.

Grabbing a pad of paper and a pencil, he headed outside to study the yard and then the house. The grass would need mowing again soon. He jotted that down. The front beds were weeded, but they wouldn't stay that way unless he put down some decorative bark or gravel. So noted. Both of the side yards needed work, nothing he couldn't finish in a long afternoon. They each got added to the list.

That left the backyard.

Which reminded him. "Come on, Mooch. Let's see if our late-night visitor left any tracks this time."

The dog bounded off toward the trees. Halfway there, he froze briefly before charging forward again, barking his fool head off. No doubt a contingent of squirrels had once again invaded his territory. Nick let him have his fun while he did some hunting of his own.

Making his way just inside the edge of the trees, he studied the terrain to pick out the optimal position for watching the house. It seemed doubtful that anyone staking out the place would stand where he could see only the back door. Nick kept moving, studying the ground and even the bark on the trees in hope that the intruder had left some visible sign of his presence.

Nothing.

Nick moved deeper into the trees. The view was more restrictive, but the thicker foliage would provide better cover. An experienced hunter weighed all the options and chose what best fit his purpose.

Even though this was the back of the property, the house was situated in such a way that it faced the thicket that ran along the shared property line with Callie's house. Since this stand of trees faced the short end of the house, it was possible to see both the front and backyards pretty much from one position.

It was what Nick would do if he were on the hunt. He slowed down to study the ground inch by inch. No footprints. No broken twigs, no overturned rocks or convenient threads caught on the rough bark of the firs. But someone had been there. Maybe. Hell, he didn't know. Granted, Mooch had thought so, too, but he could have just as easily been reacting to some four-legged varmint. All of this was new to the dog, so anything was likely to set him off.

And after living on high alert for months, Nick's own inability to shut off his hair-trigger reactions to strange noises could have him jumping at shadows. He wished like hell he could convince himself he'd imagined the whole thing. The lack of hard evidence should trump the distant sound of an engine starting, the only other indication he'd had that someone had been watching the house. Sheer stubbornness kept him moving deeper until the trees thinned out again.

"Well, what do you know."

The fresh tire tracks provided at least some vindication. He stepped out of the trees to study the narrow dirt road. A short distance to the left, it came to an abrupt end. He had to guess that in the other direction it would lead back toward one of the back roads. Either way, he'd been right about someone being back there.

He wished the knowledge made him happier, but those tracks didn't answer the questions about who had been behind the wheel and what they'd been doing there in the first place. Worst-case scenario, someone was watching the house, but it could just as easily be a couple of teenagers looking for a bit of privacy. He grinned. He and his high school girlfriend had spent a lot of quality time parked on a road just like this one.

Good times and good memories.

He'd learned all he could for the moment. Mooch sat a short distance away staring up at a squirrel. The tree-climbing rodent stared right back, its tail flicking back and forth as it chittered loud insults at the dog.

"Come on, Mooch. Ignore the little bastard. We've got work to do."

Nick kept walking, figuring the dog would catch up with him eventually. Back in Spence's yard, Nick dropped down on the back steps to work on his list. After writing down everything that needed to be done, he thought about what he could accomplish on his own. He studied the yard as it now existed and thought about what changes he would make if it were his. There was a whole world of possibilities that Callie could do without it costing too much. The place could be a real showcase. It didn't take long before he was sketching out some suggestions for Callie.

He flipped back to the list of basic cleanup work he'd offered to do. Even if the weather cooperated, it would take him the better part of a week to finish just that much, and he hadn't even gotten around to the house itself.

How long did he want to stay? He had a few weeks left before he had to report back, thanks to a combination of accrued leave and time off for his arm to heal completely.

Okay, stupid question. A better one was how long could he stay without getting even more emotionally tangled up in Callie's life than he already was.

As if he'd conjured her up from his dark thoughts, Callie came walking around the corner of the house. "So this is where you're hiding."

"I wasn't aware I was. Hiding, that is."

Although that was exactly what he'd been doing. Unwilling to actually lie to her face, he kept his focus on the paper as he finished his notes before looking up again. "Did you need something?"

"No, actually, but I thought you might. I was about to start dinner and wondered when you'd be over. It's such a nice night, I thought I'd fix some steaks and roasted veggies on Dad's grill."

Now he felt like more of a jerk than ever. "You sure you still want to feed me?"

She motioned for him to scoot over on the step to make room for her. "That was the deal, wasn't it? Grub for drudgery?"

"Pretty much." He had to laugh. "And in that case, I'd be delighted to collect my pay."

"Good." She stared into the distance, avoiding looking at him at all while she spoke. "So there are two ways we can do this, Nick. You can either fix your plate and come back over here to eat by yourself or you can stay for dinner and tell me what was going on in your head this morning. Your choice."

Never let it be said that Callie couldn't play hardball when she wanted to. "Look, I know my moods can be a bit unpredictable."

Her laugh had nothing to do with humor. "You think? One minute we're fine and the next you're looking as if you need to punch somebody. What was up with that? At the very least, I thought after you cooled off, you'd be over to talk about it."

How could he explain that he'd been fighting a bad case of jealousy without sounding like even more of a jerk? When he didn't answer, she pushed herself back up off the steps.

"Well, then. Dinner will be ready at about six. You have my number. Let me know if I should set the table for two or if you want yours to go."

Nick stared after her until she'd disappeared into the woods leading back to her parents' house, not even protesting when Mooch trotted after her. He didn't blame the dog one bit for deserting him. He didn't much like his own company right now himself.

He put a few finishing touches on the sketches before heading back inside. Maybe a cold shower would clear his head enough so that he could figure out a way to make things right between him and Callie. He hoped so.

"Mooch, I'm not sure I did the right thing by putting your buddy on the spot like that. But I hate never knowing what to expect from him."

The dog wagged his tail and bumped against her leg

in a show of support. She savored that little bit of comfort. However, as much as she liked Mooch, it wasn't his touch she was craving.

She adjusted the flame on the grill and put the steaks on to cook. While they sizzled, she set the picnic table for two, using paper plates in case Nick chose to go back into hiding. The trouble was that even if Nick couldn't come up with a rational explanation for his behavior, she already knew she wouldn't send him away.

Stupid, but there it was.

So far her cell phone had remained silent, and it was almost six. As she brushed the zucchini and asparagus with olive oil and arranged them on the grill, it finally buzzed. He'd texted instead of calling. Great. Was he afraid to even talk to her?

But one glance at the message had her popping the tops on a couple of beers. He was on his way over, bringing his explanation with him.

Mooch took off toward the woods, barking like crazy. She automatically touched her hair, hoping it still looked okay. Even though this was supposed to be another dinner between friends, she'd felt compelled to take a little more care than usual with her appearance. A touch of lipstick, a hint of blush, and a nicer shirt with her jeans.

Who was she trying to impress?

As soon as Nick stepped out of the woods, she was glad she had made the effort. His hair was still damp from a shower, and his shirt looked freshly ironed. She hoped like heck she wasn't drooling.

To her surprise, he held out a bouquet of fresh-cut roses. "I thought you might like these. They're from Spence's yard."

She breathed deeply of their sweet scent. "His

mother had a beautiful rose garden. I'm surprised they've survived after being neglected for so long."

"They're a bit ragged, but they should come back with the right care."

"I'll go put these in water. Can you keep an eye on dinner for me?"

"Sure thing."

Inside, she hunted up one of her mother's vases for the roses. Already the scent was perfuming the air. She drew one last deep breath of their rich scent as she stared out the kitchen window at Nick. He looked so at home flipping the steaks on her father's grill, like he belonged there. Too bad he'd be leaving soon. For the first time in ages, maybe ever, she was tempted to break her rule about avoiding short-term involvements.

But she had a gut feeling that a short-term fling with Nick would have long-term effects on her heart. It might be far wiser to keep things casual with him, more like the easy friendship she'd always had with Spence.

The steaks must be ready because he was reaching for one of the platters she'd brought out for them and the veggies. Time to rejoin the party.

He turned to face her, his eyes bright with emotion. "I didn't like seeing you touch Gage. I apologize for being a jerk."

Her heart did a slow roll in her chest. Well, then. She suspected she shouldn't be pleased by his explanation, but she was. Still aiming for casual, she kept her response short. "Apology accepted."

Just that quickly, the tension between them disappeared. When he joined her at the table, she passed him a baked potato and the steak sauce. "I don't know about you, but I'm starving."

"Me, too." He added some asparagus and zucchini to his plate before handing it off to her. "About Spence's house. Your house, actually. I think the whole place could end up being a real showcase. I've been working on a list of what still needs to be done to the yard if you'd like to see it. Better yet, after we eat, maybe we can do a bit of a walk-through so I can show you exactly what I'm thinking."

It would be interesting to see how closely his vision matched hers. Either way, she couldn't wait to see what he had in mind.

"I'd like that, Nick. I'd like it a lot."

Chapter 13

⚜ ⚜

By the time the two of them had cleaned up the few dishes from dinner, the sun was starting to slip away for the night. No matter. This far north, it should be light enough to navigate the yard for a couple more hours.

Nick picked up his notebook and waited for Callie to rejoin him. As soon as she stepped outside and locked the door, his pulse kicked into hyperdrive. She'd changed into a long-sleeved shirt made out of some kind of clingy fabric that emphasized all of her, um, attributes. He feigned an interest in Mooch's explorations long enough to give himself a chance to settle down.

"Come on, mutt. We're headed back next door. Play your cards right, and I might even feed you."

The dog might not understand much English, but his vocabulary definitely included every word that had to do with food. He barked happily and came running. He passed them by at a run, circling back every so often to hurry them along.

Back at Spence's house, Nick filled Mooch's bowl and gave him fresh water. He patted the dog on the head. "We'll be outside for a while."

He wanted some alone time with Callie, though being jealous of the dog was even more stupid than being jealous when she'd offered Gage the simple comfort of her touch. Stupid or not, he couldn't deal with any competition right now.

"Look, Mooch, I'll handle this patrol on my own. Finish your dinner and then enjoy some downtime. I promise to make it up to you later."

At the moment, Mooch was more interested in his kibble than he was in anyone else's problems. At least the food kept him distracted long enough for Nick to get back outside alone. He headed toward Callie, who was walking around in the circular flower bed located in the driveway turnaround.

She smiled up at Nick. "You've worked a miracle out here. I'm so glad this many of Spence's mother's roses survived, even if they're in rough shape. I'll have to add a few more to do this space justice."

He stood close enough to feel the warmth of her skin. "I think I saw a photograph upstairs that was taken out here. Maybe you could take it to one of the local nurseries to see if they can match the roses that used to be here."

The suggestion clearly pleased her. "I'll do that."

Then she looped her arm through his. "So show me what you're thinking."

They made a slow circuit around the front yard before moving on to the sides, talking ease of maintenance and color spots. By the time they reached the backyard, his list had almost doubled in length.

"If it were me, I'd put a gazebo in that back corner.

If you do turn the place into a bed-and-breakfast, it would be a perfect place for your guests to enjoy the garden, even on rainy days."

Callie's smile was a bit wistful. "I can just see it, but I doubt there'll be room for something like that in the budget, at least not right away. For sure, I'm going to get bids for having all this yard work done."

She leaned her head against his shoulder. "I appreciate all the thought you've put into this. To be honest, I'm feeling a bit overwhelmed by everything that needs to be done. I don't have any experience working with contractors at all. Would I be better off hiring a general contractor to oversee everything?"

"That's what most people do. The only downside is that you'd be paying his profit on top of all the subcontractors, too. The upside is that the best general contractors know which ones to use. That alone can be worth the price."

Unless Nick himself stuck around long enough to get it all organized for her. His father had taught him a lot over the years in the hope that someday Nick would let him add "and Son" to the name of his company. Had he pretty much given up on that happening anytime soon? Nick had.

Staring toward the back corner of the yard, he imagined how the gazebo would look there. Not only would it be perfect for any future guests Callie might have, but also he could imagine other, more private, uses for it.

Heck, it wouldn't take him all that long to build one. A few days at most. Even if he never got a chance to try it out himself, he liked the idea of leaving behind something that would bring him to mind every time Callie saw it. First thing tomorrow, he'd download a couple of patterns and then price out what the materials would cost him.

"What's got you thinking so hard?"

No way he was going to share that—not yet, anyway. "Just trying to think of anything I might have left off the list for the yard. If you'd like, tomorrow we can go through the house together. I should be able to give you a general idea of what needs to be done as far as basic repairs. Maybe that will help you prioritize the work when you pick a contractor."

"That would be great, Nick, but I still feel bad about you spending so much of your leave working on all of this stuff. Surely there's something a lot more fun you could be doing right now."

Oh, man, he really wished she hadn't said that, because all kinds of fun ideas popped into his mind, all involving her and a certain part of his anatomy that was now sitting up and begging for attention. At least it was now getting dark enough that the sudden change in the fit of his jeans wasn't obvious.

"I'm right where I want to be, Callie."

His words seemed to please her. She took his hand in hers and gave it a quick squeeze. "I'm glad you're here, too, and not just because you mowed my grass."

The light was quickly fading, but he was pretty sure she'd blushed as she said that. Could it be that the attraction he was feeling wasn't all one-sided? Even if it was, he shouldn't act on it. His conscience had him withdrawing his hand from her grasp.

"Look, maybe I should walk you home now. It will be completely dark soon, and I've got . . ."

What? To get away from her before he gave in to the impulse to kiss her? He tried again. "I've got stuff to do."

Callie's stance went rigid. "What kind of stuff, Nick? What kind of pressing engagement do you have this late in the evening? You know what? Never mind. It's obviously none of my business."

Without waiting for him to answer, she walked away. When he started to follow her, she spun back. "I'm a big girl, Nick. Believe it or not, I've managed to walk from Spence's house to mine all by myself for years now."

He coasted to a stop, watching her stalk away, caught between his duty to Spence and his hunger for Callie. Okay, he'd managed to piss her off big-time, but he wasn't about to let her walk through the woods in the dark unescorted. What if the lurker was back?

Screw this. He'd see her home if it killed him.

She'd already disappeared from sight by the time he reached the woods. A short distance in, something moved in the brush off to his right, followed by a loud screech. His mind told him it was a cat on the prowl, that there was no real danger.

But right now reality had nothing to do with how he was feeling. He charged forward, determined to reach Callie, to make sure she was safe, to make sure the enemy didn't steal another life. Once again he'd left the house without a weapon, but he'd kill anything or anyone who threatened her—with his bare hands if that was what it took.

There. He could see her moving in the shadows a few yards ahead of him. If she was aware of his pursuit, she gave no sign of it. At least, not until she cleared the woods. Then she turned to face him, her eyes glittering with anger.

"I told you I could get home on my own, Nick. What about that did you not understand?"

How could he fix this?

The minute he opened his mouth to try, the words came pouring out. "It's dark out now. Too many shadows to hide in. Had to watch your back."

He was breathing hard and fast, thanks to his

adrenaline-soaked fear. "Go inside. I'll patrol the perimeter. If everything is secure, I'll leave. I promise."

She backed away several steps. "Nick, are you all right?"

Fuck no, he wasn't. "Doesn't matter. Won't hurt you. Not ever. Go inside," he repeated. "When you're safe, I'll retreat."

She rocked back and forth, clearly waffling on how to respond. Then she surged forward, closing the distance between them. Despite his protests, she wrapped her arms around Nick's waist and laid her head against his chest. At that moment, he couldn't have said whether the full-body contact would soothe him or destroy him.

Gradually, her words made it past the roar in his head. "Nick, you run so hot and cold. One minute, we're chatting like old friends. The next you're backpedaling like crazy and making up lame excuses to get away from me."

Her scent clogged up his senses, making it even harder to think. But then he didn't need to think, only feel. He wrapped his arms around her, tightening his hold on her so that there wasn't room for a single thought between them. He nuzzled her hair, loving its silky texture against his skin.

"Nick? What's going on?"

That question had no easy answer, so he asked one of his own. "Do you want me to pack up and leave, Callie? Just say the word, and I'm gone. Right now. Won't wait until morning."

He held his breath, dreading her answer. At least she didn't immediately let go.

"No, Nick, I don't want you to leave, but you've got to quit sending me such mixed signals. I know the reason you came here was because of Spence and to find a home for Mooch. If all you want is to be just friends, fine. I can live with that, especially knowing that you'll be leaving soon."

She finally looked up at him. "But I've got to tell you, Nick, you're not acting like a man who is only interested in being friends. Tell me I'm not completely misreading the situation between us."

Resting his forehead against hers, he whispered, "You're reading me loud and clear, Callie, but that doesn't make it right."

Her eyes flashed hot and angry. "Make what right?"

He tightened his hold on her. "This. You're hurting over what happened to Spence, and I'm your only connection to him. His death left a gaping hole in both our lives."

Even in the faint light from the newly risen moon, the pain his words caused her was clear. Son of a bitch, he hated hurting her. She'd been through enough already. They both had.

He let go of her even though it was the last thing he wanted to do. "Go inside, Callie. I'll be all right. So will you. It will just take time."

"But—"

"Now, Callie, while I have the strength to let you walk away."

"Fine, I'll go, but there's one thing before I do."

Before he could ask what it was, she'd captured his face with her hands and dragged it down to plant a hungry kiss on his mouth. Instantly, all thoughts of duty, honor, and loyalty blew apart, leaving nothing behind but the need for this woman. Callie's touch and Callie's taste kept him grounded as the world around him exploded. Her arms held him steady. Her body gave him warmth. Her kiss gave him so much more.

But gradually the world around them righted itself,

and all the reasons he shouldn't be doing this came rushing back. He was visiting Spence's hometown, staying in Spence's house, and sleeping in Spence's bed. Above all, this was the woman Spence wanted to spend his life with.

The truth pounded in Nick's head over and over again like a heavy barrage of artillery fire: Spence's life, not his. And the price of admission to this roller-coaster ride?

The death of his best friend.

God, what was he doing here? Nick didn't want to hurt Callie with a full-out retreat. Slowly, he banked the fire and stepped away.

She started to follow him, but he held up his hand. "Go inside, Callie. I'll see you tomorrow."

If he was still there. Right now, even that much was uncertain. At least this time she didn't argue. He watched until the kitchen light came on. Making good on his promise to check the perimeter, he did a slow patrol around the yard, front and back, being careful to keep to the shadows. More than once he saw her at a window, tracking his progress around her family home.

He held it together until he entered the path back to Spence's place. Without either Callie or Mooch to keep him focused, the last of his control shattered. His chest ached with the need to howl out his pain, but he held it in. He'd already upset Callie enough for one night. If she heard him, she'd either call for the medics or the cops or both.

Neither of them needed that.

He'd learned to control his fear in war; he could do the same here. But once he was through the woods, he was going to do what any good military leader did in the face of overwhelming odds. He would call in reinforcements.

Chapter 14

❧ ❧

"Damn, Nick, do you know what time it is?"

He quickly did the math and grimaced. At least Leif didn't sound as if he'd been asleep, despite the three-hour time difference.

"Sorry, man. I wasn't thinking."

That much was true. He'd hit Leif's number on speed dial the second he'd cleared the woods. He kept walking, using his friend's voice as an anchor to stay focused in the moment. Right now it would be all too easy to shred the thin fabric of reality that separated the present from his past, leaving him caught up in the hell of combat.

While he listened to Leif grumbling, Nick safely navigated his way across the yard to the front porch. Objective achieved. As soon as he opened the front door, Mooch bolted outside, almost knocking Nick down as he charged out into the darkness.

"I'm assuming you called for a reason, Sarge, not to keep me hanging on the line listening to you breathe." At least Leif sounded more concerned than irritated. Although they'd talked a couple of times since Nick had hung up on him the other day, he'd made sure to keep the conversations low-key and focused on what they'd heard from the rest of the squad. Right now Nick was having trouble focusing on anything at all.

"What?" Nick pinched the bridge of his nose as he struggled to think. "Oh, right. How's the ankle doing?"

His friend's laughter rang out. "Seriously, Nick? You called me at twelve thirty in the morning to ask about my ankle? What the hell is going on? Where are you?"

Nick sank down onto the steps, relieved to have even this tenuous connection with his friend. "Yes, I called to see how you were doing. I'm still at Spence's, and I thought maybe you might be up to flying out here to help me build a gazebo."

This time the silence came from the other end of the line. Nick waited him out. It didn't take long.

"Are you serious? A fucking gazebo?"

As serious as death, but Nick rephrased it for his friend. "Yeah, unless you have something better to do these days."

He could hear Leif shifting around on the other end of the line and the soft whirr of a motor. Maybe he was using the button on his hospital bed to sit up.

"Okay, then. Let's see. My ankle is healing as well as can be expected, which isn't saying much. The docs say I'm better off if I use it, but I can't be on it for very long without it hurting like hell."

Nick grimaced at the reminder of how close he'd come to losing not just Spence, but Leif as well. He shut his eyes tight and crossed his fingers that he didn't sound as needy as he felt. After all, he'd survived that last patrol mostly intact, physically anyway. "So is that a no?"

"Not necessarily. They are planning on booting me

out of here tomorrow, so the rest of my rehab will be outpatient."

Leif's voice was sounding stronger now. Maybe he had been asleep after all. "Let me check with the powers that be on this end. Maybe they can arrange for my therapy out there, at least short term."

The knot in Nick's stomach eased up. "Thanks, man, but I wouldn't want to interfere with your rehab. If you can't swing a hammer, you can always sit and watch. As I recall, sitting on your ass was always your specialty anyway."

"Screw you, Nick," Leif said with no real heat. "We both know Spence and I did all the work."

God, he'd missed exchanging insults with his friends, missed them all giving one another a hard time. The three of them had turned it into an art form. "Fine, if you want to sign on as supervisor, that's okay with me."

"Supervisor sounds boring and beneath my skill level." Leif chuckled. "I'm thinking along the line of Gazebo God as my job title, even if I'm not quite sure what the hell a gazebo is in the first place."

Nick laughed, feeling better than he had in hours. "Well, almighty-godlike one, let me know what you find out. If you can work out the details, let me know when and where to pick you up. The nearest commercial airport is in Seattle, but the air force base is a lot closer."

"Will do. But one thing, Nick. When I get there, you're going to tell me what's really going on in that thick skull of yours. Promise?"

"Yeah, I promise. Now, get some sleep."

"I will if you will. I hope I see you soon, Sarge."

"Me, too, Leif. Me, too."

He disconnected the call and whistled for Mooch to come back inside. They could both use a good night's sleep. First thing in the morning, he'd track down a good design for the gazebo and get started. He'd have to haul ass if he wanted to have everything delivered and ready to go by the time Leif arrived, assuming he could get there at all.

But one way or the other, that gazebo was going to get built.

Callie entered the crowded Creek Café and looked around. She finally spotted Bridey in the back corner booth. Wending her way through the clutter of mismatched tables and chairs, she was stopped by several people along the way, mostly friends of her parents, but a few were ones she'd gone to school with.

A full five minutes later, she finally slid into the bench across from her friend. "Thanks for meeting me on such short notice."

Bridey shrugged her shoulders. "Not a problem. Besides, if I wasn't here, I'd be back at the shop trying to balance the books. This is a far more relaxing way to spend my afternoon off."

A middle-aged waitress stopped to take their orders. Anyplace else Callie would have asked for a few minutes to make up her mind, but here there was no need. Other than the prices, nothing much had changed on the menu at the Creek Café in decades.

"I'll have a burger, fries, and a chocolate shake."

Bridey surrendered her menu. "I promised myself I'd have the salad, but we all know that's not going to happen. Let's keep it simple. I'll have the same."

When they were alone again, Bridey gave Callie a curious look. "So what's going on, Callie? I don't mind an impromptu outing now and then, but you sounded a little frazzled on the phone. Is that new hottie you've got stashed in Spence's house causing you problems?"

Callie's cheeks burned hot. "I didn't stash Nick any-where. He showed up on my doorstep unannounced and uninvited. As it turns out, he came to pay his re-spects to Spence, but also to find a home for Mooch."

"The dog I've seen him with?"

"Yeah. Back in Afghanistan, Mooch got shot one night when he warned Spence's unit about someone waiting to ambush them. They got the dog patched up and then adopted him into their unit. I guess Spence was in the process of making arrangements to have Mooch shipped back here to the States when he was . . ."

She let her words fade away. They both knew what had happened to keep Spence from completing that particular mission himself. "Anyway, that's why Nick drove all the way here to Snowberry Creek. I suspect he thought I'd have a harder time saying no to the dog in person."

No matter what, she would have given Mooch a home. Come to think of it, she hadn't told Nick of her decision. Maybe because that would give him one more excuse to leave.

Bridey's eyes crinkled at the corners. "So if you didn't want him to hang around, why invite him to stay right next door? One night was one thing, but it sounds more like he's moved in."

That was a question with no good answer. "He of-fered to mow the grass."

This time Bridey didn't bother to hold back her laughter. "And his ability to push a mower around is all you're interested in? Because if that's true, send him over to my place. Believe me when I tell you my yard could use some work."

Then she waggled her eyebrows just to make sure Callie got the point. Bridey was most likely teasing, but then again, maybe not. Neither one of them had had a

date in a very long time. Bridey was right about Nick
being a hottie, but he wasn't up for grabs. Time to stake
her own claim.

"Down, girl. The only mower I'm interested in him
using is mine." Then she snickered. "Well, technically
it's my dad's, but that's wrong on so many levels. Besides, you live in an apartment."

"Picky, picky." Bridey laughed right along with her.
"So considering the way he looks at you, mutual attraction isn't the problem."

At least Callie wasn't the only one picking up that
vibe from Nick. It didn't do much to improve her
mood, but at least she hadn't been wrong on that point.
What to do about it was a whole different ballgame.

"I like Nick." She paused to choose her words carefully. "Maybe I could even like him a whole lot."

"So? You're single. I'm assuming he is. What's the
hang-up?"

Leave it to Bridey to go right for the heart of the matter. "Any number of things, starting with I don't do
short-term flings. Been there, done that, burned the
T-shirt."

Bridey's smile faded. "Yeah, I get that. But what
else?"

"I can't get a solid read on him. It's like he's attracted
to me, but at the same time it makes him mad that he
feels that way."

There was more, like the times he seemed to get
caught up in what had happened back in Afghanistan.
That was his private business, nothing she would share
with anyone, not even Bridey. She knew from past experience when Spence would come for a visit that it
often took soldiers time to readjust to living outside of
a war zone. He used to do his best to hide it, but she
could always sense when he was struggling.

Just like she did with Nick.

"So have you tried just talking to him? Primitive, I know, but sometimes communicating actually works."

Not so much. "We parted on pretty awkward terms last night, but he promised to see me today."

She picked up her paper napkin and began folding it into smaller and smaller squares, anything to keep her hands busy. "But when I stopped by Spence's place this morning to see if Nick or even just Mooch wanted to go on a run with me, his truck was gone. Nick still hadn't returned when I left to come here."

The waitress was back with their burgers and shakes. By unspoken agreement, they suspended the discussion while they ate. No life crisis was worth letting a Creek-burger go cold.

It wasn't until they were each down to their last few fries that they started talking again.

"So did you go inside to see if his stuff was gone?"

The thought had crossed Callie's mind, but she hadn't been able to muster up the courage to check. "No, I didn't. I guess this will sound stupid, but since Nick's been basically living there, it would have felt like I was trespassing or something."

And if he caught her snooping around, she wasn't sure if he would forgive her.

"Maybe he needed to talk to Chief Logan again."

Callie had been about to eat her last fry, but she let it drop back down on her plate. "Again? When did Nick talk to Gage?"

Bridey frowned. "It was at the end of last week. The chief stopped in my shop for his usual iced coffee on his way to meet his daughter. He bought one for Nick and said they could talk as long as Nick didn't mind walking over to the school with him."

"Did Nick say what he wanted to talk about?"

"If he did, I didn't hear it, but I was in the middle of the afternoon rush. Do you think it's important?"

"No, not particularly. On the other hand, it does explain why Nick knew Gage liked iced coffee on Saturday when we ran into him and his daughter in the park."

It was time to wrap this up. Nothing had been settled, but it had felt good to share some of this with Bridey. "Well, I should let you get back to adding your numbers."

Bridey rolled her eyes. "Thanks a lot. Some friend you are."

Callie reached for the bill. "To make it up to you, I'm buying."

Her friend protested. "You don't have to do that. Besides, aren't you unemployed right now?"

Thanks to Spence, money was the least of her problems at the moment. "I invited you, so it's my treat."

"Fine, but the next time you stop in the shop, the muffins are on the house."

"Agreed, even if it means I'll have to add more distance to my morning runs."

They stepped out into the afternoon sunshine and walked toward where Callie had left her car parked. Before they parted ways, Bridey gave her a quick hug.

"Hang in there, Callie. If you need to talk, you know you can call me anytime, day or night."

"Thanks, Bridey. That means a lot."

She managed a small smile for her friend. "I'm probably seeing issues where there really aren't any. Nick's not here to stay and is probably as skittish about getting involved short term as I am."

"Maybe, but maybe not. Let me know how it goes."

Callie climbed in the car and rolled down the window. "I will, and thanks again for meeting me for lunch. It was fun."

"We should do a girls' night out soon. Maybe call Melanie and see if she wants to join us next time she's back in town."

"Sounds good."

Callie pulled away from the curb as Bridey walked on down the block toward her shop. She waved at her friend one last time as she drove past. Still in no hurry to get back home to find out if indeed Nick had actually left, she headed for the grocery store to pick up a few things.

An hour later, Callie pulled into the driveway only to discover she had a visitor. He was just stepping out of the woods coming from the direction of Spence's house. Considering he was wearing a uniform, she could only assume that he was another one of Spence's army friends stopping by to pay his respects.

He stopped walking as soon as he spotted Callie's car, probably not wanting to worry her. On second thought, maybe that wasn't it at all. He was leaning heavily on a cane, and the lines bracketing his mouth spoke to the amount of pain he was in. She turned off the engine and hurried to greet him.

When she got within a few feet of him, she took note of the way his uniform hung loosely on his frame, as if he'd recently lost weight, and saw that his tan had a sickly gray undertone. When she coupled that with his leg injury, she was positive that she was about to meet Spence's other best buddy, Leif Brevik.

"Leif? I'm Spence's friend Callie."

His smile became more genuine. "Right on the first guess. What gave me away? No, don't tell me. I can only imagine what all Spence told you about me—well, besides my dazzling good looks and obvious charm."

She grinned and stuck out her hand. "Let's go with that and that he threw in a mention of your humility for good measure."

Leif shook her hand, his laughter sounding a bit rusty. "I'd tell you not to believe anything he or Nick told you about the three of us, but unfortunately I'm guessing most of it was true."

"Don't worry. Your secrets are safe with me. Spence made me pinky-swear that I'd keep anything he told me to myself. Something about all of it being classified, although why bar brawls would be top secret is a bit of a puzzle."

Leif winked at her. "Only because what our superiors didn't find out about couldn't hurt us."

"Ah, now, that makes sense."

She looked past him toward the path. "Did Nick send you over to say hi?"

"He wasn't expecting me to get here so quickly, but I hit it lucky and caught a flight just a couple of hours after he called me to come. He wasn't home next door, and I was hoping you might know where he is. I tried his cell, but it went to voice mail."

A bit of her earlier worry returned. What was Nick up to that he wasn't taking calls from one of his best friends?

"I haven't seen him or Mooch today, but I've been gone. Why don't we go in the house so I can put my groceries away, and then I'll try calling him again. If he doesn't answer, at least we can wait inside, where it's more comfortable."

Besides, the way Leif was looking right now, if he didn't sit down soon, she might be picking him up off the ground. He glanced past her toward the house.

"Actually, if you don't mind, I'd just as soon wait out here on that swing. I just flew in from D.C., where it was hotter than blazes. It will feel really good to spend some time outside in the fresh air."

"Make yourself comfortable. As soon as I get the perishables put away, I'll bring you out a sandwich and a cold drink. Pop or beer?"

He was already hobbling in the direction of the swing. "Pop, but you don't have to wait on me, Callie. That's Nick's job. He's the one who invited me."

Thank goodness Leif had his back to her. She wouldn't have wanted him to see how that last bit shocked her. Nick had sent for Leif without telling her? Granted, she'd given him free run of the house next door, but she hadn't expected that meant he could invite all his friends. Not that she minded Leif being there, particularly. She was more interested in what was going on in Nick's head right now.

Did the invitation mean he intended to stay longer? And why would he ask Leif to fly all the way out to Seattle from Washington, D.C., especially when it was obvious Leif shouldn't really be traveling at all?

Oh, yes, they were definitely going to be having a talk—and soon. She grabbed the bags out of the car and headed up the back steps. Before making Leif's sandwich, she dialed Nick's number. Just as Leif said, it went right to voice mail. Fine, she'd take Nick up on his invitation to leave a message.

"Nick, this is Callie. Your buddy Leif is at my house. Imagine my surprise to find out we were expecting a guest. Anything else going on I should know about? And where in the heck are you, anyway? I'm really worried—"

She caught herself before she blurted out that it was him she was concerned about. "That is, I'm worried about Leif. He looks like a stiff breeze might blow him over."

After disconnecting the call, she slipped the phone in her pocket. She threw together a couple of sandwiches, added some chips, and then grabbed a couple of cold drinks.

She rolled her shoulders, trying to shake off the tension before rejoining her unexpected guest. Even if Nick deserved the sharp side of her tongue, Leif didn't. Sooner or later, Nick would show up, and then she'd deal with him.

Outside, it looked as if it was going to be sooner. Before she'd reached the bottom step, Mooch came bolting out of the woods, heading straight for Leif. If the dog was here, Nick couldn't be far behind.

Okay, let the games begin.

Chapter 15

❧ ❧

"Mooch, damn it, get back here!"

Too late. The dog had feinted toward the porch and then veered away to haul ass toward Callie's house. Granted, the pesky animal had spent most of the day cooped up in Nick's truck and needed a good romp, but not yet.

And not right toward Callie.

He'd meant to call her, but after he'd already left the house he'd discovered that he'd left his cell on the kitchen table. If he'd known how long it was going to take to round up all the supplies and equipment he'd need to build the gazebo, he would've gone back for the damn thing.

Had Callie been over to the house looking for him? After the way they'd parted last night, maybe not, and he wouldn't blame her. Right now, he was more worried that he had missed calls from Leif. Nick ran inside and grabbed the phone off the table and then took off running after the mutt. If Callie wasn't home, the dog would have circled back by now.

No doubt she was over there waiting for him to

show up for that talk he'd promised. In between stops on his supply run, he'd played out various scenarios in his head, trying to come up with a comprehensive battle plan. Yeah, that probably wasn't the right way to approach the situation, but he was a soldier after all. Or at least he had been one.

As soon as he cleared the trees, he knew he was well and truly screwed. Out of the three pairs of eyes now turned in his direction, none seemed particularly happy to see him. Mooch was too damn excited about Leif's unexpected reappearance in his life to care much about Nick being there. Fine, he could understand that.

Leif, for his part, glanced up from petting Mooch long enough to give Nick a "WTF?" look. Nick sent one rocketing right back at him. *Yeah, same to you, buddy. How the hell did you get here this quickly?*

Nick reined in his temper, though, after he got a good look at his friend. The man looked like hell, like death warmed over, and generally like shit. Obviously Leif wasn't nearly as far down the road toward recovery as he'd led Nick to believe. Something else he'd kick Leif's ass for as soon as the man could stand up long enough for Nick to take aim.

"You're back."

Callie put enough chill into those two words to shrivel a man's pride and joy. Damn, this wasn't going well at all. Nick had always found that admitting to a screw-up sometimes bought more mercy from those higher up the food chain. He wasn't sure it worked that way in civilian life, but short of hunting down a sword and throwing himself on it, he didn't know what else to do.

"My bad, Callie." He held up his hands to signal his surrender. "I should've called you this morning. I didn't know my errands would take this long, and I left my cell phone on the kitchen table."

She jerked her head in Leif's direction and arched an eyebrow. Okay, then. Evidently he wasn't done groveling.

"I asked Leif if he could come give me a hand with a project I want to finish before I leave, something I was going to surprise you with. But I didn't know he was going to get here this soon."

He shot his friend a hard look. "He was supposed to call and let me know if the army docs would even let him travel this far. Obviously, he forgot that part of our conversation."

Leif didn't look at all apologetic. He was taking pleasure in watching Nick scramble to make things right with Callie.

"I didn't have time to call because I would've missed my flight. I hitched a ride on a cargo plane flying into McChord. As it was, they were already starting to close the door when I got there. Five more minutes and I would still be sitting on my ass back in D.C."

"Yeah, well, I'd say you barely made it anyway. You look like hell."

Callie gasped. "Nick, could you be more of a jerk right now?"

Yeah, he could, but he was also smart enough not to say so. Leif knew it, too. He smirked in Nick's direction when he was sure Callie wouldn't notice.

"Don't worry, Callie. The idiot knows how I feel about him."

It was true. War brought out either the best in men or the worst. The friendships forged in that hellfire maintained their strength and integrity through the worst life could throw at them. And God knows, the two of them had been through their own special hell recently.

Callie divided her attention between him and Leif for several seconds. Evidently whatever she saw convinced her he'd told her the truth, because some of her tension eased.

She held up her paper plate. "I left the sandwich makings out on the counter. Help yourself if you're hungry."

Nick was hungry all right, but not for bologna and cheese. Another thing he kept to himself. "I'm fine. After Leif finishes eating, we'll head next door. It's time for our afternoon nap."

Once again Callie gave him an incredulous look, her eyes narrowed in suspicion. "Really? A nap?"

Leif backed his play. Sort of. "Well, not all us big, tough army types need naps to get through the day, but Sarge here is delicate. You don't want to be around him if he doesn't get his afternoon snooze followed by a snack of milk and cookies, preferably some homemade chocolate chip or oatmeal raisin."

Callie giggled at the hopeful smile that accompanied that last part. She gathered up their empty plates and drinks. "Right. Well, you two toddle off. Be back at six, and I might even feed you a real meal."

"I'll take you up on that. The only meal Nick ever fixed for me was an MRE, and I'm not talking about when we were in Afghanistan."

Leif held up his hand as if taking a solemn oath. "Seriously, we were at his apartment in Ohio, and he hands me one of those foil packages. I tossed it back at him and ordered pizza."

She gave Leif a sorrowful look. "Oh, dear, I thought you guys loved those things, and I stocked up on them at the local surplus store this morning. Certainly Nick hasn't complained about eating them every day. Guess I'll have to come up with a better idea for dinner tonight."

Leif looked suitably horrified. Nick struggled to keep a straight face but couldn't hold it for long. When he cracked up, Leif looked both a little pissed and a whole lot relieved.

Nick held up his hands again. "Sorry, Leif, but the look on your face was priceless. Come on over next door, and I'll make it up to you with a cold beer and a comfortable bed."

"At least that's a start." Leif turned his attention back to Callie. "Thanks for putting up with me until Sarge got back. I'm glad to finally meet you in person."

"Me, too, Leif."

Nick stood back while his friend hoisted himself up out of the swing. He was worried Callie wouldn't be able to resist leaping forward to help him, which would only embarrass Leif. Instead, she planted her feet to steady the swing to give him a firmer surface to push off against.

As Leif started the long walk back to Spence's, Nick hung back long enough to mouth "Thank you," and then added, "Can we have that talk later?"

She stared after Leif, watching him as he hobbled along, each step clearly an agony. "That will be fine."

Nick called Mooch to his side. "Thanks, Callie."

As he walked away, she called his name. "Nick? Is it okay if I bring dinner over there? It would be nice to get out for a while after being shut up over here all day."

Smart woman. If she brought the food to Spence's house, Leif wouldn't have to make another trip to Callie's house. And knowing his friend, he'd insist on doing exactly that rather than allowing Nick to drive him next door. Pride made a guy do foolish things.

Like building a gazebo for a woman whose heart might belong to another man. Swallowing the sour guilt and pain that cost him, Nick sent a silent apology winging skyward to Spence's memory. For now, he needed to concentrate on getting Leif settled in.

"Thanks, Callie, if you're sure it's not too much of a hassle. I was going to ask you to come over anyway. I have something to show you, and it will be easier over there."

"What is it?"

He winked at her. "It's a surprise."

One he really hoped she'd like. "Come on, Mooch. We don't want to wear out our welcome."

Breaking into a jog to catch up with Leif, he called back, "See you at six, Callie."

Chapter 16

❧ ❧

Watching Leif struggle up the few steps to the front porch left Nick wanting to punch something. Better yet, he wanted to hunt down the bastard who'd planted that fucking IED in the first place. Granted, Leif was lucky not to have lost his foot in the explosion, but damn.

Right now it was all Nick could do not to toss Leif over his shoulder and carry him up to the porch fireman-style. The only thing stopping him was knowing Leif would rather hurt than ask for help. Pride was something they both understood.

The hard part would be fixing up a place for Leif to sleep. The bedrooms were all on the second and third floors, and right now Nick couldn't imagine his friend being able to haul his ass up all those steps. Of course, stubborn bastard that he was, Leif might just insist on trying it anyway.

Leif was breathing hard by the time he made it up onto the porch, his face covered with a thin sheen of sweat. He sagged against one of the pillars as Nick stepped around him to unlock the door. Mooch bolted inside, nearly tripping both men in the process.

"Damn it, dog, be careful."

After Leif shuffled into the house, Nick picked up his friend's duffel and carried it inside. At least Leif let him do that much for him.

"Have a seat in the living room, and then I'll grab us a couple of cold ones."

Leif slowly lowered himself into an easy chair. Nick pushed an ottoman over so Leif could prop up his injured leg. When he was finally settled, he let out a long sigh. "Better make mine nonalcoholic, Sarge. I'm overdue for my pain meds, which don't mix well with anything stronger than pop. They already knock me on my ass."

Nick grabbed two cans of root beer, a bag of tortilla chips, and a tub of salsa. After putting them in easy reach for Leif, he flopped down on the couch. Time to ask the hard questions. He studied the boot on Leif's foot. The bulky contraption was made out of some kind of heavy-duty plastic with Velcro straps. It looked like something the Stormtroopers in *Star Wars* would have worn.

"So how bad is it? And don't bother lying about it, soldier. I want the truth."

Leif focused on opening a bottle of pills he'd pulled out of his pants pocket. "Bad enough. Not as bad as it could've been. Getting better. Some, anyway."

After downing a couple of tablets with a swig of root beer, Leif laid his head back against the chair and closed his eyes. "The docs weren't sure at first they'd be able to save it, but that particular crisis is past as long as I'm careful with it."

Seriously? "And bouncing around in a cargo plane

for twenty-eight hundred miles fits your definition of being careful?"

The jerk actually smiled. "Yeah, maybe it wasn't my most shining moment. At least I'm here and in one piece. More or less, anyway."

He opened one eye briefly. "So tell me, what's going on between you and Callie? And don't bother lying about it. I want the truth."

Having his own words thrown back at him didn't help Nick's mood one bit. "Nothing is going on. I came here hoping she'd offer our boy Mooch here a permanent home, something neither one of us can give him."

Leif managed to look both disappointed and disgusted at the same time. "All of that could have been accomplished by e-mail. Even if you felt as if you had to do it person, that doesn't account for why you're still here."

The man was just like Mooch, growling as he worked hard to get every bit of meat off a new bone. Nick waved his hand around to indicate their surroundings. "Spence left Callie his family home. She's thinking about turning this place into a bed-and-breakfast but knows squat about the remodeling business. I don't have anywhere to be right now, so I've been doing some of the grunt work in cleaning up the yard. I also promised to go through the house with her to give her an idea of what all needs to be done."

That eye was open again. "Fine. That makes sense but doesn't account for why you needed me to come out or how all of that translates into a burning need to build something for her."

The pills must be fast acting, because Leif's color had improved; he was also breathing easier. Good. Maybe now he could get some rest.

Leif's smile had taken on a slightly dopey look. "And don't think I haven't already texted the rest of the squad to tell them our fearless leader has a burning desire to build a gazebo."

He snickered, shaking his head as he did. "Seriously, Sarge? A gazebo."

Great. Nick would be getting grief about this from every corner of the world once the word got out.

"Yeah, well, payback is a bitch, Corporal. Wait until I post pictures of you swinging a hammer on said gazebo."

Leif rattled his pill bottle. "I can always claim it was the drugs. What's your excuse?"

Nick shocked them both by giving an honest answer. "Spence grew up in this house. Maybe I think fixing it up will help preserve his memory or maybe I want to leave a little piece of myself here when I leave, something that you and I have built to leave a permanent mark on the place. Hell, Leif, maybe I just need to help Callie any way I can. You know, for Spence."

It was the first time since he'd returned to the States that he could admit some of what he was feeling. His parents meant well, but they'd never met Spence. To them, he was a familiar name, but nothing more. They were sorry about his death, but they had no real understanding of how profoundly it had affected Nick.

Not that he wanted them to know. It was enough that he carried the burden of guilt over Spence's death. They didn't need to share in his pain. No one did, not even Leif, although he clearly did. He hadn't said so, not in so many words, but it was there in the way Leif flinched at the mention of Spence's name.

Focusing on the faded wallpaper on the wall that surrounded the fireplace, Nick did his best to reassure his friend. "You do know that none of this is your fault, Leif. You're not the one who left Spence behind. That was all me."

No response. Nick braced himself to face the well-deserved recriminations, only to discover that Leif had drifted off to sleep. Or maybe simply passed out from the potent combination of drugs and exhaustion. Good. A few hours of rest would do him a world of good.

Leif's body needed time to heal. Hopefully, his mind would follow suit. Before he'd been transferred first to the hospital in Germany and then on to an army hospital stateside, Leif had broken down, pleading with God to explain why Spence had to die in Leif's place. What a screwed-up way of looking at what had happened, but, then, who was Nick to talk?

Spence died because Nick had left him lying defenseless in the street. Leif might always walk with a limp because Nick had managed to get them separated from the rest of their patrol. He'd been trying to lead everyone away from a withering barrage of fire, but the insurgents blew up a wall that blocked the way for the vehicles behind them. No one could have predicted that, but that didn't make it hurt any less. The bottom line was his faulty judgment had cost his friends and their loved ones dearly.

Leif stirred briefly, his face contorted in pain. Nick couldn't sit there and watch his friend hurt, so he headed back outside. Mooch could stand guard while Nick vented some of his frustration on the overgrown bushes and weeds in the backyard.

After two hours of sweating in the sun, Nick gave up and went back inside. Although he had a pile of debris big enough to fill the yard wastebin twice over, Nick's mood hadn't improved at all. After using his T-shirt to wipe the river of sweat off his face, he poked his head in the living room to check on Leif.

Mooch wagged his tail slowly and whined softly. Leif hadn't moved at all in the time Nick had been outside. He'd wait to wake him up after he took his shower. Callie would be coming over with dinner in a little over an hour. Leif might want time to clean up and change out of his uniform before they ate.

Nick headed upstairs, taking the steps two at a time. After stripping off his clothes, he ducked into the shower and cranked it up to full. The stinging blast felt great. He was tempted to linger but kicked it into high gear to make sure there was enough hot water for Leif. At least the downstairs bathroom had a small shower stall in it, forestalling any need for him to climb the stairs.

After toweling off, Nick put on some cargo shorts and a clean shirt. Slipping on his flip-flops, he headed back down to the living room. Leif was awake and talking to Mooch.

"Well, dog, you seem to be adjusting to life in the States. I think you've even put on a couple of pounds."

Nick joined the conversation. "Considering how much chow that mutt packs away every day, I'm surprised he's not the size of a small horse by now. Probably would be if I didn't take him running most mornings."

As soon as the words slipped out of his mouth, Nick grimaced. There would be no running for Leif for the foreseeable future. The trouble with sharing close quarters with someone for months at a time was that they learned how to read each other's thoughts.

"Don't sweat it, Nick. You can't watch every word you say around me."

Leif lifted his foot down off the ottoman, biting his

lip as he did so. "Is there a bathroom down here or do I need to go upstairs?"

"There's one in the utility room off the kitchen. Let me bring your duffel over to you. Once you've picked out what you need, we'll get you headed in the right direction."

After dragging the duffel over by the chair, Nick perched on the ottoman while Leif rooted through his things for his shaving kit and some clean clothes.

"Can you get that boot wet?"

"No, but I've gotten good at keeping it dry by covering it with a plastic bag and taping it closed. I brought a couple with me, but I'll need to pick up some more if I'm going to be here any length of time."

"Add whatever you need to my shopping list on the fridge."

Once Leif had laid out the stuff he needed for his shower, he scooted to the front edge of the chair and braced himself to stand up. It was damn hard to sit by and watch his friend struggle, but Nick had to trust that Leif would let him know if he needed help. That's what he would have wanted if the situation were reversed.

It crossed his mind that there was one thing he could do to help. He hustled to the kitchen to dump the odds and ends he'd brought back from the hardware store out onto the counter. Then he took the empty plastic bag back to the living room and loaded all of Leif's gear in it.

"Here, that should make it easier to carry everything."

Leif accepted the bag without comment. "Which way?"

"Through there," Nick said, pointing toward the kitchen. After his friend got up a good head of steam, Nick followed along behind.

"Don't hover, Nick. I've been taking showers by my-self since I was five."

Okay, then. "Promise me you'll holler if you need me, and I'll back off."

"Yeah, yeah." Leif kept shuffling forward. "The nurses made the same offer, and they were a lot better looking. I'll tell you the same thing I told them. Every inch I give is one I won't get back. So short of falling flat on my ass, let me muddle through on my own."

Nick had to laugh. "Okay, so we've established the ground rules. If you're flat on your ass, I'll scrape you up, but only so I don't trip over you. Besides, Callie will be coming over. Wouldn't want to damage her eyes by letting her see your nakedness in all its questionable glory."

Leif's answering laugh sounded more like a wheeze. "Sarge, if my hands weren't full at the moment, I'd be offering you a one-fingered salute."

"Fine, I'll consider myself well and truly flipped off if that makes you happy."

"It does."

Satisfied that Leif would eventually make it to the utility room on his own, Nick settled in at the kitchen table and spread out the gazebo plans. Right now, they mostly provided him with an excuse to remain within shouting distance of Leif without being obvi-ous about it.

As he studied the instructions, he could hear Leif muttering to himself and occasionally cutting loose with a colorful string of curse words. Nick figured any soldier with enough energy to be that creative was a soldier on the mend.

Feeling better than he had in hours, he grabbed a pencil and started making notes.

*   *   *

Juggling a large pan of lasagna, a tossed salad, a loaf of bread fresh from the bakery, and a double batch of cookies wasn't easy. Callie made two trips to stash it all safely in her car. She could've called Nick to come give her a hand transporting it all through the woods, but it was just as easy to put it in the backseat of the car and drive over.

She closed the passenger door and then slid into the driver's seat. It was a matter of being practical and not at all because she was skittish about being alone with Nick right now. She didn't really want to think of Leif as a chaperone, but he would provide a buffer between the two of them.

"Yeah, right, Callie," she muttered as she started the engine. "Let's not lie about the situation."

She had good reason to avoid being alone with Nick. The trouble with being honest about her feelings on the subject was that she'd have to admit he'd scared her last night. Watching him patrol the entire yard, looking for who knows what among the shadows and trees, had left her restless for hours afterward. Partly because her own imagination kept wanting to kick in with images of bad guys lurking in the woods, but also out of worry over the demons that were clearly plaguing the man.

He hadn't mentioned getting any help in decompressing from the strain of fighting in the war, not to mention the loss of a friend so close to the end of their deployment. According to everything she'd read, therapy could help. But how could she even suggest such a thing to him without hurting his feelings? If she pushed too hard, he might decide to up and leave. Another bit of truth was that she wasn't ready for him to go.

And might never be.

She pulled out of her parents' driveway and drove

the short distance to Spence's. No, it was hers now, something she needed to keep repeating over and over until she actually believed it was true. For a minute, the past was superimposed over the present, and she could see Spence with his head under the hood of that old Chevy he'd been restoring back when they were sixteen.

She slowed to a stop halfway down the driveway, not yet willing to face Nick and Leif, especially when she was lost in the past. Time sped up, and Spence was older and about to leave for his first deployment in Iraq. He'd been so handsome in his uniform, a big smile on his face but with a hint of manic fear in the depths of his pale green eyes. She was probably the only one who knew him well enough to recognize it, but she'd never doubted for a moment what she'd seen.

The next time she'd seen him, war had carved its mark on her friend. He still laughed, but not as easily. Even in the quietest moments there'd been a thread of tension running through him. It was as if he could never quite relax because maintaining constant vigilance had become second nature for him.

Her eyes burned, but she refused to give in to tears. She missed Spence so darn much, but somehow meeting his two friends had eased the pain a little. Not only were they a lot like him, but they also carried a big chunk of Spence in their hearts. Between the three of them, their combined memories would keep him alive, at least in their world.

Maybe. She hoped so, anyway. Right now the wounds were still too fresh for all three of them. Leif's literally. She'd wanted to ask him about the prognosis on his ankle but sensed the question wouldn't be appreciated.

Nick had his own scars that went far beyond that

twisted red streak on his upper arm. While that one would heal, there was no way to know if the other ones ever would. She hated what the war had done to them all.

Driving slowly as the house came into view, she was struck by how much Nick had accomplished in just a handful of days. Already the grass looked healthier, neatly mowed instead of harvested like a wheat field. The flower beds were edged and weeded. The overall effect on how the place looked was amazing. Imagine what a coat of paint on the house itself would do!

She couldn't wait to see how it all turned out, but now wasn't the time to get lost in her plans for the future. Especially since Nick and Mooch had both stepped out on the front porch. When the dog tried to charge down the steps, Nick grabbed him by the collar to make sure Mooch didn't run in front of Callie's car.

Once she was safely stopped, he released his buddy and followed the dog down the steps.

She managed to get out of the car without being bowled over by her four-footed fan. Kneeling down, she laughed as Mooch about wiggled himself to pieces in his efforts to deliver enough doggy kisses to last her a lifetime.

When he finally settled down, she stood up and dusted off the knees of her jeans. "I think he missed me."

Nick grinned. "Can you blame him? He hasn't seen you since lunchtime. In dog hours, that must seem like forever."

Callie patted the dog on the head again. "I hadn't thought about it in those terms. Poor baby!"

Nick peeked into the backseat of her car. "Let me help you with all of that."

She opened the back door and pulled out the salad

and the cookies, handing them off to Nick. After retrieving the rest herself, she shut the car door with a quick nudge of her hip.

Nick was busy sniffing the air. "I'm guessing something Italian with an underlying hint of oatmeal raisin."

"Right on both counts. Since this is Leif's first night here, I thought I should hold off on serving MREs for dinner. Tomorrow, though, all bets are off."

He stood back to let her lead the way into the house. "That's just mean, Callie. Besides, they won't taste right unless you season them with Afghan dust. Not sure the stores around here will have that in stock."

There was something in his voice that made her think he wasn't kidding about that. She couldn't imagine a steady diet of gritty food morning, noon, and night.

"Fine, then. I'll see what else I can come up with. We could grill something tomorrow night."

"That sounds great. Maybe with some roasted corn or a big salad."

"You've got it."

They headed inside the house with Mooch bringing up the rear.

Chapter 17

Leif was waiting for them in the kitchen. The two men had set the table with the dishes that had once belonged to Spence's mom. Another ping from the past. Callie set the lasagna down and peeled back the aluminum foil. Nick added the bowl of salad and then the bread Callie handed him.

As soon as Leif spied the plastic container of cookies Nick had put on the counter, he hobbled around the table to pop off the lid. His expression turned positively reverent.

"Tell me those are oatmeal raisin."

"They are."

Nick slapped Leif's hand as soon as he started to pick one up. "Down, boy. You can have cookies after you eat a good dinner."

Leif tried again. "Come on, Sarge. Just one. Call it an appetizer. You know how long it's been since I've had one of Callie's cookies."

Nick relented. "Fine, but that's it for now. Got that, Corporal?"

Callie blinked. Nick was kidding, wasn't he? Maybe

not, considering that Nick made that last part sound like a direct order. What was going on?

Time to distract them. "They're just cookies, gentlemen. I can always bake more. But right now I could really use some ice water, and the lasagna is getting cold."

Her effort to defuse the situation worked. Nick immediately fixed drinks for all three of them while Leif settled himself at the table. Callie rooted through the drawers to find some serving utensils and a knife to cut the lasagna. Soon all three of them were seated at the table and passing their plates.

Leif accepted the huge helping of lasagna she gave him with a smile. "This smells delicious. Thanks for cooking for us."

Then he shot a sly smile toward the cookie container. "And baking. Spence always shared your cookies whenever he got some, but I swear he made us beg. Believe me, we all got excited whenever he received a package from you. A couple of times we had a long discussion with our fists over how he divided up the goodies."

Okay, that was just too much. "Seriously? You actually fought over cookies? Don't tell me neither of you received packages because I know better. Especially you, Nick. Spence told me about the stuff you got from your mom."

Leif looked a bit sheepish. "Well, sure, we all got stuff, but it was from our moms. Spence was the only one who got cookies from someone who wasn't a blood relative. We wanted some of that for ourselves."

She blushed. "But Spence doesn't have any family. The only relatives he has . . ."

Had, darn it, had. Callie ignored the fresh stab of pain that idea caused her as she paused to correct herself again. "The only family he had left were his uncle and his cousin. God knows neither one of them would have thought to send Spence a package, not even for Christmas or his birthday."

Nick perked up. "Have you talked to either of them since you heard about Spence?"

"Yes."

She turned her attention to serving herself some salad, hoping to avoid elaborating, because that meeting hadn't been at all pleasant. The army had notified Spence's uncle as his next of kin. Vince had promptly come snooping around Spence's house, assuming he was going to inherit. Her father had noticed him hanging around and wandered over to see what was going on.

That was the first anyone in town had heard about what had happened. She could only imagine how Vince had reacted when he'd learned from the attorney that Callie, and not Vince or even his son, had been named as Spence's heir.

"I'm guessing they weren't happy about you ending up with this place."

She set her fork down to answer. "No, they weren't. Vince took it harder than his son, Austin, but neither one was happy. They threatened to contest the will, but the attorney Spence hired made sure it was ironclad. There was no love lost between Spence and Vince; that's for sure."

It was hard to face Spence's two friends. "I had no idea he'd left everything to me. I hope you both know I'd rather be Spence's guest in this house instead of its owner."

Nick was seated on her right and Leif on her left. Each of them reached out to take her hand. Leif gave it a quick squeeze.

"Yeah, we both know that. We're all having a hard

time getting our heads around the fact that Wheels won't be walking through the door again."

"Wheels?"

The two men exchanged an odd look before Nick answered. "Actually, that's short for Wheelman. When the three of us were out on patrol, Spence was our driver of choice."

The flatness in his tone made it very clear that there was more to the story than that. "Okay, fess up. Which one of you christened him with the nickname, and why did you choose him to drive?"

Another one of those looks. It appeared that this time Leif drew the short straw because he rolled his eyes and leaned back in his chair. "I'm not admitting anything, but I assume sometime in the past you had the questionable privilege of riding in a car with Spence at the wheel."

Okay, now she knew where Leif was heading with all of this. That didn't mean she was going to make it easy on him. "Yes, often. Did you know the cops around here used to hold him up as an example to the other teenagers whenever they talked about driving safety?"

Leif looked incredulous as he sputtered, "Seriously? Are we talking about the same Spencer Lang?"

Nick joined the protest. "No way. That boy was already crazy the day he enlisted. The army didn't make him that way."

It was hard to decide which of Spence's two friends had the funnier expression on his face: Nick trying to keep a straight face or Leif looking completely befuddled.

Nick took pity on Leif and pointed the tip of his knife in her direction. "Corporal, you might note that she didn't say what kind of example Spence was."

Giggles burbled to the surface. "No, I didn't, did I?"

Leif finally caught on and joined in the laughter. "They held him up as a crappy example, didn't they? I swear that man never took a corner with four wheels on the ground if he could manage to take it on two."

Nick nodded in agreement. "Pardon the expression, but Wheels took balls-to-the-wall driving to a whole new level."

There was no mistaking the admiration in Nick's voice. Clearly Spence's driving had made a definite impression on his fellow soldiers.

Remembering her friend's wild side had her smiling. "It's nice to know the army allowed him to hone his personal skill set. 'Be all you can be' and all of that."

Leif stared off into the distance. "Gee, I don't remember seeing 'crazy-assed driver' as one of the job descriptions when I enlisted. Maybe they do things differently out here on the West Coast."

"No, they don't." She thought back to when she and Spence were juniors in high school. "After one close call involving a late-night drive through the mountains, my father wouldn't let me back in the car with Spence for a month. Then Dad had a heartfelt discussion with the dear boy. Neither of them ever shared what was said, but after that Spence never ever exceeded the speed limit when I was in the car with him."

She remembered those summer nights when the two of them would take long drives and talk about their dreams. Neither of them expected to end up back in Snowberry Creek, and look how that had turned out. She was thinking of starting her own business here, and Spence . . . well, he was here, too.

She reached for her water to try to wash down the lump in her throat. It didn't help, and silence settled over the table for a short time. At least over the course of the discussion, the three of them had made a huge dent in the lasagna. Leif pushed his plate back.

"That was delicious, Callie. It's been a long time since I've had home cooking."

Callie managed a smile. "I'm glad you liked it."

Nick started clearing the table. "I'll put on a fresh pot of coffee before we break out the cookies. Then I've got something to show you."

Something he seemed nervous about. When his back was toward the table, she shot a questioning look in Leif's direction but got no response. Okay, then. Something was definitely up, and it had these two big, tough soldiers acting awfully skittish.

Leaning over closer to Leif, she whispered, "Give me a hint about what's going on, and I'll bake you your own batch of cookies."

She'd underestimated Nick's hearing. Despite the noise of the faucet running, he responded, "Corporal."

Leif was clearly tempted but then shook his head. "Sorry, Callie, but this is Sarge's dog and pony show. I wouldn't want to steal his thunder."

"Fine, then."

Then, while Nick still had his back to them, she winked at Leif. "I'll still bake the cookies."

"Callie, my friend, you seriously rock."

She smiled at him. "Gotta do my part to fatten you up a bit."

Damn, not only was he capable of being jealous of a dog, but now he resented the small exchange between Callie and Leif. Although she was right on the money about Leif needing to pack on some weight. He must have lost a good twenty pounds since getting his ankle almost blown off. He needed protein, not pastries, but right now seeing Leif acting enthusiastic about anything was good.

Nick wiped down the kitchen table and the counters before setting out three mugs for the coffee. When he reached for the cookies to set the plastic tub on the table, he hesitated as visions of his mother artfully arranging hers on a fancy plate popped into his head.

Sorry, Mom, but that's not happening.

As a compromise, he did pour some milk into a small pitcher. Besides, a gallon jug took up too much of the room he'd need to spread out the plans for Callie to study. He set out the sugar bowl along with a handful of paper napkins and called it good.

Leif minded his manners long enough to offer the cookies to Callie first. She took one and set it on a napkin.

Nick snagged the container out of Leif's hand and held it out to her again. "Take more than that. They won't last long the way Leif inhales cookies."

His friend didn't bother to deny it. "Yeah, well, it's not like you haven't wolfed down your fair share of them in the past."

Callie dutifully took another cookie and waved him off when he continued to offer her more. "No, this is fine. Split the rest between the two of you."

Once the coffee was poured and a few cookies consumed, Nick reached for the stack of papers he'd left on the counter. Callie followed his every movement, obviously curious about what was coming next.

He wiped his hands on his shirt twice before finally unfolding the detailed plans for the gazebo. Taking a deep breath, he slid them over in front of Callie.

"I saw this and thought about what we talked about for the far corner in the backyard."

Callie's eyes widened as she studied the picture. "It's beautiful! You're so right. This would be perfect."

Her enthusiasm quickly dimmed. "But having something like this built is going to have to wait until I find out how much else needs to be done to bring the house up to code for a bed-and-breakfast. Not to mention I found out today I have to apply for a variance in the zoning to open a business at this location."

She leaned back in her chair and sighed. "I had another talk with the clerk at city hall about building permits and all the other things that it would take to pull the whole project together. It was pretty overwhelming."

"One step at a time, Callie. Don't let it scare you. Maybe we can visit city hall together at some point and ask about what needs to be done to get the variance."

She'd started to push the paper back toward him, but he stopped her. "But back to this. I mean it to be a gift from me, so don't worry about the cost. While we're checking on the variance, we'll find out if a permit is needed for a small project like this."

"It's too much, Nick. I can't accept a gift like this from you."

And why the hell not? Guessing that wasn't the right approach, he tried a different tack. "You're planning on fixing this place up as a kind of quiet memorial for Spence. Well, this would be my part of that. It would mean a lot to both me and Leif if you'd let us build this."

Callie traced the curving line of the gazebo's roof with a fingertip, her expression more hopeful. "Are you sure? Both of you? It looks like a lot of work."

"Don't worry about that. I've been doing carpentry work from plans like these for my dad for years."

He nodded toward Leif. "And my boy here takes orders well. He won't be much of a hindrance."

Leif rose to the bait. "Hindrance, my ass. We already agreed I'm the supervisor on this project."

Yeah, right. "And remind me again, what qualifies you for that job?"

"Supervisors sit on their backsides most of the time." Leif patted the boot that reached halfway up his leg. "I've gotten really good at that lately."

Nick had to laugh. Damn, he'd missed moments like this exchanging banter with his friends. "You've been good at that as long as I've known you."

Giving Nick a superior look, Leif tidied up his stack of cookies. "We all go with our strengths. That's the army way."

Callie reentered the conversation. "So what all will you need to build this thing?"

Time to lay his cards on the table. "Most of it will be here tomorrow morning. That's what I was doing when I was gone today. The hardware store promised to make delivery by ten."

For the first time a bit of temper showed in Callie's hazel eyes. "So you two weren't actually asking me if you could build the gazebo. You were telling me it's a done deal."

Okay, so maybe it was time to pour everybody some more coffee. A little distance between him and Callie right now seemed like a good idea. "I guess you could look at it that way."

The chill of her displeasure followed him across the room and back. "How else should I look at it, Nick?"

A movement on the other side of the table caught Nick's attention. Yeah, his so-called friend was having a hard time containing his amusement. He gave Leif one of those looks that promised retribution at the first available opportunity.

"Leif, wouldn't you be more comfortable in the living room? Like right now."

The jerk actually laughed. "Yeah, probably, but then

I wouldn't have a front-row seat watching you grovel, Sarge. She's got you on the ropes."

That last crack drew some of Callie's anger in his direction. "You think this is funny, Leif?"

All good soldiers knew when it was time to make a strategic retreat, and Leif was definitely a good soldier. "Maybe stretching out on the couch would be a good idea. Sarge, can you get me a glass of water so I can take my pills?"

Nick frowned. Was he due for more already? Maybe so, considering that those lines bracketing his mouth had become more pronounced again. "Sure thing."

While he took care of that little chore, Leif kept Callie distracted. "Would you have some extra sheets and blankets? I thought I'd sack out down here on the couch rather than battle those steps tonight."

Soft touch that she was, Callie immediately leapt to her feet. "Actually, the sofa in the den is a hide-a-bed. You stay here while I get you all set up."

She was off and running before either man could respond. Leif swallowed his pills before standing up. "She's something, isn't she? No wonder Spence felt the way he did about her."

Rather than answer, Nick watched Leif stand up and waited to be sure his friend could make it to the bathroom off the utility room on his own. Leif didn't need to hear that Nick understood all too well exactly why Spence had wanted to build a life with Callie.

Because, God forgive him, Nick felt the same damn way about her.

Chapter 18

A fter giving Leif time to get settled, Callie peeked into the den. "Good night, Corporal. Can I get you anything else before I head back home?"

He mumbled something that sounded like a cross between "Good night" and "I'm fine." Either way, she suspected he was nearly asleep, which was a good thing. By the time he'd reached the den, he'd been breathing hard with the effort it took him to walk. Callie hurt for him but knew better than to let it show.

She debated over whether to close the door but, in the end, left it open. If Leif needed to get up in the night, the fewer the obstacles in his way, the better. With that in mind, she'd also dug up a couple of night-lights to leave burning in the hall and kitchen to light his route to the bathroom.

Nick was waiting for her near the front door. "I'll walk you out."

She didn't bother to argue but walked on past him. He'd do what he wanted to anyway. When they reached the car, he handed over the plastic bag that held her dishes, including the empty cookie container.

After stowing them in the backseat, she closed the door. When she turned around, it was to find Nick standing close behind her. Too close, or maybe not close enough. Her confusion on the subject had her casting about for something to say.

"You guys weren't kidding about the cookies, were you?"

He smiled for the first time since he'd told her about the gazebo. "Nope. And what Leif doesn't know is that I already squirreled the rest away where he won't find them."

Despite it all, she bet he'd be sharing them with Leif tomorrow. "Next time I'll know to make a triple batch. What do you think? Chocolate chip?"

"Oh, we're not picky."

She feigned hurt feelings, placing her hand over her heart as if his words had wounded her. "So any old cookies will do? Even store-bought?"

He wrapped his hand around hers, his eyes staring down into her face. "Not at all. I'm pretty damn selective about some things, Callie."

Were they still talking about cookies? Somehow she didn't think so. Her body didn't think so, either, as a heavy ache stole through her, starting in her chest and moving south. She could feel his body heat and wanted to lean into it. Rather than worry about where all of this was headed, she returned to their earlier topic of conversation.

"About the gazebo."

He leaned in closer. With the car at her back, she had no room to retreat. "What about it?"

"I love the whole idea, and it's sweet of you to want to do something like this for Spence. If you want to build it, that's fine with me. All I'm asking is that next time you talk to me first."

His fingers were now toying with a lock of her hair. "Next time? How many gazebos do you think one yard needs?"

"You know what I mean."

She gave his chest a soft shove, but he didn't budge an inch. If anything, he leaned closer. Enough so that there was the slightest contact between the sensitive tips of her breasts and the hard wall of his chest. Temptation and frustration all rolled into one.

"Nick?"

"Callie." He said her name in a whisper, his breath mingling with hers. "Tell me you want this."

She did. That didn't mean she should. "Are you going to get mad again if we kiss, Nick? Because if so, the answer is no."

They hovered there for a long, painful heartbeat while he thought about it. That was answer enough for her. "I should be getting home."

He backed up half a step. "Maybe you should."

She scrambled into the car and pulled away in a spray of gravel. Her pulse didn't slow down until she was back at her parents' house with the doors safely locked. What should she do next? Maybe Leif had the right idea about turning in early, with the added feature of a long soak in a bubble bath first.

When she carried the empty dishes into the kitchen, she was drawn to the back window. Staring out into the night, she knew exactly what she'd see. Sure enough, there was Nick out walking the perimeter with Mooch at his side, two soldiers on patrol.

She unlocked the door and stepped outside. It told her a lot that Mooch remained with his sergeant rather than charging over to greet her. Was it because of the mood his friend was in or had they noticed something wasn't right?

"Is everything okay?"

Nick's steps faltered briefly before he continued his determined march along the edge of the woods. "All is secure out here."

That might be true, but it was obvious not everything was okay. He kept moving even when she started down the steps. Callie aimed straight across the yard to cut him off.

"Nick, stop."

When he would have kept walking, she planted herself directly in his path. "Please, Nick. What's wrong?"

He finally stopped. "Nothing is wrong. I'm just making sure you got home safe and sound."

"There's more to it than that, Nick."

He kept staring past her into the darkness. "I needed to know you're safe. That there's no one out there."

There was a wildness about him that she'd only glimpsed before. Was this what it was like for him back in Afghanistan? Living with the knowledge that the enemy could be anywhere, anytime, hiding in the shadows or behind the nearest door? Maintaining constant vigilance, nerves on edge all the time?

She edged closer to him, not sure what his reaction would be if she were to actually touch him. "You're not downrange, Nick. You're right here with me in Snowberry Creek."

His laughter was ugly. "I know that in here," he said, pointing at his temple. Then his hand dropped to his chest. "But in here, sometimes I'm still there, still on the hunt for the bastards who wanted me dead and killed my friends. I can feel them out there, just waiting for me to make another mistake."

Her heart lurched. "What mistake did you make, Nick?"

He shook his head and moved back from her, clearly

about ready to bolt. "You don't want to know, Callie, and I don't want to tell you."

He was probably right about that, but she couldn't stand to see him hurting like this and not do something to help.

"Fine, Nick, you don't have to tell me anything, not until you're ready."

This time when she tried to approach him, he remained still, his eyes open wide enough that the whites showed all around. Her hand brushed down his arm lightly as she tried not to spook him into full retreat.

When he accepted that much from her, she used both hands this time, letting them drift slowly back up his arms to rest on his shoulders. He quivered, his breathing rough, but he stood his ground. Damn, she wished she had a better idea of what to do, but all she could do was go with her instincts.

She leaned into him, pressing her body along the length of his, but made no effort to wrap him in her arms. They stood there absolutely still for the longest time. Slowly, his stance relaxed slightly. When he finally did move, it was to pull her more fully against his chest, wrapping her in his arms and holding her close.

Nick rested his forehead against hers. "I don't mean to scare you, Callie. That's the last thing I want to do."

She tilted her head back far enough to make sure he could see her clearly. "You don't scare me, Nick. Frustrate me, yes. Confuse me, yes, but that's all."

"Well, considering you have the same effect on me, lady, it only seems fair."

When he smiled, she knew everything was going to be okay, at least for now. When she started to step away, he tightened his grip on her. "I'm going to kiss you, Callie, unless you tell me to stop."

Then he claimed her mouth before she had a chance

to respond one way or another. His kiss was hot, hungry, and demanding. His tongue swept past her lips, staging a gentle assault on her control. Her knees turned to jelly and her hands didn't know what to do with themselves. Finally, she latched onto the soft cotton of his shirt and held on for dear life.

His shorts did little to disguise the impact this was having on him. She moaned and rubbed against the rigid length of his erection. He immediately cupped her bottom with both hands and raised her up to increase the pressure enough to almost send her flying over the edge.

"Nick, please!"

She didn't know exactly what she wanted, but what she got was dragged down to the ground. The grass was cool and damp along the backs of her legs and arms, but that was a luscious contrast to the burning heat of the man stretched out above her. There might be better, more appropriate places for what they were doing, but right now she couldn't think of a single one.

His hands were everywhere. Tangled in her hair one second as he kissed her hard and deep and then kneading her breasts the next. When he tugged her shirt up to reveal her plain cotton bra, she wished she'd worn something better, something lacy. Nick didn't seem to mind, especially because with a quick flick of his fingers, he unfastened the front clasp and shoved it out of the way.

His mouth was liquid heat as he worked the sensitive tip of her breast with his teeth and tongue. She arched up, asking him without words for more. He obliged her, murmuring in approval against her skin.

She tugged on his shirt, pulling it up until she could slide her hands across the well-defined lines of his tanned skin she'd been aching to touch for days. His muscles flexed under her touch, all that masculine strength hers for the taking.

Nick surged up her body for another deep kiss, his big body settling over hers. Their mouths mated as he lifted her leg high along his side as he flexed his hips hard against hers. The sheer wonder of the powerful connection arcing between them was amazing.

This was insane, rolling around in the grass out of control and nearly out of her clothes. But right now she didn't want to think; she wanted to feel, to savor this.

Nick slipped his hand beneath her waistband, his fingers spreading out across her stomach, leaving a burning trail of heat in their wake. He eased to the side, staring down at her with eyes that glittered in the faint light from the kitchen window.

His hand had stilled, as if asking permission to go any farther along this path. She couldn't find the words, didn't know what she'd say if she could. When her own hips flexed, he nodded, accepting her unspoken answer.

Her breath caught in her throat as those strong fingers stroked lower, still short of where she thought they were headed. Hoped they were headed. His touch was slow, gently circling across her skin, leaving a trail of hungry fire in its wake.

She tugged his face down for another kiss, his skin so hot to the touch. Then she brushed her hand over his hair. Still military short, it tickled her palm. She liked it. Liked all of this.

"Nick, don't stop. Not this time."

He didn't need a second invitation. Not when Callie was his only anchor is this world. Without her touch, without her warmth, he'd slide right back into his past. He'd be trapped in the endless stench of fear mixed with adrenaline. Where death stalked the streets or out on the bare hillsides that offered no protection from the enemy.

God, her skin was soft. Warm. Enticing. As she kissed him, drawing his tongue into her mouth, he tasted her hunger for him. For this. He quit holding back and clamped his hand between her legs, brushing a fingertip across her slick folds. Callie whimpered softly, then louder when he increased the pressure.

As focused as he was on the woman in his arms, a part of him was still aware of their surroundings. The cool night air in sharp contrast to the heat pouring off her skin, warming him from the outside in. The light of the moon sweeping across them as the clouds drifted across the sky. The slight rustle of the trees in the breeze.

Callie's eyes were closed, allowing him time to drink his fill of her pretty face. Right now, her eyebrows were drawn down tight and she bit her lower lip, her expression so serious. He could feel the tension building as she strained for completion. He wanted that for her, for them both, but not quite yet.

When he backed off, stopping short of sending her over the edge, her eyes popped open to stare up at him.

"Two can play at that game, Nick."

Her threat was accompanied by direct action. She shoved him over onto his back. He could have fought back, but he wasn't that crazy. If this woman wanted to take charge, he'd let her. She quickly had his shorts down far enough to allow her easy access to his pride and joy.

As soon as she gripped him in her fist, he about exploded. The woman definitely had the touch—and knew it, too. Her mouth, still swollen from his kisses, quirked up in a superior smile. She worked him slowly, never quite as hard or fast as he wanted, but enough to hold him prisoner.

But her plan backfired. Yeah, he was so hard for her it hurt, but she wanted him even more. An experienced soldier knew when to spring into action. Any further delay in completing his mission would nearly kill him. He sat up long enough to peel off his shirt and then reached to do the same with his shorts, already down around his hips. Oh, hell yeah, this was going to be so good. Skin against skin. Her slick heat and his . . . Oh, hell. His whole train of thought derailed.

"We can't."

The two words dropped between them like a bombshell. Callie looked up at him in confused hurt. "Why?"

"I don't have my wallet. No protection."

Callie gave him a considering look before holding her hand out to him. "It's okay. I'm protected."

She accompanied the good news by tossing her shirt over to join Nick's. Then she shimmied out of her shorts, leaving him momentarily stunned by the beautiful picture she made. Then she drew him down to her, the time for teasing and tantalizing over and done.

When their bodies came together, the fit was perfect, even if their movements were awkward at first. Then they found their rhythm as Callie urged him on with frantic whispers. He wanted this perfection to last forever, but the sensations were too powerful to be resisted for long. They came together in a heated flurry, faster and faster until she keened out her release, taking him flying over the edge with her.

And then the world went to hell around them.

Chapter 19

❦ ❦

Mooch had been blissfully absent since the second Nick had kissed Callie. Hell, he wouldn't have given the dog credit for knowing to make himself scarce when a buddy hooked up with a beautiful woman. He had no idea where the mutt had been, but right now he was back and pitching a fit.

Nick hated—*hated*—having to withdraw from Callie's embrace so abruptly, but Mooch wouldn't be sounding the alarm for no reason. Surging to his feet, Nick paused only long enough to toss Callie her clothes and yank on his own shorts. The rest would have to wait.

"What's wrong, Nick?"

"I'm not sure. Lock yourself in the house while I see what's got Mooch upset."

He waited until she pulled on her shirt and shorts and ran up the steps. "Keep the outside lights off, Callie. It screws with my night vision."

"Should I call the police?"

"Not yet. Let me check it out first. It could be just a raccoon raiding the trash."

Although he didn't think so. He cocked his head to the side to try to triangulate the dog's location. There. Near the start of the path toward Spence's house. Mooch ran out of the trees. As soon as he spotted Nick, he retreated back the way he'd come, his barking fading into a deep growl.

The intruder was back. His gut said that was the only logical explanation for Mooch's agitation. The sound of breaking glass sent Nick charging back to Callie's. She saw him coming and opened the door.

"Call the cops. Tell them someone is breaking into the house next door. Warn them Mooch and I will be around. Leif, too."

Hopefully they'd give him a chance to identify himself before any shooting started. Without waiting for Callie to respond, he wheeled around and headed right back toward the path. He wished like hell he had his Beretta with him or, better yet, his rifle. Even unarmed, he couldn't wait for the police to show up, not with Leif alone and asleep in the house. The painkillers would hamper his ability to react to any kind of threat.

Nick followed his four-legged scout across the yard, dividing his attention between studying the house and watching Mooch for clues as to where the threat originated. The dog ranged out ahead of Nick, nose to the air. Old habits had them both keeping to the darkest shadows.

Mooch made it all the way to the front porch before suddenly veering off to circle around the end of the house toward the backyard. Nick followed him, going slowly, trying to hear past the approaching sirens.

Mooch yipped softly and stared up at the back porch. The window in the door was broken, the hole round as if shattered by a fist-sized rock. Nick crept up the steps, ignoring the shimmer of broken glass scattered on the porch even though he was barefoot. Luckily for him, most of the pieces had gone inside, but it wouldn't have mattered. He would have stomped across an acre of jagged shards to get to Leif.

He reached the door, which was unlocked and ajar. Had the prowler gone in or had he been scared off by Mooch's barking? Nick pushed the door farther open, moving slowly as he listened for the sound of someone moving around. Nothing. All was quiet. Outside, flickers of red and blue lights warned him the police had arrived.

Stepping around the rock lying on the kitchen floor, Nick grimaced. The corporal would not be happy to find out that he'd slept right through a direct attack on the house. There wasn't much that could be done about that. Nick flipped on the kitchen lights and headed for the den to wake him up before the cops came pouring in.

Where the hell was he? When Nick finally spotted Leif, his heart nearly stopped. His friend was sprawled on the floor next to a pillow, his face covered with a dark splash of blood. A swirl of blackness swirled through Nick's brain as the room around him disappeared.

He staggered back two steps, holding his arm, trying to stop the bleeding while he assessed the damage. Who else had been caught by the explosion? Too much blood. It was everywhere, soaking into the dirt, sprayed on the clay walls. Even the shredded metal that used to be his armored vehicle was tinged red in his mind. Spence! Where was Spence! Please, God, let Wheels be there.

Fuck no! That wasn't right. Nick wasn't in Afghanistan anymore. His arm was scarred, not bleeding. Spence was dead; Leif wasn't. Although he might be if Nick didn't get his head back in the game.

He knelt down and gently shook the unconscious man's shoulder until his friend moaned. Good. He was already coming around. Nick stripped the cover off a bed pillow lying on the floor next to Leif and used it to wipe the blood off his cheek. Damning himself for not turning the overhead light on, Nick leaned closer to assess the damage.

The bruised area looked to be the size of a fist, with a single shallow cut in the center. Best guess was that Leif had been hit once—but hard. There was a limit to how much damage the intruder could do with a single punch. If he'd used the rock, the blow could have been fatal. Nick eased back slightly as Leif's eyes fluttered open, knowing a wounded man's reactions were often unpredictable.

"Leif, come on, buddy. Wake up. The cops are here."

He made a second, more successful attempt to get Leif moving as the pounding on the front door started.

Leif blinked sleepily. "What the hell happened? I remember glass breaking."

He frowned. "Then I yelled to ask if you were getting clumsy in your old age. Nothing after that."

Nick lifted the injured man up into a sitting position. "Someone broke the window in the kitchen to get inside. You must have startled him, and he knocked you out. Callie called the cops. Stay here while I go let them in. We'll put in a call for the medics."

His story had some gaping holes in it, but now wasn't the time for lengthy explanations. With luck, Leif would be thickheaded enough not to ask many questions about where Nick had been while the intruder had been knocking the hell out of him.

"Stay still. I'll be right back."

He flipped on lights as he went to give the police a clear view of him. They might not know him personally, but they'd at least know that a thief wouldn't be the one lighting up the house.

He hadn't expected it to be the chief of police himself standing on the porch. Gage had his sidearm in his hand, his stance relaxing only marginally when he spotted Nick through the window.

Nick turned on the porch light and opened the door. "Sorry to drag you all the way out here, Gage. Whoever tossed the rock was long gone by the time I got back here. The window in the back door is broken, but I haven't seen any other damage to the house itself. But whoever the bastard was, he hurt my friend. Can you call the medics for me?"

Gage pulled out his phone and punched a number on speed dial.

"Send the EMTs out to the Lang place."

As he spoke, he gave Nick a long look, clearly taking note of his missing shirt and shoes. Damn, it might have been smarter to delay opening the door long enough to grab at least a shirt out of Leif's duffel.

For the moment, Gage made no comment other than to send his two deputies around to scout the backyard and the woods beyond. Nick was about to step back out of the way to let Gage inside when a movement on the far side of the yard had all three lawmen reaching for weapons.

Callie stepped out of the trees. They immediately relaxed, but Nick wanted to throttle her for taking such a foolish risk. He would've gone and told her what had happened as soon as the dust settled. If Gage's men were in the least bit trigger happy, she could be dead right now.

"Mooch, protect Callie!"

The dog shot past the two men on the porch straight for his friend. Contrary to his usual behavior, he remained alert and watchful as the two of them continued on toward the house. It wasn't until she started up the steps that Mooch finally dropped his guard and demanded to be petted.

Callie patted him on the head before coming all the way up to where Nick stood glaring at her. She didn't seem the least bit cowed by his expression, probably thinking the intruder was the cause of his bad mood.

Gage saved him having to straighten her out on that. His voice was little better than a growl when he said, "It would have been better for you to wait next door, Callie. What if the guy who tossed a rock through the back window is still out there in the woods somewhere?"

"I didn't think—"

Nick joined in. "No, you didn't. I would've come back for you when it was safe."

He slipped his arm around her shoulder, offering her comfort even as he made it clear that he was siding with Gage on this one. "Leif's hurt. I need to get back to him."

She shivered despite wearing his shirt over her own. At least she'd taken the time to put on shoes and brought him his flip-flops. Hopefully she'd also gathered up any other clothes the two of them had left scattered on the grass. The last thing he wanted was for the two deputies to stumble across his boxers or her bra if they did a sweep across her yard as well.

Stubborn bastard that he was, Leif had managed to stand up on his own and came limping out of the den. Gage might not have anything to say about Nick's shirtless condition, but Leif might not be as tactful once he realized that Nick had been next door when the vandalism happened. They would deal with that fallout once the medics had a chance to give Leif the once-over.

Until then, he needed to get the man to a chair before he toppled over. Callie took Leif's other side and the two of them maneuvered him into the kitchen and sat him down at the table.

"Can you stay with him for a minute? I'll be right back."

When she nodded, he took the steps two at a time to his room upstairs and grabbed a clean shirt. When he returned to the kitchen, Callie had washed the blood from Leif's face, but that didn't do anything to disguise the darkening bruise. Nick clenched his fists, wishing like hell he had a handy target for his fury.

Of course, if he'd stayed with Leif, this wouldn't have happened. Even if he hadn't been able to resist the compulsion to make sure Callie was safe, he should've come right back. He'd known the painkillers had left Leif sluggish and unable to defend himself. He'd also suspected all along that someone had been snooping around the house and had even been inside long enough to steal things.

And instead of protecting Spence's home from invasion and Leif from attack, Nick had failed them both. Again. Son of a bitch, could he be any more worthless?

Leif looked more alert now. "I think I asked you this already, but what the hell happened here?"

Nick swallowed his guilt long enough to answer. He pointed toward the glass scattered on the floor. "Someone broke in. When you first woke up, you said you heard something, because you hollered something about me getting clumsy. I figure you started for the kitchen to see what was going on and startled the intruder. That's when he coldcocked you."

Callie handed Leif a plastic bag full of ice wrapped in a dish towel. "Hold that on your cheek, big guy.

There'll be plenty of time for explanations after the EMTs are done with you."

Leif winced at the cold but did as she said. Meanwhile, Gage and one of his men entered the room. "No sign of anyone out in the yard or in the woods now. We'll take another look around in the daylight to see if we can learn more."

Then Gage cocked his head to the side as if he'd heard something. "I think the med techs are here. I'll send them in. Meanwhile, Nick, if you've got a minute."

There was nothing to do but follow Gage outside. The man obviously had questions, ones he was either reluctant or too tactful to ask in front of Callie and Leif.

The medics were just coming up on the porch. The woman took the lead. "Chief."

Gage nodded. "Angela, Jace, this is Nick Jenkins. The injured man is in the kitchen. He took a blow to the head."

Nick stopped them. "Just so you know, Leif took some heavy-caliber pain pills about an hour ago. The bottle should be on the table by his bed in the den."

The pair nodded in Nick's direction but headed straight inside. They had their priorities straight. Blood took precedence over chitchat.

When they were out of hearing, Gage turned his lawman's gaze in Nick's direction. "Okay, start at the beginning and tell me what happened. Don't gloss over anything. I'm no gossip, and if certain, um, details aren't pertinent to the case, they won't go in my official report."

Nick nodded, grateful for even that much. "My buddy Leif arrived earlier today. He flew out from D.C. to help me do some work around here."

Gage's eyebrows shot up. Obviously he'd done his

own assessment of Leif's condition. No harm in confirming it for him.

"Leif got hurt in the same attack that killed Spence. When I asked him if he'd like to help me do a few things around the place for Callie, he hopped a plane and flew out here." Nick forced a small smile. "I suspect he exaggerated how much help he'll actually be."

Gage's laugh was short but heartfelt. "There's no convincing a good soldier that it takes time for a wound to heal properly. Let's hope all of this excitement won't set him back too much."

Nick ran his hand through his hair, wishing like hell all of this would just go away. "I'll hog-tie him and haul his ass up to the military hospital if that's what it takes to make him rest. For sure, if he's going to be here for long, we'll have to look into rehab for him."

"Let me know if you need help with that. I've still got a few connections with the locals up at the army base, and there's someone at the local medical center who was military herself. She would be able to help."

"Thanks for the info."

Time to get back to business. "Callie brought dinner over for us. That's kind of the deal she and I made. She doesn't want me working around here for free, so I told her room and board would be enough."

"Seems like a fair trade. So what happened after that?"

Good to his word, Gage wasn't taking notes. That didn't make it any easier for Nick to keep talking.

"She drove herself back home, but I cut through the woods to make sure she got there safely. Mooch and I patrolled the perimeter of her yard to make sure everything was quiet."

When he stopped talking, Gage prodded him. "And what then?"

"All you need to know is that I stayed there for a while, maybe half an hour or so. When Mooch raised the alarm, I sent Callie inside and came back here to see what was going on. When I heard glass breaking, I ran back long enough to have Callie call nine-one-one."

The sick feeling in his gut got worse. "Maybe if I'd kept going, I could've stopped the guy from hurting Leif."

Gage shot him a hard look. "And maybe the guy would've shot you. I shouldn't have to remind you that second-guessing your actions is a waste of time. You did what you thought was best with the information you had."

Interesting. That sounded like the voice of experience. What decision had Gage made that he regretted? Now wasn't the time to ask.

"After we came through the woods, Mooch started toward the front porch but then charged around back. I saw the broken window and the door standing open a few inches. After gaining entry, I listened but didn't hear anybody moving around. The bastard was already gone. I went in to check on Leif and found him on the floor. The rest you already know."

"Okay, then." Gage pulled out a business card. "This is my direct number. If you think of anything else or if the bastard comes back again, give me a call, day or night. Otherwise, I'll return in the morning to take another look around in the woods out back. I'll also take the broken glass and the rock in case we can find any trace evidence."

Nick glanced back inside, hoping Callie wasn't close by. "Have you talked to Spence's uncle or his son?"

"No, but that's at the top of my to-do list. This could be some dumb teenagers looking for an easy score, but something about that scenario doesn't feel right. I plan to ask Callie to do a quick look around inside tomorrow morning to see if anything has gone missing."

"I'll help her with that."

"Okay, then, I'll go check in with my deputies and then head home. Let me know if anything else happens."

"I will."

Gage had started down the steps but stopped to look back at him. "And, Nick, I know you're pissed off about this and want to pound on somebody. I get that, but dealing with whoever was behind this is my job. Let me do it."

Fine. As long as Gage and his men got it handled. If they didn't, well, Nick and Leif would do a little hunting of their own. Not trusting himself to speak, Nick nodded. Evidently, his thoughts on the subject still leaked through his façade.

Just that quickly, the chief was back on the porch and right up in Nick's grill. "I mean that, soldier. My job. Not yours. I'd hate like hell to throw your ass in jail. Tell me you understand what I'm saying."

Nick stood his ground but nodded again. "I understand, but you'd better catch the bastard before someone gets hurt. Oh, wait. Someone already was."

And it should have been him, not Leif. Once again, the wrong man suffered because of Nick's lousy judgment.

There was a definite gleam of empathy in Gage's eyes. "Go check on your friend. Get some sleep. We'll talk tomorrow."

"Okay. And just so you know, I'm expecting a delivery of building materials in the morning. If that will screw up your investigation, I can try to put a hold on the order."

"It shouldn't. We'll make sure to be out early to take pictures, and then you should be good to go."

Nick doubted that. Hell, nothing had been good for a long time now. No, that wasn't true. Him and Callie—that had been good. Way better than good, but the price for those few minutes had been too high. Leif had already lost enough. They all had.

Chapter 20

✂ ✂

It was tempting to floor it and put some distance between himself and Spence's house as fast as possible. Especially since Austin could already hear sirens and see the flashing lights heading straight for him from just past the next rise in the road. But he knew it wouldn't be smart to speed away. He hit the brakes, backed into the driveway he'd just passed, and quickly killed the headlights.

Thirty seconds later, three cop cars went ripping past him. Damn, that had been close. Too close. It was by the grace of God that he'd already been on his way out of the house when that stupid dog had gone ballistic. Earlier, when the guy who'd moved in headed off toward Callie's place, Austin had hung back to make sure he wasn't coming straight back before approaching the back door.

Granted, breaking that window had been a bone-headed move on his part, but he'd been pissed to verify that his key no longer worked, thanks to the brand-new lock on the door. More proof that he and his old man had been screwed over by dear cousin Spence. Well, at

least the rock had proven they couldn't keep him out.
Not forever.

All things considered, he should've been content to
let the broken glass make the statement for him. All
he'd planned to do was snatch a few more things, the
kind the antiques stores would pay cash for without
asking many questions. Nothing big or traceable. Knick-
knacks, dust catchers, really. Surely Callie wouldn't begrudge him a few mementos from those screwed-up
years Spence had been forced to share his home with his
uncle and cousin.

But as soon as Austin had stepped into the kitchen,
some other guy had started yelling. Where the hell had
he come from? Was Callie running a flophouse for free-
loaders? If she wanted to open the place to boarders,
she should have called him. He'd love to crash in the
house for a while. God knows it was better than the
hellhole he lived in now.

He'd been backpedaling for the door when he'd
heard a crash. It might have been smarter to keep running, but something about the dead silence that followed had creeped him out. He'd ignored the cold
sweat of fear that had him shaking as he slowly approached the den.

The newcomer was flat out on the floor, his temple
bleeding from where he'd hit it on something as he fell.
Austin had stuck around long enough to make sure the
guy was breathing okay and the bleeding wasn't getting out of hand. Even stuck a pillow under the guy's
head. If the injury had looked worse, Austin would
have called for help himself. Probably.

As it was, the dog had already sounded the alarm.
At the first bark, Austin had bolted out through the
kitchen and not slowed down until he'd reached the
dirt road past the woods. Once there, he'd had to brace

himself with both hands against the front fender until his lungs caught up on air and the shakes had passed.

He wouldn't calm down completely until he got back to his own place. Easing the truck forward enough that he could see both ways, he relaxed, but only a little. No more sign of cops headed this way, but it was too soon to assume he'd made a clean escape. Turning on his lights again, he pulled out onto the road and drove toward Spence's house. The cops wouldn't expect the culprit they were looking for to be driving back by the scene of the crime.

At least he hoped so. Besides, he wanted to get a glimpse of what was going on. He barely slowed as he passed the driveway. He sneered. The Snowberry Creek police were out in force; three squad cars, including the one belonging to the chief of police himself, were parked at Spence's place.

Evidently their definition of "major crime" included a broken kitchen window. Even now they were probably salivating over the chance to dust the rock for prints. Well, good luck with that. He flexed his hands on the steering wheel and admired the new pair of work gloves he'd bought just for tonight.

For now, he'd head on home and let the cops do their job.

Three steps forward and one step back. Yes, it was awful that Leif had gotten hurt, but Callie put that blame squarely on the shoulders of the intruder. Nick wasn't at fault and neither was she, no matter what they'd been doing when the guy broke in.

Leif didn't look any happier with the third member of their party than she was. "Damn it, Nick, sit down. You're making me dizzy prowling around like that."

Nick continued past them both to stand by the front

window. He stared out at the night, his expression harsh and etched in pain. She'd tried to talk to him a few minutes ago when Leif was out of the room, but he'd flinched when she'd reached out to touch him.

The jerk! This evening's events—all of them, not just the break-in—had left her badly shaken and unsettled. She could use a little hug time right about now.

She turned her attention back to Leif. "Can I fix you something to eat or maybe a cup of tea?"

"No, thanks, Callie. I'm going to head back to bed here in a minute."

He'd refused to let her take him to the hospital for a more thorough exam than the EMTs had given him, saying he'd been poked and prodded enough for one lifetime. A couple of butterfly bandages had patched up the cut on his temple, and the ice pack was helping with the bruise. She was more worried about a possible concussion, but the man was nothing if not stubborn.

Probably another reason he and Spence had been friends.

"Well, if neither of you needs anything, I'm going to head back home and turn in for what's left of the night. I'd appreciate it if one of you two would call me when Gage gets here in the morning. I want to know if they find anything."

She headed for the door. "Come on, Mooch, you can probably use a trip outside. Walk me home."

Nick immediately planted himself between her and the door. "You're not going anywhere."

Okay, who elected him king?

She aimed for calm and controlled. What she ended up with was cold and cross. "Yes, I am, Sergeant Nick Jenkins. May I remind you that I'm not one of your soldiers, so don't give me orders. I'm going all the way next door, the same place I've been sleeping every night. Now, get out of my way."

Then, as a concession to the fact that the threat tonight had turned out to be real, she added, "I promise to call as soon as I'm inside with the doors locked. I left the lights on outside and in the kitchen."

It was a standoff. Nick didn't move an inch, and she wasn't going to back down. She stared up into his eyes, so icy and cold. So different from when he'd kissed her. Earlier, he'd used his strength to make her feel special, cherished. Now he was using it as a weapon to control her.

"Nick, she's not yours. Let her go."

Great. Nick had been upset before, and his friend had to go and pour gas on the fire. Leif had moved up behind her, leaving her sandwiched inside their anger.

"It's not your call, Leif. Back off."

"Not happening."

The injured man did his best to shoulder his way in between Callie and Nick. "You can't keep her. You know I'm right about that. Now, let her go."

Maybe tired trumped intelligence. She was only just now realizing that there was obviously more to the conversation than the two men arguing over whether she could go back to her parents' house. Lord, save her from testosterone-fueled posturing.

She left them glaring at each other and beat a fast retreat toward the kitchen. Mooch had been standing beside the door, watching the two men with interest. His tail was normally in constant motion, but not now. He remained frozen in position, probably unsure which side to take in this particular skirmish.

Callie knew the answer to that. She needed him on her side. Despite her determination to return to the other house, she wasn't thrilled about walking through the woods alone. She couldn't ask Leif to accompany her, not with his injuries. But she wasn't about to ask Nick, remembering how his last patrol around her parents' house had ended up.

When she patted her leg, Mooch immediately broke formation and led the charge out the back door. "Good boy. With luck I'll be home with the door locked and the covers pulled up before either of them notices I'm gone."

Yeah, that worked for all of thirty seconds. She'd barely cleared the steps when Nick came charging after her. Fine. He could provide escort. She snickered. Maybe she was spending too much time around soldiers if she was starting to use their vocabulary.

Evidently he wasn't interested in conversation, either. She also noticed that he was carrying his pistol. He stayed on her right side, maybe hoping she wouldn't notice the weapon. No, that wasn't it. He wanted to make sure his gun hand was free and clear if any threat presented itself.

When she shivered, it had nothing to do with the cool temperature of a Northwest summer night. At least they'd come to the end of the path. A few more steps and she would reach the sanctuary of her mother's kitchen.

"Are you all right?"

Nick's concern for her well-being sounded gruff, but the soft touch on her shoulder told her it was sincere.

"I will be once I'm inside and asleep. The sooner I can put this whole night behind me, the better."

Nick jerked his hand away from her shoulder and dropped back behind her. Had he picked up on another threat? No, his body language wasn't on high alert like it would have been if that were true. If anything, he looked hurt. What had she said that would have had that effect?

Oh, God, did he think she meant she was unhappy about the two of them having sex? But, then, what else was he supposed to think? It wasn't like she'd qualified her statement to exclude it.

"Nick, I wasn't talking about what happened between us. I don't regret that. Not at all."

He clearly wasn't buying it. "Go on inside, Callie. I need to get back to Leif."

"But, Nick, I want—"

"Not now, Callie. It's late, and we're both tired. I'll see you in the morning."

He continued to watch her as he retreated toward the path. With the mood he was in, there was no use in arguing with him. He'd made up his mind and wouldn't listen to reason right now. But soon she would carve out a few minutes alone with him and set the record straight.

Depending on how that conversation went, she might not be getting that gazebo after all. She could live without it, but doing without Nick? That was a whole different ballgame.

Waving one last time, she shut the door and flipped the lights on and off as proof that she was safely inside. She just wished there wasn't more than the solid thickness of the locked door between her and Nick right now. The wall of anger hung heavy on her heart. The only good-bye she got was from Mooch, who wagged his tail one last time before following his friend back into the woods.

She took some comfort in knowing that at least two of the three males next door were still on good terms with her. It was a start.

*   *   *

Nick hadn't expected to sleep, but emotional overload combined with exhaustion had kicked in and knocked him out. He'd dragged himself out of bed at nine to take a cold shower, hoping to jump-start his brain. It had helped, but this was going to be one of those days when he'd have to mainline caffeine to burn away the cobwebs in his head.

Leif was already sitting at the kitchen table eating cold cereal when Nick came downstairs. Evidently he wasn't in the mood for conversation, either, but at least he'd started the coffeemaker. Nick filled two of the biggest mugs he could find and set one in front of Leif before taking his own seat.

"That cop named Gage called while you were in the shower. He'll be here in about fifteen minutes."

Nick had been considering making scrambled eggs and bacon, but there wasn't time for that. Cereal would have to do.

"The guy from the hardware store said he'd be here soon, too." Leif shot him a narrow-eyed look and shoved Nick's cell phone across the table. "And just so you know, my job description doesn't include the word 'secretary.' "

That pretty much exhausted any need for conversation. The cereal was passable, and the coffee tasted like battery acid, just the way Nick liked it on rough mornings like this one. They'd practically lived on the stuff back in Afghanistan, drinking it strong and pitch-black. As soon as he'd hit stateside, he'd made a point of adding real cream and three teaspoons of sugar minimum to each cup he drank. He needed those little reminders to keep him focused on living in the moment and not getting lost in the past.

It even worked sometimes.

Leif dumped a healthy dose of cream into his coffee, too. Maybe for the same reason. As he stirred it, he asked, "Think Callie will be speaking to either one of us this morning?"

Not a subject Nick wanted to discuss right now, especially with him. He ignored the question, hoping Leif would take the hint. Yeah, right, like that ever worked. The only one who'd been worse about not backing off and giving Nick some space had been Spence. The man had been blind when it came to reading body language, verbal hints, or even the occasional strong right hook. Idiot.

And damned if Nick wouldn't give anything to have him sitting right here giving him grief over the mess he'd gotten himself into with Callie. Of course, if Spence were there, Nick wouldn't have been the one rolling around in the grass with her last night. As amazing as that experience had been, he would have given it up in a heartbeat to have his friend back.

The rumble of a truck derailed that downward-spiraling train of thought. Nick picked up his dishes and Leif's and dumped them in the sink.

He headed for the front door, leaving his friend to follow at his own pace. Nick wouldn't have wanted to hold anyone back if he couldn't move quickly and figured Leif felt the same. If not, he'd let Nick know.

A big flatbed truck was parked out on the driveway. It was the owner of the hardware store himself who stepped down out of the cab. Nick had to hide a smile as he walked down to shake hands. In all the years of working with his dad, Nick had never seen a man who looked less like he belonged in the construction business than this one.

Mr. Reed stood about five foot seven and weighed in at about one-thirty. It wasn't his size that set him apart, though. Some of the toughest SOBs Nick had served with weren't big men. A lot of them walked around with a chip on their shoulder the size of a tank, just looking for a chance to prove how tough they were.

No, it was the starched, short-sleeved shirt, bowtie, and sweater vest that had him looking at the man with a "what's wrong with this picture?" reaction. Add in the half dozen hairs neatly combed over the top of the man's shiny scalp, and he'd look far more at home in a bookshop or maybe teaching Latin at the local college.

But the minute Mr. Reed had opened his mouth, any doubt about him knowing his way around joists and plumbing parts disappeared. He greeted Nick with a smile. "Good morning. Where would you like me to unload this stuff?"

Nick pointed toward the far end of the house. "As close to the backyard as possible."

"Sounds good." He looked past Nick, his smile brightening considerably. "Hey, Callie girl, how are you?"

The woman in question walked right past Nick to give Mr. Reed a big hug. Nick never thought he'd see the day he'd be envious of a man half his size and twice his age, but he was.

"I'm fine, Clarence. How's that lovely wife of yours doing?"

He grinned and patted his slight potbelly. "Still trying to fatten me up."

Callie laughed. "Seriously, if I ate Marcy's pie as often as you do, I'd have to ride on the back of that flatbed because I wouldn't fit inside the cab."

The older man flushed with pride. "Let me know when you've got a free night, and we'll have you over for some of that pie. Blueberries are in season, you know. Bring your young man with you."

Then he glanced toward the porch with a puzzled look on his face. "Both of your young men."

Nick waited to see what she had to say on that situation. Her happy smile faded into one that was tinged with sadness.

"Nick and Leif are Spence's friends. They served in Afghanistan with him. I'm sure they would love to sample Marcy's cooking. They've been living on my meager fare for days."

Clarence straightened his shoulders as he met Nick's gaze and then Leif's. "It would be our pleasure to have two of our nation's heroes join us for a meal. Thank you both for your service to our country."

Nick appreciated the sentiment but never knew how to respond when people said things like that. Luckily, the corporal spoke up.

"It is our privilege and our honor, sir."

Leif held on to the railing and slowly eased himself down the steps. "Callie's cooking is great, and she bakes a mean cookie. However, you had me at the mention of blueberry pie. I'd love to come. We both would."

Clarence nodded. "I'll check with my wife and get back to you to set a time and date."

"Sounds good, sir. I'll look forward to it."

While Nick was grateful Leif knew how to turn on the charm, enough was enough. Now that the social crap was out of the way, he was ready to get down to business.

"Can we start getting this stuff unloaded?" He belatedly added a smile to soften the edges of his question.

Clarence walked past him. "Good idea. I'm sure you're wanting to get started on your project. Let's find the best place to offload the lumber. Callie, want to show me where the gazebo is going to be built?"

She walked around back with him, with Mooch providing escort as usual. Clarence bent down to pick up a stick and threw it. The goofy dog took off after it and pranced back to his new friend with his prize.

The trio returned a few seconds later. Clarence studied the yard. "If you're sure it won't tear up the lawn too much, I'll drive around back."

"That will be fine, Clarence, and it will make it easier for Nick if his materials are close at hand. There's other work that needs to be done on the place, so I'm sure there'll be other contractors driving in and out for a while. Fixing the yard up is pretty low on my list right now."

"Sounds good. Guess I'll get right to it."

The truck rumbled to life as the police chief pulled into the driveway. He pulled off onto the grass, probably to give Clarence enough room to maneuver.

When he joined Nick and the others, Gage asked, "Is that Clarence driving the truck by himself? Usually he has a couple of the high school football players with him to do the heavy work."

Well, crap. Nick had been wondering about that himself. "I had expected him to have one of those little forklifts with him."

Gage fell into step with Nick. "Doubt he can afford one right now. With the housing market tanking around here, it's hit his business hard. I'll give you a hand pulling stuff off the truck after I take a quick look around. Doubt I'll learn anything new about your intruder, but I wouldn't want to miss anything."

"Sounds good."

So did having something physical to do that would help Nick work out the kinks in his muscles and his attitude. He hadn't missed the way Callie was tracking his every move as if she were waiting to pounce the second she thought he wouldn't bite.

That was going to be a fun discussion. Rather than worry about it now, he started unfastening the ties that held the lumber in place.

Chapter 21

Callie made a thermos of lemonade and a big stack of sandwiches and waited for the crew outside to take a break. Gage, Leif, and Nick had been working in the yard all morning doing all kinds of manly things, the kind they evidently didn't want a woman's help with, or at least not hers. Ordinarily, she would have put on her work gloves and ignored their protests.

The only reason she hadn't was because of Leif. He was doing his best to keep up with the other two, but it was a struggle for him. When she'd tried to help him lift down some two-by-fours, he clearly hadn't appreciated her efforts. Nick had caught her attention and shook his head. Okay, fine. She could take a hint.

Evidently it was supposed to be Gage's day off, and he had pitched in to help after the two of them had walked through Spence's house together. He'd given her the okay to clean up the rest of the broken glass. Clarence had measured the broken window before he'd left and promised to call Nick when he had the glass cut. Evidently, there wasn't any kind of house repair that Nick couldn't handle.

She supposed she should be grateful. Well, she was, but it would be way too easy to get used to having him around to take care of things like that. As she swept up the last of the shards of glass and tossed them in the trash, she hoped her heart didn't end up shattered just like the window. It wasn't as if she could order a new one from the hardware store, and patching it back together wouldn't be any fun at all.

She wiped down the counters next and set the table. It didn't look as if the guys were going to quit anytime soon, so she straightened a few things and then moved on to the den. Leif had already made the bed, square corners and all. It made her feel guilty about the mess she'd left in her own room.

Meanwhile, she'd give the den a quick dusting since she hadn't had a chance to do more than throw the sheets on the bed last night. As she swiped the cloth across the end table next to the sofa bed, it snagged on a sticky spot. Maybe Leif had spilled something. When she went to wash it off, the wet paper towel turned red.

Bloodred.

On closer look, she could see where the liquid had soaked into the wood. It was Leif's blood, had to be. Poor guy, he was lucky that he wasn't hurt worse than he had been. She'd like to get her hands on the jerk who'd dare attack an injured man or, better yet, let Nick have at him.

Unfortunately, from what Gage had told her, it was unlikely they'd find enough evidence to pin the break-in on anyone. From the questions he'd asked, she had to guess that Spence's uncle and cousin were high on his list of suspects. But with no proof, there wasn't much he could do.

The back door opened. The rapid footsteps meant it wasn't Leif, which left either the police chief or Nick.

The latter had been avoiding being alone with her all morning. Maybe this would be her one chance to corner him for a little talk.

The kitchen was empty, so he must have ducked into the bathroom off the utility room. No way she wanted to talk to Nick badly enough to confront him in there. Instead, she checked the backyard to make sure it was him. The last thing she wanted to do was get caught lying in wait for the wrong man.

Sure enough, Gage and Leif were busy measuring some lumber. The men had set up a power saw on a table to cut the wood. Earlier, Nick had dragged a tall stool outside for Leif to sit on, giving his friend a way to be useful without putting undue stress on his injured ankle.

That was thoughtful of him, especially when it was obvious that Leif refused to cut himself any slack. He had to be hurting since he hadn't taken his usual pills this morning. She hated to see him in pain, but at least he was smart enough to know that power tools and strong drugs don't work well together.

The bathroom door opened. She drew a slow breath before turning to face Nick. Her heart immediately jumped in her chest. He'd stripped off his shirt while working outside, leaving his chest bare. The faint dusting of hair on his chest narrowed down to disappear underneath the waistband of his low-slung jeans. She'd thought him sexy before, but after last night she knew exactly how all that warm, tan skin felt.

She hungered.

Rather than give in to the urge to step toward him and unwilling to retreat, she dug her nails into the palms of her hands, planted her feet, and stood her ground. Nick froze in the doorway, neither in the utility room nor in the kitchen, watching her with a wary look in his dark eyes. Why? What did he think she was going to do to him with his two good buddies within shouting distance?

Pointing out the door, she said, "Now isn't the time to have that little talk I warned you about, so you can relax, Nick. Go tell your buddies that lunch is ready. You've been at it all morning, and I'm betting at least Leif needs a break."

Then she stepped back to give him room enough to pass. At the last second, she blocked his way long enough to kiss him on the cheek. "And nice job setting him up with the stool, big guy."

Hours later, Nick was more than ready for the day to be over. It had been productive, and they'd made good progress on the gazebo. They'd gotten the footings in place and framed in the floor. At the rate they were going, it would be finished and ready to paint in two more days, three tops. Then he'd be packing up and driving back to Ohio.

Unless he found another excuse to stay longer, which might be the stupidest thing he'd ever done. The more time he spent around Callie, the harder it was going to be to walk away and not look back. Or worse yet, come crawling back.

Stepping into the shower, he cranked the dial all the way to freezing. When the blast of frigid water failed to cool his temper or his raging erection, he gave up and adjusted the water to a more tolerable temperature.

He wouldn't need to resort to such extremes if that damn woman would stay out of sight and out of his head. But all day long, there she'd been. Bringing out cold drinks and snacks. Digging up an old boom box and cranking up some classic rock for them to listen to while they hammered away.

She'd even coaxed Leif into taking a nap, pointing out that he'd cut enough lumber to keep Nick and Gage busy for a couple of hours. Rather than nag at the man about taking it easy, she'd made it sound as if he was doing everybody else a favor by giving them a chance to get caught up. She'd said flat out that Leif was making Nick look bad because he couldn't keep up with him.

He smiled up into the stinging spray. Granted she hadn't fooled any of them with that line of bull, least of all Leif, but he'd let her persuade him to go along with it. Pride was important, especially when that was all a man had left. The corporal had planned on making the army his career, and right now all of that was up in the air. Everything depended on how well his ankle mended. With all the screws and plates that had gone into patching it up, they all knew it added up to one big question mark.

Time to get moving. Nick was running out of both hot water and excuses. If he didn't seek out Callie for that talk she was hell-bent on having, she'd come looking for him. Considering he expected her to rip him a new one, he'd prefer some privacy.

What was she so upset about? She was the one who said she wanted to wish away everything that had happened yesterday. How was he supposed to know she hadn't meant to include what had happened between the two of them?

He had mixed feelings about it himself. Satisfaction was a big part of it. Even allowing for how long it had been since he'd last taken a woman to bed, coming together with Callie had been amazing. Not that her parents' lawn was technically a bed. Pride definitely added its own spice. He'd bet his last dollar she wasn't the kind of woman usually given to rolling around naked in the grass with a man she'd known only a few days.

But the overtones of guilt colored everything else. She'd belonged in Spence's life, not Nick's. He could write it all off to two people finding solace over their mutual loss, but that would be a lie, at least on his part. He'd taken Callie because he'd wanted her. Plain and simple.

The worst part of his guilt came from the knowledge that he'd do so again in a heartbeat. Some friend he was.

He put on a clean pair of jeans and a short-sleeved shirt. It looked like hell from being crammed in his duffel, but it was the best he could do. Bracing himself for Leif's disapproval, he headed downstairs.

It came as no surprise that his friend was waiting for him in the living room. He stared at Nick long and hard before speaking.

"For the last time, Nick, what's going on between you and Callie? And don't feed me any more crap about building the gazebo in Spence's memory. Lie to yourself all you want, but don't bullshit me."

Nick toyed with marching right on out the door without answering, but Leif was here because Nick had asked him to come. He'd known he needed a buffer between him and Callie; that didn't mean he could look his friend in the eye and confess all his sins. Maybe the best course was a little honesty—or as close as he could come without blurting it all out. The truth about what had happened last night was between him and Callie. Period.

Staring out into the yard, he said, "Out there is Spence's hometown, and this is Spence's house. Everything you see belongs to him."

Before he could continue, Leif said, "Including Cal-lie."

He was stating a fact, not asking a question. What could Nick do but nod? It was a truth that stabbed Nick right in the gut. He forced himself to agree. "Yes, Leif, including Callie."

"So why the gazebo?"

Did he really have to lay it all out for him? "Because maybe I'm a selfish bastard. When I drive out of Snowberry Creek for good, I want to leave something of myself behind, too. Something permanent."

Because right now he was rootless. No home, not even a rented apartment, just a few boxes stuck in a storage unit someplace. The room started closing in on him as the guilt and shame in his chest expanded until there was no room to breathe. He had to get outside. Immediately, before he lost it completely.

He made it to the door without letting the panic show. Outside in the yard, Mooch caught up with him, whining softly in concern. Nick knelt down to wrap his arms around his four-legged therapist. Soft fur and a warm body went a long way toward dragging him back from the edge.

"Nick?"

Okay, so he hadn't disguised his pain as well as he'd thought. As the iron band of panic around his chest gradually eased, he stood up.

"Sarge, are you okay?"

Hell no, but he was as okay as he was going to be for now. He forced himself to look back toward his friend.

"I'll be fine, Leif. We both will."

Then he walked away, desperately hoping that he was right about that.

*   *   *

The last thing he wanted to do was show up at Callie's house all fucked-up in the head again. That meant he had to get through the woods without jumping at shadows and imagined threats. Last night his gun had made her skittish, so he'd settled for carrying his combat knife this time.

Gripping it hard enough to make his knuckles ache, he walked with measured treads, neither rushing nor dragging his feet. Mooch was cool, calm, and collected, which helped Nick's own mood stay level. Before stepping out into Callie's backyard, he paused long enough to stick his knife on the back side of a Douglas fir. There was no reason to freak her out by showing up on her back porch toting an eight-inch blade. He'd retrieve it later on his way back to Spence's.

He headed across the yard and up the steps to the back door. Would she invite him in or keep him outside? He didn't much care as long as she was still talking to him. His biggest fear was that she'd remain on the wrong side of the door, leaving him alone on the porch.

He'd hate that but wouldn't blame her if she did. Not much, anyway. He rapped on the doorframe and waited to see which way the wind was blowing.

At least she didn't keep him waiting for long. Callie opened the inside door but didn't immediately open the screen door, as she studied him for several seconds.

"Do you want to come in?"

All things considered, maybe it would be better if he didn't. "It's a nice night. Want to go for a walk instead? I'll even spring for some ice cream if you're interested."

Her smile was slightly happier. "When it comes to ice cream, I'm always interested. Let me put on better shoes and lock up."

While he waited, he called Mooch to his side. "Listen, dog. You make a great wingman, but not this time. You head back to the house and watch over Leif for me."

The dog plunked his backside down on the porch and stared up at Nick, his head tilted to the side as if thinking it over. "Go on and go, Mooch. Leif needs you, too, and I'm all right for now."

Still not moving. Nick squatted down to meet the dog's gaze head-on. "Listen, soldier, that was an order. Go keep an eye on things for me while I'm away from my post. I want to iron out some things with Callie, and I have to know that things are under control while I'm gone. Stay, Mooch."

Finally, the dog yipped softly and took off running back toward the other house. That didn't mean he'd stay there, but it was a start. If he showed back up again, Nick would carry him back to Spence's house and lock him inside, if that was what it took to have some time alone with Callie.

She joined him out on the porch. "Ready?"

Was she talking about the ice cream or the talk? Either way the answer was the same.

"I am."

Nick slunk past the entrance to Spence's driveway and then picked up speed until they were some distance down the road. Callie managed to keep pace with him but had to ask, "Are we in a particular hurry?"

He immediately slowed down, looking a bit guilty. "Not at all, but I told Mooch he couldn't come with us. He headed back to the house when I told him to, but I'm not sure he'll stay there, especially if he realizes I'm with you."

"I wouldn't have minded if he tagged along."

"I figured you wouldn't." Nick reached out to take

her hand in his with a quick squeeze. "I feel better knowing he's there to keep an eye on things, especially because Leif promised to take some of his meds soon. Once that happens, he'll probably zone out on the couch in front of the television. Mooch can sound the alarm on the off chance our visitor is stupid enough to come back tonight."

She tightened her hold on Nick's hand. "Do you think he will?"

"No, at least not so soon. Having the cops show up so quickly after he broke in last night had to have spooked him a bit. He also knows the house isn't empty all the time."

She hoped that was true.

Nick dropped her hand to wrap his arm around her shoulders instead. "Let's not give the bastard the power to ruin an ice-cream run for us."

"Fair enough."

And truthfully, she felt safe from the whole world when Nick held her close like this. Well, safe from everyone but him. For now, though, she'd enjoy their walk. There would be time for the hard stuff after ice cream.

As they continued on, Nick seemed to relax, and gradually his almost hypervigilance disappeared. Her house was located on the outskirts of Snowberry Creek, barely within the city limits. As they drew closer to the business district, the houses were closer together and the yards smaller. A fair number of her neighbors were out on their front porches enjoying the evening air.

They waved as she and Nick passed by, several calling out for her to tell her folks hello for them. No doubt the local gossip mill would be in full swing within minutes. It was too much to hope that no one would e-mail her mother about seeing Callie out walking with a handsome man.

Nick picked up on their interest, too. "Why do I feel as if we're on display, kind of like we're the chimps at the zoo on parade for all the local humans?"

She giggled at the analogy. "Aren't you from a fairly small town, too? If so, you know how all of this works, and don't tell me that folks there don't live to gossip."

"That they do, but I haven't been subjected to it for a while. I'd almost forgotten what it was like. Think we should stop and fill in some details for them? Like where I'm from or how we met?"

Then he gave her a sly smile. "Or, better yet, give them something to really talk about?"

Images from last night's encounter in the backyard filled her mind. Oh, yeah, anything along that line would certainly set the tongues to wagging.

"As tempting as that is, Sergeant Jenkins, I'm pretty sure some of the older folks have heart conditions. I wouldn't want to jeopardize anyone's health. Besides, I'm not sure Gage would appreciate having us be at the heart of another emergency call so soon."

Nick looked genuinely disappointed. "Too bad."

They'd finally reached the business district. There was a line at the ice-cream shop, but it moved quickly. She snickered when Nick didn't even bother to check out the flavor choices, settling for plain old vanilla.

"What? I've always liked vanilla."

Even if he sounded a little defensive, she tweaked his nose about it. "Not very adventurous for a big, tough soldier like you, is it?"

"I've had enough adventure for one lifetime." He grimaced as if regretting his response. Then he lightened the moment by adding, "And maybe I'm saving today's allotment of adventure for something better than ice cream."

Her cheeks flushed hot. "Good answer, Sergeant."

Back outside, they headed for the same small park where they'd shared muffins and coffee with Gage and his daughter. All of the picnic tables were taken, so they followed the path along the creek for a short distance until they found a small clearing that would afford them some privacy.

They settled down in the grass in companionable silence while they finished their cones. Nick leaned back on his elbows and stared up at the sky.

"Ready for that talk you wanted to have?"

Not really. In fact, she wished they could skip it altogether, but they needed to set some rules. Maybe come up with some guidelines about where this relationship was headed or even if it was headed anywhere at all.

"Nick, what I said last night was thoughtless. When I wanted to wish away everything that happened, you've got to believe I was talking about the break-in and Leif getting hurt, not you. Not us."

She drew her knees up and wrapped her arms around them. "As I tried to tell you last night, I don't regret what happened between the two of us. I still don't."

He rolled onto his side to face her but kept his distance. "I know that now. I should have known it last night, too."

She wished he'd tug her down beside him or even take her hand in his like he had just a short time ago. But she sensed it wouldn't be wise to push him too hard right now. There was a question she had to ask, especially because he hadn't volunteered the information himself.

"Now we both know how I feel about last night, but do you regret it, Nick?"

More silence, which gave her at least a partial answer. Her blood ran as cold as the ice cream had been as she waited for him to answer. "Can't you at least tell me why?"

He rolled onto his back again, studying the stars overhead as if the answer were written up there in the sky. Fine.

"I'm a big girl, Nick. Just spit it out. And don't try to sell me that usual guy line of crap that the problem is with you and not me, because I won't buy it."

That had him sitting up. "How do you figure?"

She wanted to punch something or, better yet, him. "Oh, please, Nick. You weren't alone out in my folks' backyard last night. That was me you were—"

He abruptly sat up and stopped her tirade by putting his hand over her mouth. "Believe me, I know it was you. And if you keep talking that loud, everyone in the park will know it, too."

She'd had enough. "I'm out of here."

"Don't go. Not yet."

Nick caught her arm, tugging her back down. When she didn't struggle, he released his hold on her. He drew his legs up and rested his head on his arms, staring down at the ground this time.

"I'm sorry for screwing this all up."

His frustration echoed hers. "Nick, I don't even know what *this* is. Obviously something about our relationship is a big-time problem for you. If it's too much too fast, fine. We'll slow it down."

He looked up at her briefly. "For both our sakes, aiming for just being friends might be the smartest move."

"I'm not even going to ask why that is, Nick. Obviously, you've already made up your mind that's how it has to be."

This time when she moved to stand up, he didn't stop her. Before she could leave the clearing, he blocked her way. "I don't want to hurt you, Callie."

"You already have, but I'll get over it. I thought there was a chance for something special between us. Obviously I was mistaken about that. But regardless, I'm more worried about you, Nick. I hate seeing you in such pain and not being able to do anything about it."

He winced as if her words had struck a physical blow. "I'm sorry, Callie. I really am."

And God help her, she believed him. It would be smarter to tell him to pack up and leave. That she'd pay someone to finish the project he'd started, and he could get on with his life without Mooch and without her. She wasn't going to do either of those things for the simple fact that he'd probably do just what she asked if she pushed too hard.

As frustrated as she was, she wasn't ready to stand in Spence's driveway and wave good-bye to Nick.

"I should get back home."

He nodded. "Me, too."

They headed back down the path, this time careful to maintain a safe distance from each other. As they walked, it occurred to her to wonder about one thing. When he said he should go home, did he mean Spence's place or back where his folks lived in Ohio?

She'd have to wait and see, because right now she didn't have the courage to ask.

Chapter 22

❧ ❧

"How did it go?"

Nick pulled one of the wicker rockers closer to Leif's and sat down. "Better than expected. Worse than I'd hoped for."

His friend kept rocking, his expression relaxed and calm, although that could be the drugs. "So should I be packing my bag anytime soon?"

"Not yet, although it was close."

The jerk actually laughed. "Man, you must have taken your talent for offending people to a whole new level. What did you say to Callie that pissed her off that bad?"

"I said we should be friends."

Another round of Leif's laughter rang out in the night. "Damn, Nick, what were you thinking? You're lucky she didn't gut you with your own knife. I admit I'm not an expert with women, but even I know that's like waving a red flag in front of a bull."

"Tell me something I don't know."

Leif took a long swig from his root beer. "I can tell you this much: I like Callie, Nick. A whole lot, actually.

I can see why Spence wanted to hook up with her when he got back."

But Spence hadn't gotten to come back, not like Nick and Leif. Hell, even Mooch had survived life on the brutal streets of Afghanistan. Everybody had gotten home safely except Spence. And Nick's gut was tied up in a knot of guilt and grief over it.

Leif kept right on talking. "Maybe they could have built a good life for themselves here, but I've got to say I'm having a hard time imagining Spence sitting still long enough to be happy in a small town like this. From the way he used to talk about his past, it was clear he couldn't wait to get the hell out of Snowberry Creek permanently."

Nick shrugged. "I felt the same way about my own hometown."

And that hadn't changed. The whole time Nick had been at his parents' house, it was as if his clothes were all two sizes too small. Nothing fit right. Nothing felt right. He didn't belong there anymore.

On the other hand, here in Snowberry Creek, he could breathe. It wasn't just because Callie was next door, although that was part of it. A big part. The whole area, with its mountains and towering trees, was beautiful, so unlike the hellholes where he'd spent so much of his time since joining the army.

He could see himself building a life here, but that wasn't going to happen. It would feel too much like he was an imposter, trying to pass himself off as Spence somehow. Even so, his instincts were screaming that this place had what he needed in order to heal from the inside out.

He kept rocking at a steady pace, trying hard to hide his churning nerves. "You should know that I'm going to talk to Callie about doing more than building the gazebo for her. I want to act as the general contractor on all of the work she needs done on this place."

He threw it out there as if he'd put a lot of time and thought into the idea, although he hadn't. It was as if the plan had simply sprung into existence fully formed, all the bits and pieces fitting together perfectly.

Leif stopped rocking to stare at him in total shock. "Seriously, Nick? What in the hell put that craziness into your head?"

"It's not crazy. You know damn well my dad is a general contractor, and I put myself through school working for him summers and holidays. By the time I enlisted, I had been writing up estimates and hiring the subcontractors for years."

His friend let out a long, slow breath and resumed rocking again. "Okay, maybe it's not completely insane, but have you talked to Callie about this?"

"Not yet. I wanted to see how things went with a small project first, to see if I still liked the hands-on part of it. I'm planning to do most of the work myself and only subbing out stuff like the plumbing and electrical."

"So why not go back and work for your dad?"

Good question, one Nick had no easy answer for. Maybe because he needed to do something on his own. Something for himself.

He stared at his combat knife, hating what it represented. "I need to fix something."

Starting with himself, patching up a few of the holes the war had ripped in his heart and soul. Maybe someday he would even rediscover the man he used to be.

Leif stared at Nick for a long time, maybe trying to decide how serious he was about the idea.

Finally, he stood up. "You should have a couple of beers if we're going to keep talking about this. That way when Callie tells us we're out of our heads, we can truthfully say you were drunk and I was on pain pills at the time."

Nick laughed and followed him inside. "Let's work at the kitchen table. The light's better and the beer's closer."

"I like the way you think, Sarge."

"Thanks, Corporal. I live to please."

Callie hadn't been sure what to expect from Nick the next time she saw him. As far as she could tell, their awkward encounter hadn't affected him at all. On the other hand, she'd tossed and turned most of the night, leaving her crabby and spoiling for a fight.

Considering how hard he was working on the gazebo, she couldn't very well complain. Of course, that probably meant he was trying to get it finished as fast as possible so he could get back to his real life. She could hardly stand the thought of him deploying again, not when the last one had cost him and his friends so much. She'd already lost one friend in the war; she didn't want to lose another.

Since she couldn't use Nick as a target for her bad mood, she would've settled for nagging at Leif about overdoing it. That didn't work, either, because he had dragged one of the lawn chairs into the shade and was supervising the project. Evidently his duties consisted of consuming cold drinks and offering worthless bits of advice to Nick in between naps.

They were both jerks.

She'd delivered lunch but hadn't stuck around to share it. Instead, she'd spent the afternoon working on her inventory in the rooms upstairs, avoiding Nick's bedroom. The last thing she needed was to hang around in there.

After a couple of grueling hours, she finished two of the smaller bedrooms and moved up to the third floor. She hadn't spent much time at all on that level of the house, but it was obvious that three things had gone missing recently. Nothing big, though, judging by the size of the empty spots in the dust.

She clenched her fists and stamped her foot in frustration. Gage wanted her to let him know if she discovered anything had been taken. What good would that do when she had no idea what had been there in the first place?

Maybe rather than dragging Gage all the way back out to the house, she'd pay him a visit. She needed to stop at the store anyway, not to mention she had a craving for something wicked and bad for her waistline from Bridey's shop. Maybe she'd even take pity on Leif and his friend and bring something back for them.

Should she tell Nick about the missing items? Would he even care? Okay, that wasn't fair. Of course he'd care. She gathered up her camera and notes and headed back downstairs. The men were right where she'd left them. Well, not quite. Leif was now sitting on the stool wielding a paintbrush with wild abandon, considering the drips of primer on his pants and the grass.

He smiled when he saw her. "It's really coming along, isn't it?"

She dutifully admired the gazebo, honestly loving its graceful lines and open design. "Yes, it is."

"Nick does quality work, that's for sure. I try not to stroke his ego too much, but he sure knows a lot about this kind of stuff."

The third member of the party joined in the discussion. "Leif, thanks for talking me up like that, but seriously, I don't want to think about you stroking anything of mine."

Leif responded by flicking paint at him. "Fine, you big jerk."

Callie couldn't help but laugh at their good-natured sniping. "I'm going to make a run into town. Do either of you need anything from the store?"

Leif went back to his painting. "I could use another twelve-pack of root beer. Nick, how about you? Need anything?"

For the first time all day Nick looked directly at her. She truly hoped that it wasn't a desire for beer that put that hint of heat in his dark eyes. Her skin flushed hot as she waited for him to answer.

"I'm good."

Yes, he was, even if she was thinking of something completely different than he was. He was way better than just good, but she kept that to herself. After all, they weren't going there again. More's the pity.

"Any preference about what I fix for dinner tonight?"

Nick stepped down off the ladder he'd been working on. "Let's keep it simple. Maybe grill something."

That sounded good to her, too. "I could pick up some salmon while I'm in town. How does that sound?"

It was Leif who answered. "Perfect. I haven't had fresh seafood in a while."

Before leaving, she walked over to where he was sitting. "Give me the brush. You missed a spot."

When he handed it over, she dabbed it on his nose and then danced back out of reach.

"Hey, what was that for?"

She giggled and surrendered the brush. "You have that stuff splashed on your forehead and both cheeks. I wanted to complete the look."

Leif rolled his eyes and used a rag to swipe at his face. All he succeeded in doing was smearing the paint even more. He tried to look fierce but couldn't quite hide his grin.

"You'd better get going, woman. I might not move as fast as Nick, but I'm sneakier. There will be retribution."

He waggled his eyebrows in a halfhearted attempt to look evil; instead he only looked playful. She offered him a deal.

"Forgive me, and I'll also pick up something for dessert."

"It's a deal."

"I won't be gone long."

As she spoke, she happened to look at Nick. He was watching the two of them with the oddest look on his face, a little fierce mixed with a touch of temper. When he realized she was watching him, his expression changed, once again the amiable guy she liked so much.

It took too much effort to keep track of his shifting moods, so she left. She had enough on her plate at the moment without burning up all her energy on figuring out Nick.

Callie slid a ten-dollar bill across the counter. "I'll take those pastries and my iced coffee to go."

Bridey bagged up Callie's choices and mixed her drink. As she made change, she asked, "You still have those hunky soldiers hanging out at your place?"

"Yep, both of them."

"And keeping them both all to yourself? Doesn't seem fair." She handed over the goodies. "I'm just saying."

Callie could take a hint even when hit over the head with a sledgehammer. "I'm going to grill salmon for dinner tonight. I'm aiming for easy, so I'll fix a tossed salad and roast some corn on the grill. Would you like to join us?"

Then she held up the bag. "And if you say yes, I'll be needing another one of these."

Bridey immediately picked up another raspberry turnover with her tongs and dropped it into the bag. "I'll tell you what: Save those for tomorrow's breakfast, and I'll bring a cheesecake. I've been experimenting with a new recipe that's topped with a blackberry compote. I'd love a chance to try it out."

Callie licked her lips. "Whoa, that sounds decadent. I'd be a fool to turn down an offer like that, and both of the guys have a serious sweet tooth."

Bridey frowned. "The only problem is that I can't be there until seven. I hope that's not too late. I've got to make the bank deposit on the way home, and I'll need time to shower and change clothes. I'd just as soon not show up smelling like yeast and coffee."

"Seven will be fine." Then Callie added, "But seriously, I'm thinking if you could bottle that scent as a perfume, men would be following you in droves."

Bridey wasn't buying it. "It hasn't worked so far. Besides, I don't need droves. I'd settle for one decent prospect. See you at seven."

Ten minutes later Callie paused outside Gage's office to take a deep breath. Now that she was there, she wished she'd gone straight to the store. She felt foolish taking up so much of the police chief's time. It wasn't like he could do anything about empty circles in the dust.

Maybe there'd been nothing there in the first place and she was imagining things. No, the empty marks in the dust spoke for themselves. Heck, as far as she knew, the missing objects were probably worthless, the kind of things people held on to only because of the memories they evoked.

Yeah, this was silly. Time to go. Before she could retreat, Gage opened his office door. Callie froze, caught between the need to tell him what had happened and feeling foolish for talking about a phantom stealing unknown objects.

"Callie? Did you need to see me?"

There was no way he'd let her walk away without an answer. "Yes, if you've got a few minutes."

"Always." He stepped back into his office and motioned her toward one of the two chairs in front of his desk. "I was on my way to get a cup of coffee. Want one?"

"Sure. Cream and sugar."

He wasn't gone long. While he settled back in at his desk, she wrapped her hands around the mug he'd handed her, taking comfort from the warmth. When she forced herself to look at Gage, he was watching her with the same kind of patience a cat had when stalking its prey. She didn't feel threatened by him but recognized that he was a hunter on the trail.

"I've been working on my inventory of Spence's house again. I started off on the first floor, but today I moved upstairs. Once I finished two of the bedrooms, I headed up to the third floor."

"And," he prompted when she fell silent.

"As soon as I walked into the front bedroom, I noticed marks in the dust." She paused for a long drink, her throat as dry as that dust. "I know this sounds crazy, but it looks as if something has been taken or maybe moved. But here's the problem: it's been years since I spent much time in Spence's house. Even then, I didn't go up to the third floor much at all."

He'd started to fill out a form but stopped and laid

down his pen. "So you don't know what belonged in those rooms."

Good, he did understand. "That's right, I don't, which is why I started the inventory in the first place. I can't even tell you when the last time was that anyone cleaned those rooms. The dust was pretty thick, so I'm thinking it was at least sometime before Spence was deployed, maybe a year or even longer. That's why the marks were so clear."

She pulled out her digital camera and brought up the snapshot she'd taken of the marks. "This is what I saw."

Gage studied the picture for several seconds before handing the camera back. He leaned back in his chair, its springs creaking in protest. "Well, obviously we can't do much with what you've told me or that picture. Even so, I don't like the idea that someone has been in and out of that house on multiple occasions."

He linked his hands behind his head and stared at a spot over Callie's head. "It could have been teenagers making use of an empty house. That's what I told Nick when he came to talk to me last week after the night he and that dog of his thought someone was prowling out in the woods."

Then he looked straight at her. "But my gut doesn't buy that, and neither does his. For one thing, kids leave more in the way of evidence. Beer cans, trash, stuff like that. No, I think it's much more likely that someone was looking to make a quick score off stuff no one will miss."

He paused, maybe waiting for her to respond. At the moment, it was all she could do to get her head around the idea that Nick had been talking to Gage about prowlers on her property without telling her. The idea had her fuming. What was he thinking? He should have come to her first, or at the very least told her what he'd done. Nick would get an earful when she got back home.

After several seconds, Gage sat up straight. "Here's what I'm going to do. First, I'll check with the neighboring towns to see if they've had anything similar reported. If it's a pro working the area, there's bound to be other similar instances. Right after that, I'm going to track down Spence's uncle or his son and have a talk with him."

At least Gage was taking her seriously and even had an immediate plan of action. "I appreciate this, Gage. It may turn out to be nothing, and I have to admit that wouldn't upset me. But after the incident with the rock and Leif getting hurt, I thought it best to let you know."

She wished she felt better about it, though.

"You did the right thing by coming to see me, Callie. I know you're hoping that it wasn't Vince or his son. However, they seem to me to be the most likely culprits. When the news hit town about Spence, they both made it abundantly clear they thought they should've been entitled to a little something from the estate or, better yet, all of it. Considering what I've heard about the way Vince treated Spence, though, it came as no surprise that he cut them out of not just his will but also his life."

Memories of how truly bad it had been for Spence had her wanting to kick his uncle even after all these years. "Austin was just a kid when Spence's folks died, but Vince was already a mean drunk. He hated everything about Spence. It's hard to imagine how he and Spence's mom came out of the same family. She was so warm and loving. The only thing Vince has ever loved is a bottle of cheap booze."

Her eyes burned, but she blinked until the sting of

tears faded. "Sorry, Gage. Guess I'm still not dealing with losing Spence all that well."

"Not a problem, Callie. His death should be hard to deal with, not just for you but for all of us. He wasn't only your friend. He was a real hero."

The sincerity in Gage's voice eased Callie's pain enough that she could breathe. It was time to go.

"Thanks again for listening. I've taken up enough of your time, and I still have errands to run."

Gage walked her to the front door of the police department. "I like your friends, Callie. They've been dealt a tough hand, but they're both good men. The town could use a few more just like them."

"That's true."

And if the thought of Nick settling down in Snowberry Creek caused her pulse to race, well, that was her own little secret.

Chapter 23

Callie was glad Bridey arrived before the guys came over. Nick had called to say he and Leif were making a beer run and to see if she needed anything from the store. Then he'd lowered his voice to admit that it was really his way to save wear and tear on Leif's leg by driving him over to Callie's.

She was still aggravated about him keeping secrets from her, but it was hard to stay mad at a man who went out of his way to protect his friend's pride.

Bridey helped set the picnic table. "Are you sure the guys won't mind me being here? Especially Leif?"

Callie had been checking the coals in the grill. "Why Leif?"

Her friend looked a little uncomfortable. "I didn't think about it until after I'd already agreed to come, but it feels kind of like a fix-up. You've made it clear that you have your sights set on Nick, so that leaves Leif and me unattached. I wouldn't want him to think I was expecting to be paired up with him."

Callie hadn't thought that far ahead. "To be honest, I'm not sure what's going on between me and Nick these days. I wasn't thinking about this like a date night for any of us."

Bridey looked only marginally happier as she pointed toward the top of the driveway, where Nick had just pulled in behind her car. "Well, either way, it's too late now."

Callie's pulse sped up as the two men made their way to where she and Bridey were putting the finishing touches on the table. She was glad she'd taken a little more care with her appearance since both Nick and Leif were wearing something other than their usual T-shirts and jeans. She wasn't sure brightly colored Hawaiian shirts could be considered dressing up, but both guys looked good in them.

"Love the shirts, guys."

Leif looked down at the splash of red and white flowers on his. "They were Nick's idea. What do you think?"

Bridey answered before Callie had a chance. "I think they look great."

She stepped forward holding out her hand. "I'm Bridey, by the way."

Leif shifted his cane to his other hand to shake hers. "It's nice to meet you. I'm Leif Brevik. And if my boy Nick here told you anything about me, I swear it was all lies."

Then he winked at her. "Unless he said something good, of course. It would still be all lies, but I'll stand by whatever he said."

The exchange set the tone for most of the evening. Nick and Leif took turns entertaining them with hilarious stories about their exploits in the army. They included Spence's contributions to the scrapes they'd gotten into, but for once the mention of his name brought more smiles than sorrow. Callie suspected they all needed a bit of that.

In return, she and Bridey shared a few memories from high school. One of her favorites was when Spence and the rest of the football team were ordered to perform a musical number in the high school talent show. The coach hadn't been too happy when they'd dutifully shown up, all wearing dresses, makeup, and heels.

She smiled. "I'm sure I've got a picture somewhere. You've got to wonder where they found so many pairs of high heels for size thirteen feet."

Nick laughed and shook his head. "Wish I could have been there. If we'd known such a picture existed, we would have given Wheels all kinds of grief over it."

Nick looked more relaxed than he had in days. So did Leif, for that matter. Unfortunately, Bridey had started checking her watch.

"I hate to break up such a great party, but morning comes early for me. Nick, can you move your truck for me?"

"Sure thing."

But when he started to get up, Leif stopped him. "Why don't you give me the keys? I should be getting back to the house."

Nick tossed him the key ring. "I'll catch up with you soon."

"See you in a few minutes, Sarge. Don't keep me waiting too long. It's past our bedtime." Leif was already in motion. "Callie, thanks for dinner. The salmon was great."

He fell into step with Bridey. "And that cheesecake was flat-out amazing. If I keep eating like this, I'm going to need bigger uniforms."

Bridey paused. "Oh, that's too bad. I left the rest of the cheesecake with Callie. Maybe I should take it back home with me."

Leif caught Bridey by the hand before she could act on the threat. "No way, lady. I promise to share the leftovers with my man Nick and maybe Callie."

"If you're sure, Leif."

The two of them kept up the discussion all the way to her car.

Nick watched as his friend climbed into the truck and then backed out of the driveway. "It's good to see Leif acting more like himself."

Callie sat down on the swing, careful to leave some space between her and Nick. "I think Bridey had a good time, too. The coffee shop keeps her pretty busy."

Nick set the swing in motion, rocking it slowly back and forth. "That's true for anyone who owns their own business."

"I know."

But that's not what she wanted to talk about right now. "Nick, Gage told me today that you'd talked to him last week about someone prowling in the woods. Why didn't you tell me about it yourself?"

He went rock still. "I guess I should have, especially once I mentioned it to Gage."

"Why didn't you tell me? That seems like something I should have known about." She fought to sound more curious than accusatory.

After several more seconds of silence, Nick finally turned in her direction. "Because all I heard was a vehicle starting up a couple of times. Because I searched the woods and couldn't find evidence that anybody had really been there. And because sometimes I don't know if I'm in Snowberry Creek or back in Afghanistan."

He pushed himself up off the swing. "I'd rather not worry you needlessly if it turned out that I'm jumping at shadows that don't exist."

He stared out at the surrounding trees. "Thanks again for dinner, Callie. I had a great time."

Right up until she'd ruined it all with all her questions. Even in the darkness, the pain and embarrassment he was feeling was all too clear. Rather than let him walk away, she started after him.

"Nick, wait."

He kept going for another few steps before he finally stopped. "Did I forget to apologize? If so, I'm sorry I didn't keep you in the loop, Callie. Now, I'd better get back to Leif in case he needs anything."

"Damn it, Nick. I'm not mad, and I wasn't fishing for an apology. Next time just tell me what's going on even if it turns out to be a false alarm. That's all I'm asking."

She thought maybe he jerked his head in a quick nod, but she couldn't be sure. "I had a great time, too, Nick. Thanks for sharing your memories of Spence with me."

"Anytime."

Then he was gone.

It had been two days since that awkward discussion in the dark. In the intervening time, Callie had acted as if it had been no big deal, so maybe she'd meant it when she said she wasn't mad. At least he hadn't totally freaked her out with his confession that sometimes he wasn't sure which world he was in at any given moment.

Even so, it was taking all the courage he could muster to hunt down Callie to give her the estimate he'd been working on in secret. Right now he was running on little sleep and a whole lot of nerves. He'd started off the day taking Mooch for a long run, but now it was time. No more delays or excuses.

After banging on her parents' back door for ten minutes, he'd headed back to Spence's place. Leif hadn't seen her in a while, but she'd told him she was going to be working on the inventory again. Nick finally located her sitting on the window seat in a room tucked up under the eaves on the third floor.

He thrust the papers toward her and stepped back after she took them from him. "This is for you."

"What is it?"

Damn, he hadn't been this nervous since he'd been given his own patrol to lead the first time he'd been deployed to Iraq. How stupid was that? No one's life was at risk if he'd misjudged this particular situation. Well, maybe that wasn't exactly true. If Callie turned him down, he'd have no choice but to pack up and leave.

So, yeah, waiting for her to read over his proposal had a lot in common with waiting to see if that promotion was coming through.

"It's my detailed evaluation of what needs to be done to Spence's house to bring it up to code for a bed-and-breakfast. I went to the city planner's office and got their specs. You'd still need the variance in the zoning, but the man I talked to didn't think that would be a problem. He said the mayor was pushing everybody to encourage folks to bring new business to town."

He watched as she quickly scanned the pages, her eyebrows drawn down in a frown. Then she started over at the top, this time reading more slowly.

"Wow, Nick, I'm impressed. This is way more thorough than I expected. You must have spent hours on it. This will really help me when I talk to contractors."

He shifted restlessly, wondering what was the best approach to use. Might as well just lay it all out there.

"Well, about that. You should talk to several contractors. It's important to get more than one opinion on what needs to be done. However, what I'd really like is if you'd give me a chance to bid on the job."

Okay, wide-eyed shock wasn't exactly the response he was hoping for, although he didn't really blame her. Watching him assemble a gazebo from someone else's plans was no proof that he could handle a project as big as refurbishing an old house.

"Are you sure, Nick? Don't you have to report back to duty soon?"

Not exactly. With the muscle damage to his arm from the shrapnel, he wasn't even sure the army would want him back long term. He hedged his bets.

"I'd like to do the work."

When she didn't immediately respond, he told her a little of the same thing he'd told Leif. "I'm only good at two things, Callie: fighting a war and remodeling. I've had enough of the former to last me a lifetime."

Not that he wanted her pity. He walked away, retreating as far as the small room would allow. "So call the other contractors you have in mind. If you don't know any, your buddy Clarence would be able to suggest some. See what they have to say, figure out how much you can afford to spend, and go from there. I'm not asking for favors, Callie, only that you let me stand in line with the others."

He'd either made his case or he hadn't. "I'll leave that with you. Think about it, and then let me know if anything is unclear. If nothing else, it should give you some guidance as to what any bids should include. I also prioritized each item according to what has to be done versus what can either wait or is strictly cosmetic."

Before he made it out the door, she stopped him. "Nick, wait."

She crossed the small distance between them and gave him a quick hug, the kind two friends might exchange. Not that his body responded to it like that. No, his reaction to her touch was intense and painful. Nick wanted far more than a quick embrace but had no right to ask, not when they were limiting their relationship to being friends and not lovers.

His rules and his regret.

"Thank you for doing this for me, Nick. I've been feeling a little overwhelmed by the prospect of figuring out what all needs to be done."

"You're welcome. Now I'd better get back to work. That lawn won't mow itself."

She followed him out of the room, still studying the paper he'd given her. "Nick, I appreciate that you're willing to do all this work for me, but—"

He knew what she was going to say and didn't really blame her. She had no way of knowing if he'd stick around to make sure the job got done. It was hard to remember that the two of them had known each other for only days, not months. To her, he'd been someone Spence talked about, but his name had been only one of many.

Callie had been so much more than a name to Nick. He'd heard dozens of stories of her childhood with Spence living right next door. He'd heard her laughter when she and Spence connected over the Internet. Her goodie boxes had helped all of them get through the hellish days and long nights of their deployment.

He held his hand up to stop her. Obviously it was time to cut bait and start packing. "That's okay, Callie. I understand."

She crowded closer to him. "Understand what exactly?"

"That you'd rather go with someone local, someone who already has roots here in Snowberry Creek."

Callie shot him a look of pure disgust. "No, Nick, that wasn't what I was going to say at all. When you're done putting words in my mouth, let me know. I'd like to finish what I was about to say."

He fought the urge to grin. For some reason, at that moment she reminded him of one of the first sergeants he'd served under, a tough old bastard with twenty years under his belt. The man had no use for idiots and showed little mercy when he encountered one.

Nick snapped to attention and executed a salute. "I'm sorry, ma'am. I won't interrupt again."

Her mood didn't improve. Yep, just like the sergeant, minus the cuss words.

"What I was wondering about is if you'd have to get a business license and all of that stuff if you're going to work in this state. Maybe a permanent address?"

He'd already thought about that. "I can hold off doing anything about it until you decide which direction you're going to go. If you decide to step off the cliff and let me do the work, I could maybe list Spence's house for my address since I was sort of hoping you'd let me stay in the house for the duration. However, if you'd rather I rented a place in town, I will."

"Okay, then."

She hesitated a few seconds longer. "If I seem reluctant, it isn't because of you, Nick. Going ahead with this will be a huge change in lifestyle for me. The thought of getting estimates is making it a little too real all of a sudden. My whole working life has been spent moving from one place to another, sometimes three times or more in one year. I don't know if I'll be happy staying in one place long term, but I'm awfully tired of living out of suitcases in short-term rentals. I also miss my friends and family when I'm gone for months at a time."

He could sympathize. "And if I take the discharge the army offered, I'll need to stop moving sometime, too. It's a scary proposition."

"It is, isn't it? But for now, I guess I'll get cleaned up and go talk to Clarence. That seems to be the next logical step. Getting a few names isn't like I'm totally committed."

But he really hoped she was. "One step at a time, Callie. That's all any of us can do."

Then he kissed the tip of her nose. "And like I said, the grass won't cut itself."

The temperature outside was pleasant, especially compared to summers in Afghanistan or even back in the Midwest where he'd grown up. Even so, Nick had worked up a good sweat by the time he finished mowing the yard. After a short break, he'd move next door and take care of Callie's yard, too.

For now, he sat down on the front porch and enjoyed a cold beer and the afternoon breeze. After a few minutes, Leif joined him. He lowered himself into the next rocker with a soft grunt of pain.

"Think I could run her dad's lawn mower? I'm tired of sitting on my ass watching you work."

Nick understood the need to feel useful. "I don't see why not. It has hand controls, so you won't have to worry about using your boot for anything."

"Good. I'd like to give it a try next time you mow."

"No time like the present. I was going to do the yard next door while I have the mower out. I'm only too glad to get you started and hang out on the swing and watch you do all the work. When you're done or even if you just get tired of riding around in circles, you can ride it back over here. I'll need to hose the mower down and refill the tank before I put it back."

He added that last part mainly to give Leif an excuse not to walk back from Callie's house. Cutting through the woods was shorter, but the path was pretty rough. Walking up the driveway to the road and around to Spence's driveway would be easier going, but the distance would be tough for him.

The jerk tried to pretend he was stronger than he was. Nick could only hope that Leif wasn't doing further damage to his leg or at least wasn't jeopardizing his long-term recovery. Maybe it wouldn't hurt to ask a few questions.

"So for real this time, what did the docs say about your ankle?"

Leif's lips instantly went hard and thin, and his hands gripped the arms of the rocker tightly enough to make his knuckles white. Okay, they'd had nothing good to say, or Leif wouldn't be so angry. The real question was how bad the verdict had been. Rather than push, Nick waited him out.

Finally, Leif let out a big sigh as he stared down at his leg and slowly flexed his hands over and over. "I need long-term rehab on it. They said if I follow the right therapy plan diligently I might eventually walk without a cane and only a bit of limp."

He shot Nick a quick look. "Of course, those bastards always make things out to be worse than they really are. I'm hoping to be back up to speed in a couple of months and ready to deploy again."

Nick didn't believe that and figured Leif didn't, either, even if he wasn't ready to admit it. They'd both set out to make the army their careers. Now they were both damaged goods. Nick could probably hang on, depending on how much residual damage he had from the shrapnel that had ripped his arm open.

Nick remembered all too clearly the mangled mess Leif's lower leg had been after they'd hit that first IED. Hell, he'd been surprised to find out that they'd managed to save Leif's ankle and foot. Leif had been in shock and too doped up to have gotten a clear look at it.

Nick still had nightmares about the bloody mess. Another secret he kept to himself.

"So when do you need to get back to the hospital to get started on that therapy?"

"That depends."

Nick leaned back in the wicker rocker and closed his eyes. "On?"

"When you're heading back to Ohio. I thought I'd ride along and keep you company since I'm guessing Mooch will be staying here in Snowberry Creek with Callie."

That was news to Nick. "Has she said that in so many words?"

"No, but she's crazy about that damn dog, and he clearly loves her right back. After all, that's the life Spence wanted for both him and the mutt."

Like Nick needed Leif to remind him of that. Now he was the one curling his fingers up in a fist, but Leif didn't deserve his temper.

"I won't be heading back to Ohio until Callie makes up her mind about what she's going to do with this place. Once she decides that much, she'll let me know if I'm in the running to do the work for her. I've already told her that I'll understand if she chooses to use someone else, someone who'll be here for her long term."

Leif stood up and stretched. "Just to be sure, you are talking about contractors, aren't you?"

Maybe. Maybe not. For the moment, though, that was the story he was going with.

"What else would I be talking about, Corporal? We both know this is Spence's place, not mine."

Even if he wanted it to be.

Evidently Leif was satisfied with his response, which was all that mattered at the moment.

"Okay, I'll hang out here until you know for sure what you're going to do. If you're going to stay, I'll see if I can get my therapy scheduled out here rather than heading back east for it."

Was he doing that because he needed Nick's support through the painful process of rehabbing his ankle or because he thought Nick needed a chaperone if he was going to hang around Callie for any length of time? The answer didn't matter. He wanted to be there for Leif regardless, which reminded him: "Gage says he has connections with the bases out here. He said to let him know if you wanted him to make a few calls."

"Will do. Now, let's get that lawn mowed."

When Leif started down the steps, Nick stood up and stretched, using the maneuver as a pretense to be ready in case his friend took a header. Once Leif safely reached the ground, Nick followed him.

"Climb aboard, and I'll show you how this thing works."

He'd be glad when they fired up the lawn mower. The noise of its engine would preclude any more discussion about whether Nick belonged in Snowberry Creek.

* * *

"Mooch, I know it's silly that I brought you along for moral support while I talk to Clarence about contractors, but there you go. Hope you don't mind."

The dog offered no complaints but happily did his doggy thing, sticking his nose out the window to drink in the myriad of smells that rolled past them as she drove. What did he make of this new world he was in? Was it starting to make sense to him? Of the three males camped out in Spence's house, Mooch seemed to be having the easiest time adjusting to life in Snowberry Creek.

She reached over to pat him on the back, loving his soft fur although the jagged scar from his bullet wound gave her the shivers. He didn't even flinch, so that was a good thing. "I wish your two buddies weren't having such a hard time of it, Mooch, but I guess these things take time."

As she drove into the parking lot at the hardware store, Clarence was just getting out of his small pickup truck. She pulled into the spot next to his and rolled down her window.

As soon as he spotted her, his face lit up. "Callie girl! How are you?"

"I'm doing fine, Clarence. I was wondering if I could pick your brain for a few minutes. If you're too busy, I can come back later."

"I always have time for friends. I've got about an hour before I have to relieve my assistant manager."

Mooch crawled into Callie's lap and stuck his head out of her window in an effort to reach Clarence. The older man gave him a quick scratch. "Hey, there, Mooch. Good to see you, buddy."

Clarence stepped back to give her room to open the door. "Why don't we walk around back? There's an old picnic table by the loading dock where we can sit, and Mooch can stretch out in the shade. I've got my laptop with me, so I can access any information from it."

"Great! Come on, Mooch."

She snapped on the dog's leash before letting him out of the car. It was unlikely he'd wander off, but this was a busy parking lot. The dog was adjusting pretty well to this new world, but there was no use in taking any chances with his safety.

When the three of them were seated at the picnic table, she handed Clarence the paperwork Nick had given her.

"You already know that I'm thinking about turning Spence's home into a B and B. Nick used to work for his father, who is a remodeling contractor back in Ohio. He went through the house and gave me this list of what needs to be done. It looks pretty comprehensive to me, but then what do I know about such stuff?"

Clarence studied the evaluation for several minutes, flipping back and forth through the various pages. After a few minutes, he set it aside.

"That boy has a good eye for detail, and it sure reads as if he knows his business. So what can I do to help?"

She hid a smile over Nick being described as a boy. Not exactly the image she had of him, but then she had firsthand knowledge of how much of a man he was. Okay, this wasn't the time for that line of thought, though. Back to business.

"I'd like to have at least one more contractor look at the house and give me his take on it as well. It only makes sense to get more than one opinion on what needs to be done and how much it should cost. The trouble is I don't know any contractors who do this kind of work."

Clarence nodded. "I can give you a few names to

call, but it's a shame your young man can't stick around and help with the work. We could use some fresh blood here in Snowberry Creek."

"He's not my young man." More's the pity. "Besides, I suspect the army figures they have first claim on his time."

"Yes, I suppose they do. Well, let me get those names for you. I'll run inside and print the list for you and be right back. After you call these guys, let me know if you have any questions, and I'll do what I can to help.

"Thanks, Clarence. I appreciate it."

When he returned, he handed her the list. "I have to tell you that any of these men will be happy to get the work. I hope you'll have them order as much of their supplies through me as they can."

"I'll make that part of the deal."

"Don't think I've forgotten about having you, Nick, and Leif over for dinner. The missus said she was going to give you a call about setting a date."

"I'll look forward to it, and I know the guys were excited about the mere mention of the word pie."

Clarence looked pleased. "I'll tell her she'd better bake two just to be safe."

"See you soon, and I'll keep you posted on what I decide about the remodel."

"Do that. And tell your folks hi for me when you talk to them."

"I will."

If she called them. In truth, she'd been avoiding it, but that would work for only so long. She was surprised they hadn't already called her. The rumor mill worked far too well in Snowberry Creek for them not to have heard all about her walking hand in hand with Nick, not to mention having added a second soldier to her list of houseguests.

Yeah, she should phone them and explain what was going on. But how could she when she wasn't sure herself? There was no use in making the call until she had some answers. That was her excuse, and she was sticking to it.

Chapter 24

Well, Callie certainly hadn't wasted any time. It was just yesterday that Nick had given her his list of the jobs that needed to be done. Now, less than twenty-four hours later, she was in the process of getting her third estimate for the job.

He shouldn't be mad about it. Hell, he'd even told her she should talk to other contractors. Still, it pissed him off, even if he had no cause to be angry. It didn't help to remind himself that experience had taught him that a man couldn't expect to win every job he bid on. Win some; lose some.

But damn, he wanted to win this one. Needed to win this one. It was Nick's duty to make sure Spence's woman was taken care of, because the man couldn't be there to do it himself.

Rather than watch Callie trailing along behind the contractor, Nick turned his attention back to painting the gazebo. He had only a little more to do. Once this first coat dried, he'd be able to start the final one. Unless it rained, he'd be done tomorrow. So maybe it was time to start making plans for the long drive back to Ohio.

His parents had left him another message asking when he'd be coming back home. How could he tell them the truth—that home really wasn't home anymore? Not for him. Until he figured that out, he ignored both the call and his conscience, which was telling him he shouldn't be worrying them like this.

The sound of an engine starting told him the contractor was leaving. He forced himself to keep painting, figuring Callie would seek him out when and if she wanted to talk about anything. After a few minutes, he looked around but didn't see her anywhere.

Instead, Leif was headed his way, holding up his cell phone, wiggling it in the air, and mouthing, "It's your mom." Rats. She had obviously done an end run and called Leif since Nick wasn't answering. He climbed down off the ladder and held out his hand for the phone.

"Hi, Mom."

Leif looked apologetic before retreating to sit on the porch steps, probably thinking Nick wanted privacy. He appreciated the gesture, but there wasn't anything he needed to say to his parents that he hadn't already told Leif. He then realized Mom was already talking, and he'd missed everything she'd said.

"Whoa, Mom, slow down. I was climbing down off a ladder and missed that."

She sounded exasperated when she repeated herself, speaking slowly to make sure he didn't miss a word this time. "I asked when you were coming home. My friend from church has a daughter your age who will be in town for a visit week after next. I thought it would be nice if you showed her around the area."

He closed his eyes and prayed for patience. Even if he was in town, he had no interest in being fixed up with some random woman.

"My plans are still up in the air, Mom. I'll have to get back to you on when I'll have time to stop by for another visit."

Normally, his mom was pretty easygoing, but evidently she'd lost all patience with him. "Sorry, Nick, but that's just not acceptable. And for your information, this isn't where you visit. This is where you live. Besides, I've already told my friend that you'll be glad to have dinner with her daughter. I'm not sure why you're hanging around out there in Washington, but this is your home. This is where you belong. I want my son back."

Then she stopped for a second, and he heard what he was convinced was a sob coming from the other end of the line. His anger melted away, leaving him floundering for a response that wouldn't hurt her even more.

He couldn't tell her the truth about what had happened back in Afghanistan. That was his burden to bear, not hers, not his father's.

"I know you do, Mom. I'm trying. I really am."

Another sob, but then her voice grew stronger. "When will you be here, Nick? And I won't settle for some vague promise. Give me a date."

"I can't, Mom. Not yet. I should know more about my plans in a few days. When I do, I promise I'll call."

"But, Nick—"

Okay, now he was choking on the words he needed to say. "I'm doing fine. Okay, not fine, but better. Leif and I are doing some work on Spence's house for Callie. It feels really good to be swinging a hammer again. Tell Dad all that time working for him is finally paying off for me."

The silence from the other end of the line dragged on for several seconds. Finally, it sounded as if she was handing the phone off to someone.

"Nick, it's Dad. What the hell did you say to your mom? She's crying."

"I told her I couldn't promise to be back in time to escort her friend's daughter around. I'm doing some work on Spence's house for his friend Callie, and I'm not sure how long it will take. I promised to call more often and to let her know when my plans are set."

"Damn it, Nick, she can't sleep nights for worrying about you. Get your ass back here where it belongs."

Okay, so much for controlling his temper. "Dad, I'm not some sixteen-year-old kid you can order around for breaking curfew. I'm a grown man and have been for a long time. I'm sorry I'm making Mom unhappy, but trust me when I tell you that I'm not ready to come home. It isn't that I don't want to. It's that I can't."

He'd run out of breath and anger. Breathing in slowly, he hunted for the right words to make everyone happy. He couldn't find them.

"Dad, tell Mom I'm sorry. I love you both, but right now I need to be here. When that changes, I'll let you know."

When he disconnected the call, he turned off the phone so he wouldn't hear it if his dad tried to call right back. Later, when he had time to think things through a bit, he'd e-mail rather than call. It was easier to break their hearts when he didn't have to hear his mom quietly crying in the background.

Right now, he needed a beer, or maybe several. He also needed to return Leif's phone. Would he think Nick cowardly if he asked him to leave it off so that he wouldn't have to deal with his parents right now?

Too effing bad if he did. Right now Nick's nerves were raw, bleeding with the knowledge he was failing everyone who mattered. His parents were hurt and confused by the stranger wearing their son's face. Leif wasn't complaining, but he needed Nick to be strong enough to help him deal with what those plates and screws in his ankle really meant.

And Spence—well, it was too late to do right by him. Nick had made the choice that had gotten his friend killed. All the man had wanted was to come home to Callie. So in effect, Nick had failed her, too.

Standing here wasn't accomplishing anything. Even knowing he couldn't outrun the shadows on his soul, he needed to be moving. He'd hand off Leif's phone and then hit the road. This time he'd walk away from town, losing himself in the beauty along the two-lane highways that wound through the foothills of the Cascades.

The idea might be spontaneous, but he wasn't stupid. He'd take his phone just in case he got lost and bottled water to help wash the cobwebs of guilt and pain down his throat. His plans made, he finally turned around to face Leif, only to find his friend was gone.

In his place sat Callie and Mooch. Son of a bitch! How much of the one-sided conversation had she heard? Enough, considering the way she was staring at him with wide eyes, her expressive mouth turned down at the corners. Even Mooch watched him with that amazing stillness he sometimes had when he sensed someone was hurting.

Nick's feet were nailed in place, just as unable to step forward as they were to make a run for it. So calling his parents back wasn't the only thing he couldn't muster up the courage to face.

This was ridiculous. He forced himself to move forward, knowing delaying the conversation wasn't going to make it any easier. He stopped a few feet short of the steps where she sat, wanting at least that much distance between them.

"I'm going for a walk."

She turned her attention to petting Mooch. "I'll hold dinner until you get back."

He didn't want any favors. Didn't deserve them. "I don't know when that will be. You and Leif go ahead and eat without me."

Callie gave the dog a quick squeeze and stood up. "Then I'll keep your dinner warm, Nick. It will be here for you when you get back."

She came down the steps, moving slowly as if worried she'd spook him into running. As tempting as it was, he held his ground because this was Callie, and on some instinctive level he knew he had nothing to fear from her.

"I'm going to hug you, Nick; then you can go on your walk. I'll be waiting up for you."

She meant it, but, then, she didn't know the truth of what he'd cost her. That no matter how many gazebos he built or walls he painted, he could never give back the one thing she deserved to have. He turned away, unable to bear the burden of her innocent gaze.

But still she came, her hands coming to rest on his back, their warmth seeping through the thin cotton of his shirt to his skin. He shivered but held his ground, needing the benediction of her touch. She slid her hands down to his waist and then around him until her body gently pressed against his, her face resting against his back.

He had no sense of the time that passed, his whole world consisting only of an acute awareness of this woman and the gift of comfort she was offering him. That he didn't deserve it didn't make it any less welcome, but enough was enough.

"I'll call you when I'm back."

She gave him one last quick squeeze before stepping

away. "Do that. Let Leif know I'll bring over dinner at the usual time."

In other words, don't leave without letting Leif know where he was going. "I will."

He marched up the steps as she crossed the yard, heading back to her parents' house. "And, Callie, thanks."

Her smile was a bit rueful. "You're welcome, and if it's any comfort, I've been ducking my parents, too."

Her confession didn't change anything, but at least it made him laugh.

Nick pounded the pavement. Each step that took him away from Callie was harder than the one before. He wanted to turn around and head straight back to her. The knowledge that he had no right to feel that way kept him moving forward long after his driving need to walk had disappeared.

Up ahead he spotted a flashing neon light. *Please, if there's a god in heaven, let that be a bar.*

It was. All the sign over the door said was BEER. Perfect. That was exactly what Nick was looking for. The parking lot was filled with some serious motorcycles and beat-up trucks with oversized tires. In his current mood, probably not the wisest choice of places to be without any backup. He'd have a quick beer, maybe a burger, and then start the long hike back to Spence's place.

As soon as he stepped inside the door, he paused long enough to pull his dog tags out of his T-shirt. In the past, he'd found that even the toughest bastards in a biker bar were willing to accept a stranger in their midst if he was military. Sure enough, the two men at the nearest pool table straightened up and made a pretense of chalking their cues while they made up their mind whether to challenge his right to share their space.

The one on the left spoke first. "Where'd you serve?"

Nick rolled his shoulders, forcing himself to look far more relaxed than he was. "Two tours in the sandbox. I'm just back from my latest in Afghanistan."

The other man gave the scar on Nick's arm a pointed look. "You get that over there?"

"IED."

He didn't need to say more. Couldn't have even if he wanted to. Besides, the expression on the man's face made it clear he knew exactly what Nick was talking about.

"Cowardly bastards."

The taller of the two walked around the pool table and stuck out his hand. "I'm Tim. He's Kevin. We both did a couple of stints over there with the army rangers. Let me buy you a beer."

Nick grinned and shook Tim's hand. "Only if the second round is on me."

"It's a deal. You any good at pool? I can't remember when I last had a decent opponent."

Kevin protested. "Hey, moron, who won three out of five last night?"

"You did, but only because I took pity on you."

Okay, so maybe this was Nick's kind of place after all. A few beers, a couple of games of pool, and he'd head back home. He didn't want to make Callie worry, and Leif would be pissed if Nick had too much fun without him.

He put his hand on his new best friend's shoulder. "Rack 'em up, Tim, and we'll see who really knows how to play."

Tim lifted his beer in salute. "It's a deal."

*   *   *

Callie checked her watch for the millionth time. The hour hand had just edged past midnight. Nick had been gone for close to eight hours, and still no sign of him. She'd given up on keeping his dinner warm and tossed it in the trash. "If he's not back in half an hour, I'm calling Gage."

Leif was already shaking his head. "Nick is a big boy, Callie. We would have heard by now if something was wrong. He'll come dragging in sooner or later. When he does, I'll kick his ass for worrying you like this. Or better yet, maybe I'll use that hammer he's been swinging to knock some sense into that thick skull of his."

She laughed but didn't really mean it. "You'll have to stand in line. I want first crack at him. He has to know I'd—no, we'd both be worried sick by now."

Leif shifted restlessly, obviously having trouble finding a comfortable position for his injured leg. "Yeah, well, our boy wasn't thinking too straight when he left. He'll feel really bad when he gets back and realizes what he's done."

He reached over to pat her on the shoulder. "Sometimes the memories get to be too much, and he needs to blow off some steam. Soften the edges with a few beers. We all do. You spend enough time over there, it gets to be your normal. Makes it hard to adjust to life back here."

There wasn't much she could say to that. From what little she'd heard of Nick's conversation with his folks, it didn't come as a surprise that he needed to get away for a while. She suspected he'd been more than a little embarrassed that she'd overheard his end of the conversation.

His parents wanted him home, and she didn't blame them. Was she being selfish because she didn't want to hurry him along the way back to his parents and what they saw as his real life?

Yeah, she was, but she couldn't seem to help herself. He and Leif had wormed their way into her life like they both belonged there, not just for a couple of weeks, but long term.

She was about to check the time again when a truck pulled into the top of the driveway. It didn't come any farther, but the passenger door opened and closed before the truck backed out and took off with a loud spray of gravel. Mooch charged down off the porch raising hell before Callie could grab him.

The dog came to an abrupt stop as a familiar figure began meandering his way down the driveway, stumbling slightly before catching his balance with exaggerated care. Her first two reactions were relief that Nick had made it home safely and anger that he was obviously drunk.

"Looks like Nick must have made himself some new friends." Leif pushed himself up out of the rocker. "I think I'll leave him to your tender care. I'm overdue for my meds and my leg isn't happy about it. Be sure to tell him he'll be the guest of honor at an ass-kicking party in the morning. I'd take care of that little chore tonight, but I'm guessing he wouldn't remember it. Better to do it tomorrow when he's sober and hungover."

Callie laughed. "You have a mean streak, Leif. I like it."

She gave him a quick hug before heading down the steps to confront the man still wending his way down the driveway. The door slammed behind her as Leif went inside, leaving her alone with Nick. As aggravated as she was with the man, she couldn't help but laugh when Nick stopped to pet Mooch and almost toppled over.

When he heard her coming, his face lit up. "Callie! I was just about to call you. Hey, Lucy, I'm home."

He held out his arms and twirled, clearly proud of himself for having accomplished that particular feat. Leif was right. There was no use in trying to reason with Nick now. Tomorrow, though, they'd have a long chat about disappearing for hours and worrying his friends. For now, she caught his arm and wrapped it across her shoulders while she put hers around his waist to help keep him steady.

"Come on, big guy. It's time for you to call it a day."

He belched really loud. "Oops, sorry about that. Too much beer. Not enough food. But, hey, guess what! I won five bucks on my last game of pool."

Cute. He sounded so darn proud of his accomplishment. "And how much did you lose on all the ones before that?"

Nick froze for a few seconds, his face screwed up in a frown as he tried to come up with an answer. "Doesn't matter. I ended the night on a high note."

And to demonstrate that, he started singing one of those charming ditties the army used for keeping cadence. She suspected Nick would be embarrassed to find out he'd shared such a colorful one with her, but she couldn't help but laugh. He was definitely in rare form.

"Up the steps, Nick. Then I'm going to pour you into bed. That's the safest place for you right now."

They managed to reach the front door without mishap. Good, but the steps to his bedroom on the second floor presented a whole new set of challenges.

"Come on, Nick, we can make it."

Leif wandered back in from the den to check their progress. "I'd offer to help, but then Callie would have two of us to haul up there. So tell me, Nick, did you have a good time tonight?"

The man in question nodded, looking like one of those bobble-headed toys they gave away at ballgames. "That I did, Leif. Drank beer. Played pool. Won five dollars."

He'd been about to start up the stairs but wheeled around at the last second to speak with his friend. "Sorry you weren't there. The name of the bar is 'Beer.' Our kind of place."

Then he frowned. "Well, not quite. No pretty women."

Well, that was a relief. Callie tried to get him headed back in the right direction.

"Maybe next time you can take Callie to this fine establishment. I'm sure she'd have a great time at Beer."

She shot the other man an exasperated look. "Thanks a lot, Leif. Don't encourage him."

The jerk only laughed. "See you in the morning. Knowing Nick, it will be noon or later before he surfaces after a bender like this one."

Then Leif's expression turned serious. "I meant what I said earlier, Callie. He needed this."

She believed him. "I know, Leif. That's the only reason I'm not taking Spence's old baseball bat to him right now."

"You're good people, Callie Redding."

Leif disappeared back into the den. At least she now had Nick headed in the right direction. When they made it to the top of the steps, she all but shoved Nick into the bathroom he was using while she waited out in the hall. At least he was sober enough to take care of that much on his own.

When he came back out, he'd stripped down to his boxers. Her mouth went dry at the sight of all that tanned skin and sleek muscle. Thanks to that one night they'd lost control out in the yard, she knew exactly how wonderful his body felt next to hers, and she wanted that again. At the moment, though, he was clearly not up for anything other than crawling into bed. She sternly told herself she wasn't disappointed. No, not at all, especially since it wouldn't be fair to take advantage of the man while he was in this condition. The moral high ground and all that.

When he yawned big enough to have his jaw cracking, she could only laugh. "This way, Nick."

He took her hand and let her lead him in the right direction. She didn't bother turning on any lamps in the bedroom; there was plenty of light spilling in from the hallway to get him tucked into bed.

She turned back the covers for him and hoped he wouldn't have many clear memories of how she'd fussed over him tonight. Well, technically, this morning. Unfortunately, she suspected the buzz from the copious amounts of alcohol he'd consumed was already wearing off.

Right now, he stood facing her, their hands still tangled together. "I'm sorry for worrying you, Callie."

She kept her eyes focused just south of his, not wanting him to see the hunger in them, the effect of being this close to him in this setting. "That's all right, Nick. What are friends for?"

He bent his forefinger and used it to lift her chin, forcing her to look at him. "I'm going to kiss you, friend, so if you're not interested, better leave now."

As if.

His smile was sweet with a spicy touch of predatory just as his lips settled over hers. God, it felt like coming home, like taking a victory lap, like all things good and beautiful. He kept it gentle, not crowding her at all, as he feasted on her lips, tasting and tempting and teasing.

At the moment, she felt as wobbly as he had looked coming down the driveway. The air around them was perfectly still, yet she felt buffeted by the waves of passion that were burning through her veins.

"Callie girl, you'd better go while I'm still strong enough to let you walk away."

And if she didn't want to walk away? Before she could think that through, he made the decision for them both. He kissed her again and then turned her around and gave her a soft shove. As much as she hated it, he was right. She needed to put some distance between them, both physically and emotionally.

"Good night, Nick. Sleep well."

She made it all the way to the door before looking back. He was still watching her, his dark eyes shadowed and inscrutable.

"Call me when you get home, so I know you made it okay. Better yet, take Mooch with you."

Great idea. "We'll be fine, but I'll call if that will make you sleep better."

"I'll be waiting."

That promise warmed her from the inside out. She practically danced down the steps, calling for Mooch. "Well, dog, you're with me tonight."

Uncomplicated male that he was, Mooch wagged his tail and followed her out into the night.

Chapter 25

❧❧

Nick shifted on the bed to stare out the bedroom window as he waited for the phone to ring. It shouldn't be but another minute or two. Maybe he should've gone with her, but right now he couldn't have trusted his legs to get him down the stairs safely, much less back up again. He shouldn't have had so much to drink, but that was water under the bridge.

Or actually, beer. Tim and Kevin had introduced him to several of their favorite local microbrews.

He also shouldn't have given into the impulse to kiss Callie again, at least not like that. As if his life depended on it, on her. Damn, but touching her skin, holding her close, however briefly, had felt so damn good.

Before he could pursue that line of thought, his cell phone started blasting out reveille. Damn it, Leif! He'd forgotten his supposed friend had reprogrammed Nick's phone to do that. He grabbed the phone and hit the button.

"Callie?"

"Sorry it took a little longer than expected for me to

call. Mooch was hungry, and then I got ready for bed before I remembered I'd left my cell downstairs."

Nick stifled a groan, picturing Callie curled up under the blankets all snuggly and warm. "Is Mooch there with you?"

She laughed softly. "He was stretched out on the bed before I finished brushing my teeth."

So the dog was right where Nick would give anything to be. For a mutt, Mooch sure had a knack for landing on his feet.

"I don't want to disparage a fellow soldier, but you should know he snores and has a bad habit of chasing rabbits in his sleep. Although I'm not sure why. I don't think I ever saw a single rabbit in Afghanistan."

Not exactly brilliant conversation, but it was the best he could come up with. Besides, it was only an excuse to keep Callie on the line.

There was laughter in her voice when she spoke. "Maybe he's chasing goats. I'm pretty sure I've seen pictures of goats on the news in Afghanistan."

He hated thinking about that place, especially right as he was about to go to sleep. That could be enough to trigger the nightmares.

"Mooch also likes to steal pillows. Boot him off if he tries anything."

"Don't worry, he's fine, Nick. There's plenty of room in my bed for him."

Was it big enough for three, or at least two humans and a dog? Not that Nick had the guts to actually ask the question.

"I should hang up. We both need our sleep."

She was right even if he wasn't ready to let her go. And he wasn't just thinking about tonight. "I wish I was there to tuck you in."

Silence.

Then she whispered, "I wish you were, too, Nick. Good night."

"Sleep well, Callie," he whispered back and disconnected the call.

Because he sure wouldn't. Sleep well, that is. Not with images of what it would be like to crawl under the covers next to Callie and hold her all night long. But as he imagined every detail, his eyes grew heavier until at last he could no longer keep them open. Finally, he turned to face the direction of Callie's house and drifted off to sleep.

Austin hunkered down in the far back corner of the Creek Café, but that didn't keep the police chief from walking in and heading right for him. Damn, who had ratted him out? Someone must have called Gage Logan and told him right where Austin could be found. It wasn't like he came in here all that often.

The lawman slid into the booth without waiting for an invitation. When the waitress started toward him, he waved her off. After dropping his cop hat on the table, he leaned into the corner of the booth, making it clear that he was there for as long as it took.

The only question was why. Rather than ask, Austin sipped his coffee and waited for Logan to tell him. It didn't take long.

"Where's your dad holed up these days, Austin? Haven't seen much of either one of you around town lately."

He made the question sound as if he were only making small talk, polite conversation. Austin wasn't buying it. Not when the tension lines framing Chief Logan's mouth and eyes made it clear the question was anything but casual. What had the old man gone and done now?

"He has a room a couple of towns over. I'll tell him you were asking about him, Chief. I'm sure he'll be touched by your concern."

Okay, smarting off to the man wasn't a good idea, but Austin didn't give a damn. The officer was nothing but a small-town cop with a big-city attitude. If he was any good at his job, he wouldn't have had to settle for working here in Snowberry Creek.

"We both know your father didn't take it well when he found out that your cousin Spence left his house and everything in it to Callie Redding."

Gage Logan stated it as a fact, one Austin couldn't dispute. "So? He had every right to be pissed. That house has been in our family for generations. Spence knew it, too. He left it to Callie just to spite Dad."

Logan sat up straighter, the abrupt change forcing Austin to reassess the man's capabilities. "Even if that's true, it doesn't change the fact that Spence had the legal right to do whatever the hell he wanted to with the house and everything in it. Besides, from what I've heard, there was never any love lost between your father and Spence."

That much was true, but Austin wasn't about to side with an outsider against his father. He didn't have much use for his old man himself, but blood stood up for blood.

The lawman kept right on talking. "I'm putting you on notice. If I catch you anywhere near Spence's place, I'll arrest your ass. Same goes for your father. Let him know."

It occurred to Austin that an innocent man would be asking what brought all this on. "I'll be glad to pass along the message, Chief, but he'll want to know why you brought this up now. He made his opinion clear to Spence's attorney when the will was read. As far as I know, my father hasn't been anywhere near the place since you kicked us off the property right after Spence fucked up and got himself killed."

Logan lunged forward, snagging Austin by his shirt from across the narrow span of the table. "Show some respect, you little prick. Your cousin died for his country. Got that?"

Austin nodded. "Yeah, I got it."

"Good." Logan shoved Austin backward. "But we were talking about Spence's place. It was vandalized the other night, and one of Ms. Redding's guests was attacked. If I find out you or your father was responsible, it won't go well for either of you. The judge takes a dim view of greedy bastards, especially stupid ones."

Austin forced himself to look the police chief right in the eye. "I never attacked nobody, and my father hardly ever leaves his room. You're barking up the wrong tree."

Which was nothing less than the absolute truth. Yeah, he'd broken the window, but that guy had been out cold on the floor when Austin had found him. Of course, if he told Logan that, he'd have to admit that he'd been in the house in the first place. Son of a bitch, he should have known that night would come back to bite him on the ass.

"But okay, I'll deliver the message. I should warn you, though, he's likely to go ballistic if you're accusing him of something he didn't do."

Again, the truth. Dad was a mean drunk, always had been, and drinking was about all he did these days.

The police chief's expression remained hard and cold. "He might also want to know that the two guys staying at Spence's house are trained military. If he goes messing with them, he might not last long enough for me to arrest him."

With that comment, Logan picked up his hat and slid out of the booth. He stood beside the booth long enough to make one more promise.

"And just so you know, I'm not convinced that it's your dad who was behind the break-ins. He might be at the top of my list, but you're right up there with him."

Logan walked away without looking back. Clearly he didn't view Austin as any kind of real threat to anyone. Yeah, they'd see about that. One more good score and he'd have enough money to leave town.

The last antiques dealer he'd talked to had been willing to discuss what kind of items he was looking for. When Austin had brought him that blue-and-white vase, the man's eyes had glittered with pure greed. He'd asked if there was more where that had come from.

So far, he'd found only one like it, which was part of the reason he'd broken into the house the other night. He'd have to stake the place out again and watch for an opportunity to make one last shopping trip through the house.

Once he moved the goods, he'd take off to parts unknown and start over where no one had ever heard of his old man or cousin Spence. His plans made, Austin finished his coffee and headed out the door. For now, he needed to follow his normal routine by going to work and keeping his nose clean here in town.

As he got into his truck and started the engine, he spotted the police chief's car parked a block farther down the street. Was that jerk planning on following Austin? If so, he was in for a long night, because he was heading straight to work. The only thing more boring than Austin's job flipping burgers would be watching someone else do it.

He smiled as he pulled out into traffic. Sure enough, the cop followed him. Fine. All he'd learn was where Austin parked at work. If he stuck around until after Austin's shift ended, Logan would see the crappy apartment where Austin lived. If he was hoping to find proof that Austin was behind the thefts, the cop wouldn't find it there.

He was almost disappointed when Chief Logan made a left turn a couple of blocks later. So much for being hot on Austin's trail, at least for the moment. That didn't mean the cop was giving up. Not by a long shot.

Well, he would deliver the cop's message and then lay low for a couple of days. If the cop didn't bother him or his dad after that, then Austin would start his final stakeout. It was time to be moving on, and a few hundred dollars more would go a long way toward making that happen.

The next morning Austin stood in the parking lot outside his father's apartment for nearly fifteen minutes arguing with himself about whether he really needed to deliver Chief Logan's warning at all, much less in person. However, since his old man was too cheap to buy an answering machine and didn't own a cell phone, there really wasn't any other option. It just pissed Austin off that he was the one who had to do it at all. If the cops wanted to tell Vince something, they fucking well should do it themselves.

He caught himself rubbing his jaw as he ran through a list of all the reasons why he shouldn't just get back in the truck and leave. Jerking his hand back down to his side, he let loose with a string of curses. How many times over the years had his father's right fist connected with that side of Austin's face? And it was just one of many remembered bruises, welts, and broken bones that were memorials to his father's alcohol-fueled temper. He looked back toward the highway. Maybe he should keep right on driving as far as a tank of gas and five hundred dollars would take him.

God knows, he'd dreamed of doing exactly that for . . . well, as far back as he could remember. This time, though, Austin was going to do it. He'd stockpiled almost enough money and knew how to get some more. There was no reason for him to hang around Snowberry Creek any longer. The family home had passed into other hands, a final "fuck you both" to Austin and his old man from Spence when he died. As much as Austin hated his cousin for cutting them out of his will, he really couldn't blame the guy, either.

It was all water under the bridge, and Austin needed to get moving. He'd worked all night and needed to crash soon, but he'd sleep better without this particular chore still hanging over his head. Even though he'd been the one who'd lifted the stuff from Spence's place, that didn't mean his father hadn't been up to something on his own. The last thing Austin needed right now was for his old man to bring the wrath of Gage Logan raining down on both of them, especially when he still had a bunch of stuff left to sell. One look in the boxes in the back of his truck, and the police chief would slap on the cuffs and haul Austin's ass off to jail.

He forced himself to approach the building, one that had once been a crappy motel before being converted to even crappier apartments. The exterior was straight out of the seventies, done up in a hideous combination of faded green, orange, and gold. The plastic plants in the window boxes were gray with dust. Damn, he hated this place, but each visit only made him more determined to build a future that didn't end up with him living here or someplace just like it. The breakfast sandwich and coffee he'd eaten after getting off work stirred uncomfortably in his stomach, but he kept walking.

Austin could smell the cigarettes, alcohol, and despair from thirty feet away. He rapped on the gaudy orange door and stepped back in case his father was in a fighting mood when he opened the door. Austin could pretty much count on Vince being either in a drunken stupor or pissed because he wasn't. There was never much in the way of a middle ground when it came to his father's moods.

The door opened just far enough for Vince to peer out with one bloodshot eye. "What the hell are you doing here at this hour, boy?"

At twenty-two, Austin wasn't a boy, not any longer, but his father would never see him as anything else. "We need to talk, but not out here."

Vince stepped back, leaving Austin to follow in his wake. His father headed for the makeshift kitchen in the corner and poured himself a cup of coffee and added a healthy shot of whiskey from a half-empty bottle. From there, he headed for the old recliner where he spent most of his waking hours. They'd found the chair sitting by the curb at least ten years ago. Over time, it had gradually been reupholstered with duct tape, leaving it a dull gray with only a little of the original dark brown peeking through.

"Well, you came here to talk, so start talking. I don't have all day to sit around waiting for you to get to the point. I've got places to go. Things to do."

Yeah, right. The farthest Vince ventured from home these days was the closest store that carried his favorite brands of whiskey and cigarettes. God, think what they could have done with even half the money Vince had spent on alcohol and tobacco over the years. There was no use in crying over spilled booze, though.

Unwilling to sit on the filthy sheets that covered the unmade bed, Austin leaned against the wall and stared down at his train wreck of a father. "Gage Logan, the chief of police over in Snowberry Creek, paid me a visit."

His father had been in the process of leaning back in the chair, but he shot back upright. "What did that bastard want with you, boy?"

"Seems they've had a prowler out at Spence's place, and he figures one of us for it. Said if the problem continued, he'd be looking in our direction first."

Vince slammed his fist down on the arm of the chair. "Damn it, boy, I told you to be careful! I haven't set foot on the place since we found out about Spence's will. I've been talking to an attorney. He says we've got a good case. Since that mongrel Spence was adopted, he has no right to give my family home away like that. I'm going to give the lawyer some money to get started on getting the place back from that woman who stole it from me."

Austin had to laugh, and not just at the thought of his father spending money on anything but his addictions. Any attorney who would do business with the likes of Vince wouldn't stand a chance against the law firm that had tied the estate up in a pretty bow and handed it over to Callie Redding. Besides, Vince didn't have enough money to buy even half an hour of any attorney's time.

Might as well pour gas on the fire. "Callie has moved a couple of guys into the house now. They've changed the locks and started fixing the place up some."

Vince sputtered and choked on his coffee. Austin pounded on his back until the old man was breathing again. He glared up at Austin with his rheumy eyes. "If anybody should be living there, it should be me. I deserve better than this shithole."

Then he shot Austin a guilty look. "I mean us. We both should be living there."

Like Vince would share anything with Austin besides his temper and endless demands for money. He was surprised the subject hadn't already come up, but then of course it did.

Vince took another long sip of his coffee. "You got my share of the take?"

How predictable. He took all the risks and did all the work, but Vince still wanted his cut. Austin pulled out a small wad of bills. He'd asked for ones at the bank, thinking they added up to a more impressive stack than the ten twenties he planned on giving his father. If Vince was careful, the money would carry him until his next disability check came. Good luck with that happening. The old man snatched the stack of bills out of Austin's hand and did a quick count.

Austin's ruse hadn't worked. "Where's the rest of it? You better not be holding out on me, boy."

Austin stared his father straight in the eyes and shrugged. "It's harder to sneak stuff out of the house with those guys living there."

Harder, but not impossible. "I'll have to wait awhile for things to cool down before I try again, especially with the police chief watching me."

Vince shoved the money in his shirt pocket. "If he comes poking around here, don't think I won't set him straight on your trail."

The attitude shouldn't have come as a surprise, but his father's willingness to sacrifice his only son still hurt. "You do that, Dad. Now, I'm out of here."

His father caught up with him before he made it out

the door. The old bastard could still move quickly when it was in his own best interest. He latched onto Austin's arm and tried to yank him back inside. "Not until you give me the rest of the money you owe me."

Austin stared down at his father's knobby hand for a heartbeat before yanking free of his grasp. "I don't owe you a damn thing, old man."

Then he walked away, wishing like hell it was for the last time. Unfortunately, his gut told him he'd never be that lucky.

Callie stuffed the estimates into her file folder, intending to head next door to talk to Nick. It was pretty much a done deal that eventually she would fix up the house next door, but there was more she needed to know before deciding when to move forward on the project.

After talking to Nick last night, she'd stayed awake for a long time in the darkness discussing her options with Mooch. The dog kept his opinions to himself, but he'd proven to be a real good listener. Talking it all out had helped crystallize her plans for the future.

At least until she'd checked her e-mail earlier that morning, and everything had blurred out of focus again. She printed the e-mail and added it to the stack of papers she was going to take next door. No matter what, though, she was going to award the contract for the remodeling job. She wanted the house restored to its former glory regardless of where life took her next.

A list maker at heart, she quickly made notes about things she would need to learn about if she was going to start her own business: advertising, food preparation, pricing, laundry service, liability insurance, and so much more. When she talked to Nick, she'd see if he had any other thoughts on the subject.

"Come on, Mooch. Let's go check on the guys."

She piled her files on top of the basket that contained the sandwiches and salad she had made for lunch and headed next door. The first thing she noticed was that Nick's truck was nowhere to be seen. Where had he gone? The front door was open, so Leif must still be at home. She'd drop off their lunch with him and ask if he knew when Nick would be back.

Mooch bypassed the front of the house and ran for the backyard. She caught up with him a few seconds later. To her surprise, Nick was hard at work putting the final touches on the gazebo.

"Did Leif get tired of watching you work and take off?"

Nick set his brush down on the open can of paint and wiped his hands on a rag. "He drove up to the army hospital to pick up a prescription and maybe talk to the docs about further treatment for his leg. He didn't have an appointment, but he thought going in person might hurry things along."

She frowned. "Was he okay to drive? I would've taken him."

"He knew that. I offered to ride along, but he insisted he needed to go by himself."

Nick stood staring toward the mountain peaks in the distance. "If I had to guess, Leif feels as if his life is out of control right now. Everything he has to ask someone else to do for him is one more indication of how much he's lost. I get that."

He finally looked directly at her. "Besides, it's his left leg, so he should be okay to drive."

Callie hurt not just for Leif, but for Nick as well. They were both struggling to put their lives back together. She wished there was some magic wand she could wave to make it all better for them.

She'd have to settle for what she could do. "I wanted to talk to you about the remodel job. Would you rather I came back later?"

"No, you caught me at a good stopping point. Why don't we work at the kitchen table? Let me close up the paint, and I'll be right behind you."

She nodded and headed inside. Now that the moment was upon her, an entire flock of butterflies had taken up residence in her stomach. But second-guessing herself wouldn't accomplish anything. Either Nick would accept her decision or he wouldn't. She had some tough questions to ask, and she wanted answers before she laid it all out for him.

When Nick came in, he'd pulled on his T-shirt. Too bad, but then this was a business meeting of sorts. He grabbed a beer for himself and a soft drink for her before pulling out a chair. He turned it around to straddle it, resting his arms on the back.

"Let's see what you've got."

"Before we get that far, I want to ask you something, Nick. Please think about your response, because I want the truth, not some pat answer."

He sat up straighter, looking a bit insulted by her words. "I've always been honest with you, Callie."

She held on to the files, needing something to help ground her as she stepped out onto this emotional ledge. "I didn't say you weren't. I'm just asking that you give me the straight scoop, no matter what it is, even if you think I won't like it. In fact, especially if you think I won't like it."

"O-kay."

He didn't sound all that convincing, but she'd take him at his word. Trust was a tricky thing. Right now, her gut instinct said she could trust Nick even if he wasn't sure of that fact himself.

"Your original reason for coming here to Snowberry Creek was to find a home for Mooch. Specifically to see if I'd adopt him."

Nick nodded, shifting his gaze from the stack of papers to the dog sprawled on the floor next to their feet. "That's what Spence wanted for the fur ball. He couldn't stand the thought of abandoning Mooch in Afghanistan when our deployment was up. To be honest, none of us could. Spence was determined to get him shipped stateside before our deployment ended, but then . . . well, you know."

Yes, she did. She leaned down to pat the dog on the head. "It should be obvious I've grown quite attached to Mooch. He has a permanent home with me as long as you're sure that's what you want for him."

Nick's smile was a little shaky around the edges, but he was already nodding. "That's good, Callie. Real good. He'll be happy here."

Sensing he was the object of their discussion, Mooch clambered to his feet and laid his head on his buddy's lap. Nick's big hand stroked the dog's fur softly, his expression looking a whole lot closer to sad than to satisfied that his mission had been accomplished.

"So that leads me to my next question, Nick. Why are you still here?"

He flinched in response to her question but continued petting Mooch. Even though his attention was focused on the dog, there was a new tension in the set of his jaw. When he didn't immediately answer, she had to wonder if it was because he was afraid to admit his reasons or because he didn't know the answer.

When the silence became too much, she tried again. "Don't get me wrong, Nick. Lord knows you're welcome to stay here as long as you want. I appreciate all the work you've done on the yard, and I truly love the gazebo."

She shoved the file toward him. "But why do you want to stick around long enough to do all this work on the house? Really. I need to know."

When he looked up, she gasped at the pain etched in his face. She started to take his hand in hers, but he jerked it back out of her reach. The rejection stung, but she was far more worried about him than about any hurt feelings.

"Nick? What's wrong?"

At first she thought he wasn't going to answer her at all. He looked around, his dark eyes unfocused, his face stark and scared. Right now she had no doubt Nick was back in Afghanistan. He lurched up off the chair and stalked away to stare out at the backyard. After several seconds, he pounded his fist on the wall before whirling back around to face her. "I'll tell you what's wrong. Here's the bottom line: I'm here because Spence isn't and never will be again."

Did he think she didn't know that last part? "But, Nick—"

He cut her off with a wave of his hand. "Let me finish, Callie. You say you want the whole truth, fine. I'll give it to you."

He stood with his hands clenched in fists at his sides, his voice gravel rough and low. "We all knew Spence planned to come back here and build a life with you. Hell, to be honest, I was jealous as hell about that. I suspect Leif was, too, at least a little. Spence was the only one with a real good reason to want to leave the army and settle down."

What was he talking about? "No, Nick, Spence and I were—"

"Let me finish, Callie!" Nick snapped. "On that last patrol, we got separated from everyone else. It's easy enough to do when things are all going to hell at once. Spence was our wheelman and doing his best to get back to the others. We'd almost made it, too, when our vehicle hit an IED and the whole fucking world exploded around us."

He jerked up the sleeve of his shirt to show her the fresh scar on his upper arm. "I ended up with this. The dust was so thick, I could hardly breathe much less see more than a couple of feet in front of my face."

He pointed toward the floor.

"Spence was facedown in the dirt, not moving." His next words came on a sob. "I begged God that Wheels wasn't dead."

Nick looked around the room, but she couldn't tell if he even knew where he was. "He was alive. Unconscious but breathing. What a fucking relief that was "

Then Nick pointed toward the floor about five feet away. "Leif's poor leg. I bandaged it but had to get him the hell out of there fast."

He looked around, his desperation and fear palpable in the kitchen. "I knew I couldn't take them both at the same time and that I'd have to come back for one of them. Leif might have bled out if I didn't get him to the medics as soon as I did, even though he wanted me to take Spence first."

It was like watching some macabre play, one she was trapped in, unable to make it stop and afraid of how it would end. She'd never heard how Spence had died, hadn't wanted to know, but there was no doubt that Nick was about to tell her.

"I dragged Leif about a block before I spotted the rest of our patrol. I yelled for the medic."

He retreated a couple of steps as if getting out of someone's way. "He wanted me to stay with Leif because my arm was bleeding, but I had to go back. I'd left Spence behind, and we don't do that. Not ever. He was my man; my friend; my responsibility."

Nick slumped against the wall and held her gaze for the first time, finally really back in the kitchen with her. He rubbed his arm as if remembering the pain. "I'd promised him, you see."

Callie risked standing up, wanting and needing to help him, but there was no way to protect Nick from his own past. As jagged and awful as those memories were to hear, he'd actually lived through them. If sharing them with her eased his burden and his pain at all, she would listen.

The agony in Nick's expression warned her the worst part was coming. She could already guess what had happened next, but she'd come this far. For Nick's sake, and Spence's as well, she would go the rest of the way.

"We almost made it back. Hell, he was only a couple of blocks away. But before we reached him, there was another explosion."

By now, Nick's voice was flat and cold, as if he were speaking from the depths of a deep well. He stared at his hand. "We found his dog tags, bent up and bloody. That's all. Just his fucking dog tags. Spence died all because I left him behind."

The horror of it all left her chilled straight through to the bone. She wanted to reach out to Nick, but her body refused to cooperate. Before she regained enough control to actually move, he was gone. Out the door with Mooch loping along beside him.

She made it to the back porch just as he reached the edge of the trees. "Nick! Wait for me!"

He either didn't hear her or didn't want to. She watched as he plunged into the trees with Mooch loping along at his side. A few seconds later, the dog reappeared. Her heart leapt, hoping that Nick had changed his mind about running off. But no, Mooch was alone and clearly unhappy about his master's disappearance. Every few steps, he'd stop and look back toward the trees.

Was Nick watching to make sure Mooch didn't try to follow him again? If he didn't even want the dog with him, she had to think he wouldn't be any happier if she were to try to trail along behind him. Damn the man, did he like making her worry like this?

No, of course not. He couldn't think straight right now. Her questions had inadvertently ripped open a wound that had obviously been festering for weeks. She wanted to drag him back home and do her best to reassure him that she didn't blame him for Spence's death. Obviously, he wasn't ready to hear that, not yet, so she settled for staying right where she was. Maybe when Leif returned he'd have some idea of what she should do next.

Chapter 26

❧ ❧

A few minutes after Nick left the woods behind, an approaching car slowed and pulled up across from him. Normally, he wouldn't have minded running into Gage Logan, but right now he was too twisted up inside to be fit company for anyone.

The driver's window rolled down. "Need a ride, Nick?"

Maybe the police chief happening by was a coincidence, but there was also the possibility that Callie had gotten worried and made a call. Yeah, he'd get why she might do that, but he was a big boy and capable of taking care of himself.

"Don't tell me Callie called you."

"Is there some reason to think she would have?"

Gage frowned big-time, pulled off onto the shoulder of the road, and turned off the engine. Okay, maybe that had come out more harshly than Nick had intended. Since it was obvious the cop in Gage wouldn't leave now without some kind of explanation, Nick crossed the street.

"Sorry, Gage. Callie and I had, well, not exactly an

argument, but something I said definitely upset her. I needed to get away from her long enough to clear my head."

There was a hard edge to Gage that Nick hadn't seen before. It was definitely the lawman, and not the friend, who was speaking now. "Did this almost argument get physical?"

Nick stepped back from the car and shook his head. "Hell no! I'd never lay a hand on a woman, and especially not Callie."

Gage looked a little more relaxed and maybe willing to give Nick the benefit of the doubt, at least for the moment. That didn't mean he wouldn't check back with Callie at some point to make sure he was telling the truth. Nick shouldn't begrudge the man for doing his job.

Even so, Nick slammed his hand down on the roof of the car. "Damn it, Gage, I screwed up big-time and told her about the day Spence died. I didn't mean to, but it all came pouring out. I even told her that all we found were his dog tags."

His chest hurt from trying to get past the pain of what he'd done. "Son of a bitch, I never meant to hurt her like that."

Gage took off his sunglasses to look Nick straight in the eye. "Callie is stronger than you're giving her credit for, Nick. And you have to know she's been wondering about what happened and didn't know who to ask or even if she should. One way or another, she'll figure out how to deal with it."

Gage turned to stare out the windshield. The harsh expression on his face made it clear he was seeing something other than that country road stretching out in front of him. Dollars to doughnuts, Gage had a few memories of his own that were hell to live with. He didn't offer to share and Nick didn't ask.

"I'm guessing you haven't had lunch, and neither have I. Get in. I know a little joint near here where we can get some burgers to go."

Nick looked up and down the empty road. Right now his only other option was walking himself into exhaustion. Maybe it would help to spend time with another man who'd seen more than his fair share of what life threw at both soldiers and lawmen.

He walked around the front of the car and climbed in. "Lunch sounds good, but I'm buying."

As Gage started the car, he asked, "Do you have your cell phone with you?"

"Yeah." Why would he care?

"Call Callie and tell her you're all right. No matter what happened back there, she's going to worry until she knows you're not lying in a ditch somewhere."

Nick couldn't argue with Gage's logic and reached for his phone. But instead of calling her, he took the coward's way out and texted her instead: "Sorry. I'm with Gage. Back later."

If he expected the other man to give him grief, he was wrong. Gage glanced at the cell phone. "I used to hate texting, but there are times it comes in real handy."

"I need some time to get my head back on straight before I talk to her again, but I will."

"That's good, Nick. If I had to guess, I'd say Callie can handle about anything except a lie. In my experience, that's the one thing that will piss off a woman big-time."

He glanced over at Nick. "She reminds me a little of my late wife. I was twice her size, but she was the strongest person I've ever known."

"What happened to her?"

Not that it was any of Nick's business, but something about the moment told him Gage wouldn't mind him asking.

"Cancer. She went fast."

The lawman lapsed into silence for a few seconds while he waited for a break in traffic to pull out onto a busier stretch of highway. "Too fast. I hardly got to say good-bye to her. In a lot of ways that was the worst part. Even now, a year and a half later, I keep thinking of things I should have said to her, should have told her."

Nick knew exactly what he meant. Well, not exactly. He hadn't had to sit and watch someone he loved lose a battle with cancer, but he had the same kind of regrets. The two of them rode in silence, both lost in memory for the moment.

Luckily, a few minutes later they pulled into the drive-in restaurant Gage had mentioned. After calling in to tell his office he was off the radio for lunch, Gage asked, "What sounds good to you?"

The menu had been painted on the side of the building. It wasn't very long, mostly burgers and fries. "I'll have a double cheeseburger, large fries, and a fresh strawberry shake."

Gage pulled up to the window to order. "Hi, Gary. Nick here will have a number six, I'll have my usual five, and we'll each have a strawberry shake."

Nick pulled out his wallet and passed the money over. Once Gary handed off their burgers and shakes, Gage turned down a narrow road that ran alongside the drive-in and back into the woods. A short distance later, it ended at the edge of a small clearing next to a stretch of Snowberry Creek. There were two old beat-up picnic tables. Nick was glad to see he and Gage had the place to themselves.

They both sat on top of the closest table and dug in

to their food. Nick hadn't realized how hungry he was until he opened the sack and caught that first whiff of fresh French fries.

He took one bite of the burger and moaned. "Gage, this was a damn fine idea."

His companion laughed. "I don't come here nearly as often as I'd like to; my daughter has it in her head that I need to watch my cholesterol. I swear sometimes she's the adult and I'm the child. That's how she treats me, anyway."

Having met the girl on two occasions, Nick believed him. "Well, if she finds out about this time, blame it on me."

"Don't think I won't."

Listening to the water rippling over the rocks soothed Nick's spirit. For the moment, he was content to enjoy the sunshine and Gage's undemanding company, even though the man would have to go back on duty soon. Nick couldn't expect him to spend the afternoon baby-sitting him.

Gage broke the silence. "What set off the discussion about Spence today?"

"Callie wanted to know why I was still hanging around. She knows the original reason I came to Snow-berry Creek was to see if she'd be able to give Spence's dog a permanent home. That was pretty much a yes-or-no answer. Even if she'd needed a couple of days to get to know him before she made a decision, I could have been long gone by now."

"Why aren't you? There has to be another reason you stuck around this long, and then there's the fact you sent for Leif, too. It sure as hell doesn't take two highly trained soldiers to feed one dog. Not to mention you could have either e-mailed Callie or even called her about Mooch in the first place."

Gage softened his words with a bit of a smile, but he was still asking the hard questions. The same ones Callie had wanted Nick to answer. Maybe he'd do a better job explaining himself to Gage.

"You're right. I could have called. Before coming here, I'd been staying at my folks' place. And while they were glad I was back, it wasn't easy for them or me."

He stood up, needing to move around. "I hadn't decided yet whether I wanted to reenlist or not, and they were making their joint opinion on the subject all too clear. They want their son back, the one they used to know. I'm not that man right now, and I'm not sure I ever will be again. So I used the excuse that I needed to find a home for Mooch to get the hell out of Dodge. Long story short, I ended up on Callie's doorstep."

He sat back down. "Much to my surprise, I really like it here. The people are friendly, and they don't keep looking at me as if I'm a stranger wearing their son's face."

Gage nodded. "I'm guessing the problem with your folks will improve over time. At least it did for me. Mine had to deal with me first being an army ranger and then a cop. Mom still worries, but she says that's just part of her job description. I moved here so they could help me with Syd. She needed more attention than I could give her and still work. This job isn't nearly as stressful as working in the big city was, but the hours vary a lot. I'm not sure what I would have done without their help."

Nick had to ask. "Do the nightmares go away?"

The lines bracketing Gage's mouth deepened. "Yeah. At least most of them. Even the bad ones get better if you find someone to talk to about them. As a matter of fact, there's a veterans' support group that meets at the church a couple times a month. If you were to decide to stay here long term, I'd suggest dropping in and getting to know some of the members. The wars we fought in might vary, but the problems we all face don't."

"I might just do that."

Nick cracked his knuckles and stared down at his hands. "I feel like my skin is too small about half the time. There's too much quiet, not enough action. Funny, whenever I was deployed, I was always counting the days until I could get out of whatever hellhole I was serving in. Now that I'm back in the States, I don't have any sense of purpose, like I'm drifting in the water."

Gage started collecting their trash. "How did it feel to build that gazebo thing for Callie?"

"Good. Real good. She knows I want to stay and fix up the house for her. I also told her to get bids from some local contractors, too."

"So I heard." Gage paused as if carefully weighing his next words. "I liked being in the military, but it was hard on my wife and family. She finally drew a line in the sand and forced me to choose between her and the army. Harsh, I know, but she had the right to have a say in how our lives played out together. Bottom line, after years of being a good army wife, she was ready for her husband to come home every night."

He smiled. "At first, it really pissed me off, but I finally realized she was right. I had to decide for myself what I really wanted. In the end, the answer was easy. I wanted her. My only regret was that I didn't make the decision sooner."

He started back toward the car but stopped to lean against the fender. "So, bottom line, Nick, ask yourself this. What is driving you to fix up that house? Is it only because you don't have anything else to do with your time, or is it a way to avoid facing your parents again?

Are you developing some strong feelings for Callie and want to stick around to see where that leads? Or maybe you figure you got Spence killed and in some twisted-up way are trying to atone for it by stepping into his life?"

Without waiting for an answer, Gage got in the car and patiently waited for Nick to join him. It took him several minutes to sort through Gage's words, to make sense of them and the situation he'd gotten himself into.

When he finally got in the car, Gage called in to let the dispatcher know that he was still off the grid for a few more minutes unless there was an emergency. "So do I drop you out on the highway or take you back to the house?"

"I've worried her enough."

"Smart decision."

Ten minutes later, Gage pulled up in front of the porch. "When you figure out your answers, let me know if I can do anything to help."

"Will do." Nick started to get out but stopped. "And thanks, Gage. I appreciate it."

"Not a problem. I was going to come looking for you this afternoon anyway. I finally tracked down Spence's cousin last night and had a heart-to-heart talk with him. Told him he and his old man were at the top of my list of suspects for the other night. Not sure how well Austin listened, but the warning was delivered."

Nick stared out at the woods. "Let's hope he took it to heart."

Because if he didn't, Nick would make sure he got the message the next time. Right now, he needed to get cleaned up and then go next door and try to make peace with Callie. Because in the end, he suspected there was only one final answer to the questions Gage asked.

He'd originally come to town because of what had happened to Spence, and he'd stayed on because being useful felt good. But now he wanted to make a place for himself here in Snowberry Creek, but only if he could convince Callie to be part of that life.

After taking a long shower, Nick stretched out on the couch, intending to rest his eyes for a few minutes. He woke up three hours later, but feeling better than he had in days. The house was quiet. Leif must still be gone. He checked his phone and found a voice mail saying that Leif had to stay overnight on the base and wouldn't bring the truck back until sometime late tomorrow morning. He hoped that wasn't a problem.

It wasn't as if Nick had any burning need to be anywhere. He only hoped that things were going smoothly for Leif. His friend's voice sounded tired, but that wasn't much of a surprise. Just to cover all bases, he dialed Leif's number.

The call went right to voice mail. "Not a problem about the truck, man. Just take care of yourself. Call me if you need anything."

Now it was time to go see Callie. If he'd had the truck, he might have considered driving into town long enough to pick up a bouquet of flowers or maybe some of Bridey's pastries. On the other hand, he wasn't sure how the lady next door would react to any form of bribe.

Maybe it was better to go empty-handed and hope for the best. He cut through the woods, forcing himself to walk at a normal pace, not wanting to arrive short of breath and jittery. As he crossed the yard, he could hear Mooch announcing Nick's arrival from inside the house.

Callie opened the door to invite him in before Nick reached the top step. He took that as a good sign.

Or maybe not. He wasn't sure what to think about the suitcase and carryon bag that sat in the middle of the kitchen floor. He stared at them for several seconds before he looked at Callie, needing to know why they were there and afraid to ask. She trailed her fingers over the top of the larger suitcase and answered his unspoken question.

"After you left earlier I realized that you weren't the only one who needed to think everything through more clearly."

She turned away to stare out the window toward the backyard. "I came back to Snowberry Creek expecting to stay just until I took another contract job. Then this whole thing with Spence, the house, and now you happened."

He regretted his part in putting that sad note in her voice. "You have to know that I never meant to be a problem for you, Callie."

"I do know that, Nick, and I didn't mean to complicate your life, either."

She twirled a strand of her hair around her fingers. "About the suitcases. I've been offered a job interview in Portland. It's a company I've worked for before as an independent contractor, but they said this time it might turn into something permanent. All things considered, I think I should go. Mooch will be all right here with you for a couple of days, won't he?"

Did she even have to ask? "Of course. How long will you be gone?"

"Two days, three tops. It will all depend on whether they actually offer me the job. If they do, I'll need to look for a place for me and Mooch to live."

How could she even think about leaving Snowberry Creek? The very thought made him want to shake some sense into her. Considering how unstable his control was at the moment, Nick retreated several steps before he did something really stupid. He leaned against the counter, hoping he looked and sounded calmer than he felt.

"If I might ask, what changed, Callie? It was only a few hours ago that you were planning to remodel Spence's house and turn it into a bed-and-breakfast. If you're leaving because of me, say so. I'll pack up and be ready to go as soon as Leif gets back with my truck tomorrow morning."

He willed her to turn around, to look at him, to let him see the truth for himself. When she did as he'd hoped, he immediately wished she hadn't. The stark pain in her eyes ripped a hole right through his heart. God, he never meant to hurt her like this.

"Aw, Callie, honey. I'm so sorry." Although he wasn't sure what it was he apologizing for, he repeated himself. "I truly am sorry."

Callie offered him a poor excuse for a smile. "It's not you, Nick, or at least not entirely. It suddenly hit me that maybe I am doing all of this out of some misguided idea that I owed it to Spence."

She waved her hand in the direction of the house next door. "Somehow I got it in my head that doing something with Spence's house would be like some kind of memorial to him. But what if I wouldn't be happy staying in one place? Living in that house out of a misguided sense of obligation is the last thing Spence would have wanted for me."

Callie drew a deep, shuddering breath. "So the bottom line is that I need to explore all of my options before I commit to anything."

Or anyone, especially him—not that Nick blamed her. After all, she was right. Spence's death had hit her hard, knocking her life off course the same way it had his. Both of them had a lot to consider.

She echoed his thoughts. "I think we need some time apart to figure out what it is that we actually want."

Her words sent a chill straight through him. That didn't mean she wasn't right. "When do you leave?"

"First thing in the morning."

Which meant they still had tonight. Could he convince her to spend as much of it with him as possible? Maybe not, but he had to try.

Casting around for any idea, he finally asked, "Are you up for a walk tonight?"

She blinked, clearly surprised by the change in topics. "I could be. That is, if you're not too mad at me."

Had she expected him to fight her about her decision? Even if he had the right, he understood far better than anybody the need to find his own way back to normal.

"I'm not mad, Callie, although I won't lie to you. I hate to see you go."

He forced a smile. "Listen, I haven't had dinner, and I'm guessing you haven't, either. Why don't we walk into town and grab a quick bite? I'll make sure we get back in plenty of time for you to get a good night's sleep."

It was a relief when Callie didn't hesitate. Picking up her keys, she started for the door. "Tell you what: Let's get something to go and then eat by the creek so Mooch can go with us."

Nick followed her outside, promising himself he'd do everything possible to make sure she enjoyed the outing. If it was to be their last night together, he wanted it to be memorable.

Chapter 27

ǝǝ ǝǝ

Callie couldn't remember the last time she laughed so much. By unspoken agreement, she and Nick both set aside their problems and kept the tone of the evening light and fun. They'd picked up a pizza for dinner for simplicity's sake, although they'd argued a bit about what kind to order. He wanted sausage and pepperoni while she held out for the veggie special.

Finally, they'd flipped a coin, and she'd won. Then, in the spirit of the evening, she ordered one of each kind, figuring Nick and Leif would take care of any leftovers. After the two of them had eaten their fill, she sat back and watched while Nick entertained Mooch throwing sticks for him to fetch. For a dog that had grown up alone on the streets, he took to games with surprising gusto.

Callie had promised to give Mooch a good home with her, and she'd meant it. However, watching the two of them play so happily together made her heart hurt. The bond between the man and the dog was painfully clear, and both would suffer if separated. What was she supposed to do about that?

Nick turned as if to tell her something, but his smile quickly faded. "Callie, is something wrong?"

Nothing. Everything.

She managed a small smile. "No, I'm fine. I should be getting back to the house. I still have a few things left to do before I can leave in the morning."

Now his expression mirrored hers. He called Mooch back to his side and clipped on the leash. "Come on, boy, we need to go."

Great, now even the dog's tail was drooping, but the two males joined her. Nick handed off Mooch's leash and picked up the pizza boxes from the picnic table. Then he took her hand in his, giving it a quick squeeze as they started the long walk back to the house.

After a bit, Nick released her hand and put his arm around her shoulders, pulling her in closer to his side. The evening air had a slight chill to it, and the heat from Nick's body felt good. For the moment, he seemed content to walk in silence.

But as they approached the driveway to Spence's house, he slowed to a stop and stooped down to unclip Mooch's leash. "Go on home, boy. I'll be along in a minute."

The dog woofed softly and trotted off into the woods. Nick then set the pizza boxes on top of the mailbox. Callie watched and waited to see what he'd do next. Her pulse picked up speed when he stepped in front of her and ran his big hands up and down her arms, leaving a lot of heat in their wake.

She offered up no resistance when he closed the small distance between them to enfold her in his arms. "Mooch will miss you while you're gone."

He'd whispered the words close to her ear, his breath tickling her skin. She whispered back, "And I'll miss him."

Nick gave her a stern look. "He'll expect you to call every night, so he can know you're all right alone in the big city."

Callie laughed but only because Nick expected it. "You won't mind taking messages for him?"

He pressed a soft kiss to her temple. "Not at all. You know how much the fur ball worries."

"Well, we can't have that, can we?"

But when she lifted her face to respond to his teasing, her smile died as Nick stared down at her with hot, stark hunger in his dark eyes. Whatever she'd thought to say disappeared in a rush of desire.

Nick brushed her hair back from her face, his touch gentle. "Stay with me, Callie, just for tonight."

There were probably a dozen reasons why that wasn't a good idea. Not a single one came to mind. "It won't change anything."

"I know."

There was such powerful truth and understanding in his simple statement. They both knew the risks and the rewards of sharing the night together. She'd known from early on that Nick could break her heart, but she wasn't going to miss this chance to assuage the constant ache for his touch.

She cupped the side of his face, trailing her fingers along the lines of tension in his jaw and down to the thrumming pulse at the base of his neck. He might have sounded calm, but he was feeling the same hunger, the same need.

"Take me to bed, Nick."

Rather than immediately rush down the driveway to the house, Nick kissed her with such sweetness, but with an added spice of heat. He broke it off abruptly and glanced back toward town. A car was coming their way, and soon its headlights would find them hovering on the side of the road. After grabbing the pizza, Nick took her hand, and the two of them ran down the driveway, laughing as they dove into the dark shadows like a pair of teenagers desperate for a bit of privacy.

By the time they'd reached the porch, she was a bit breathless. Nick quickly unlocked the door and stood back as Mooch ran inside just ahead of Callie. Nick led her straight up the staircase without bothering to turn on any lights. When they reached his bedroom, he closed the door, shutting out the world, including Mooch. The last vestiges of the sunset gave his room a rosy glow as the two of them tumbled down onto the bed.

God, what was he doing? Did he really need to remind himself that he was in Spence's hometown with the woman who had meant everything to him? Not only that, but Nick was about to make love to her in Spence's house. That was wrong on so many levels, but at the moment Nick couldn't find the strength to stop himself, not when time was running out for the two of them. Tomorrow would be time enough to deal with a new layer of guilt.

Doing his best to ignore the grumble of his conscience, Nick forced himself to go slowly, to savor the moment. He wanted to memorize every second, every touch, every kiss the two of them shared. For the longest time, they lay together, arms and legs tangled, as they kissed and fanned the flames between them with simple touch.

His lady wasn't as patient. She was the one who grew frustrated by the layers of clothing between them. Callie tugged his shirt up and off, tossing it to the floor. Her kisses left a hot trail down his chest until she reached the waistband of his cargo shorts. Her smile was wicked as she slipped the button free and then worked the zipper down. He lifted his hips to assist Callie in her mission.

She peeled down his shorts, taking his boxers with them. Next, she made quick work of his shoes and socks before sitting back as if to admire her handiwork. When he reached for her, she slapped his hands away.

"No way! Let me."

"Okay," he said as he reached back to hold on to the headboard, content for the moment to be her willing prisoner.

"You're looking pretty hungry there, Callie girl, although I'm thinking you have a few too many clothes on right now."

His comment seemed to please her. "Well, we can't have that, can we?"

She took her time, letting him look his fill as she gradually revealed each luscious inch of her skin. God, he hoped he wasn't drooling, but she was so damned beautiful. When her clothes had joined his on the floor, she straddled his thighs and slid her hands up his chest until she was stretched out on top of him.

The simple contact felt good but wasn't near enough to satisfy his need for her. "Damn, woman, you're killing me here."

She kissed him slowly, deeply, the whole time rocking her hips, stoking the fire between them. He moaned when she broke off the kiss, but his disappointment was short-lived. She reached between them and firmly gripped his penis in the warmth of her hand.

Her smile was all vixen as she teased him with a sliding massage. She kept her eyes locked on his as she bowed her head down to follow the trail her hand had blazed. He arched up off the bed, begging her to take more, to take everything he had to offer.

But then the teasing was over. She rolled to the side, pulling him with her. Between one heartbeat and the next, he took control and then took her. When their bodies joined, it was heaven. He reined himself in long enough to savor the moment, but when she lifted her legs high around his hips, taking him even more deeply into her body, his control snapped.

He thrust into her hard and fast, over and over. Callie dug her nails into his shoulders, encouraging him, demanding everything he had to give her. Despite the near frenzy, he recognized this moment for what it was: a claiming, marking Callie as his, maybe not forever, but at least for tonight.

All too quickly, she reached her climax, taking him with her. He held on tight, pouring out everything he had to make it as good for her as he could. A few seconds later, both of them were breathing hard and totally spent. Nick mustered up enough strength to move to the side, spooning along the length of Callie's body before tugging the sheet and quilt up to cover them both.

For the moment, he would be content to simply hold her, to fill his senses with her scent and soak in the warmth of her skin. They weren't done yet, not by a long shot. He'd give both of them time to recover, and then he'd coax Callie into a repeat performance or maybe two. He couldn't lose sight of the fact that she'd need some rest for her long drive to Portland tomorrow. But one way or another, the memory of this time together would follow her down the highway.

He hated the whole idea of her leaving, but he would watch as she drove away. Hell, he'd even smile and wave. But even as he gave her the space and time she needed, he'd despair every minute she was gone. His patience had limits. If Callie didn't realize that her place was right here in Snowberry Creek, especially with him, he'd have to figure out some way to convince her.

That was something for him to work on later. For tonight, he had her exactly where he wanted her.

A scratching at the bedroom door followed by something breaking downstairs dragged Callie up from a deep sleep. She stared up at the ceiling, trying to decide whether she'd really heard a noise or if it had been part of a dream.

Nick answered the question for her. "It's Mooch scratching at the door trying to tell us somebody else is in the house. Stay still and stay quiet."

His words came in a soft whisper near her ear just before he rolled up to sit on the edge of the bed. Fear tasted sour in her throat as Callie watched Nick pulling on his cargoes. "What are you going to do?"

He put his finger across her lips, reminding her not to talk. The scratching at the door resumed, this time accompanied by a soft growl. Nick reached for something on the dresser and approached the door, calling softly, "Stand down, Mooch."

Nick returned to the bedside long enough to toss Callie her shirt and jeans with his free hand. The other one held a handgun.

"Get dressed, Callie. I'm not sure how this is going to play out."

Her fingers fumbled with even the simplest task, but she managed to pull on her shirt and zip her jeans. "Shouldn't we call the police?"

Nick nodded and handed her his cell phone. "Warn them I'm armed and that I'm going downstairs to see what the hell's going on."

Callie followed him across the room. "Why can't you stay up here and wait for the police?"

His eyes glinted in the darkness, and his voice was steel hard and cold. "I'm tired of this bastard playing these games, and he could be gone before the police arrive. This ends tonight."

She wanted to argue some more, but he'd already opened the door and stepped out into the hall. The way he moved in total silence was startling. He looked far too at home with that gun in his hand. Gone was her gentle lover; in his place was the highly trained soldier. Knowing that was what he was and seeing Nick in action were two very different things.

She hated being left alone, but someone had to call the authorities. The dispatcher answered on the second ring; her calm voice and businesslike attitude went a long way toward calming Callie's badly frayed nerves.

"They'll be there inside of ten minutes, Miss Redding. Where are you in the house?"

"I'm on the second floor, but my, uh, friend Nick went downstairs to investigate. He's a soldier and took his handgun with him. He wanted me to tell you that."

The dispatcher didn't try to hide her disapproval. "I'll warn the officers, but it would have been better if he'd stayed with you."

Callie wasn't about to argue that point. "What should I do?"

"Stay where you are. Lock the door to your room if it has one. The officer says he's within two miles of your house now."

Thank goodness. Callie held on to the phone like it was a lifeline, praying the police would get there before anything happened downstairs. She didn't even care if the intruder made good on his escape as long as no one got hurt, especially Nick.

What was going on down there, anyway? She pressed her ear against the door, hoping to hear something, anything that would let her know that Nick and Mooch were all right. Nothing but an ominous silence. She crossed the room and carefully peeked out the window to watch for the police.

The first set of lights she saw flickering through the trees kept on going. She held the cell phone in a death grip, praying the next car would herald the arrival of the cavalry.

What was happening downstairs? Nothing, she prayed.

But then a crash and a cry of pain shattered any hope of that. The smart thing to do would be to stay right where she was, but what if Nick was hurt? She was out in the hall and poised at the top of the steps in a heartbeat.

A weapon. She needed a weapon. The big vase on the table in the hall would do. There was no use being stealthy, not with all the banging around going on right below her in the dining room. At the bottom of the steps, she debated whether to turn on the lights. Since Nick had obviously already confronted the intruder, she flipped on the switch, hoping to give the police a clear view of whatever was going on.

The front door was ajar. Had she and Nick left it unlocked? She couldn't remember. And it really didn't matter now. Creeping forward on wobbly legs, she risked a quick peek around the corner into the living room. Sure enough, Nick had the other man cornered, holding him at bay with his gun.

"Hey, man, let me go, and you won't see me again."

The voice was vaguely familiar, but it took her a second to place it. As soon as she did, her temper flared hot. "Austin Locke, is that you? What are you doing here?"

But she knew. The doors to the china cabinet stood

open, and there was a pile of silver serving pieces scattered across the floor. Seeing it all made her sick.

"No way you're walking out of here, you little prick!" Nick's voice was almost unrecognizable, his entire demeanor radiating a murderous rage.

Austin held his hands up. "Look, man, don't shoot. I'm not armed."

There was already blood trickling down the side of his face. He looked past Nick toward Callie. "For mercy's sake, Callie, call him off."

"There's no mercy for scum like you," Nick sneered.

Austin threw the handful of forks in his hand straight at Nick's face and tried to bolt past him.

In a lightning fast move, Nick had a terrified Austin by the throat, lifting him up on his toes with one hand. He shoved the barrel of his gun up under Austin's jaw hard enough to bruise and growled, "I should do the whole world a favor and end you right now."

"Stop him, Callie!"

Austin was choking as he desperately tried to pry himself free of the death grip on his neck. Callie wasn't sure which man had her more worried. Yes, Austin might deserve to go to jail, but she didn't want Nick to do something he'd regret forever.

"Nick, let go of him. Austin isn't going anywhere. The police will be here any second. Let them do their job."

Nick was breathing hard, his jaw working with tension as he shook his head. "My friends and I fought to protect this country, and for what? So scum like this little prick can terrorize people in their own homes? So he can rob you blind because he thinks he's entitled to profit from Spence's death? Not on my watch."

It was hard to keep her own fear out of her voice, but it was imperative that one of them remain calm. "No,

Nick, you and Spence served our country to make sure that even criminals get their day in court. Austin's actions have already ruined his life. Don't let him ruin yours, too."

She gently tugged on Nick's wrist. "Please let go. If not for your sake, then for mine."

He finally looked at her hands on his arm. His grip on Austin eased up enough for the man to draw a deep breath.

"That's it, Nick, loosen your hold. He's not going anywhere."

Nick's hands finally dropped back down to his sides, and his shoulders slumped. Austin slid down the wall to the floor and scooted sideways into the corner. He rubbed his throat and stared up at Nick as if he were a rabid dog poised for another attack. Maybe he wasn't far off the mark, but right now she was more worried about Nick than she was Austin.

When she tried to wrap her arms around Nick, he backed away shaking his head. "No, don't. Not now."

Before she could change his mind, Mooch barked from out in the hall. She reluctantly left the two men alone long enough to greet the police. Gage Logan and two deputies filed in, their weapons drawn. The three men relaxed only slightly when she waved them inside.

"We're in here," she said as she led them into the other room. Nick was right where she'd left him, staring down at Austin with his hands clenched into white-knuckled fists. It was a relief to see that he'd set the gun down on the table.

"Just as you suspected, Gage, it was Austin. He's in the far corner on the floor."

Gage's eyes flicked back and forth between Callie and Nick, his expression grim. He glanced back at his two companions. "Secure the prisoner and transport him to headquarters. I'll be along in a while."

When he spotted the bruises on Austin's neck, he leaned in closer for a long look. After shooting Nick a hard look, he added, "Have the EMTs check him over once you get him processed."

While the two deputies dealt with Austin, Gage motioned for Callie and Nick to follow him into the kitchen. He pulled out a chair for her and motioned for Nick to take a seat, too. When he refused, Gage simply stared at him until he gave in.

"Okay, tell me what happened."

Nick remained grimly silent, leaving it to Callie to do the honors. It took longer than she liked, but it was hard not to stumble a bit on explaining why the front door had been left unlocked. Her cheeks were burning hot by the time she finished explaining that they'd been in a bit of a hurry.

Fortunately, Gage merely nodded and didn't ask for any details about what had happened once they'd gotten upstairs. But then considering her hair was a mess, Nick was missing his shirt, and they were both barefoot, maybe no details were necessary, especially since it wasn't the first time he'd seen them like this.

His interest increased when the story picked up again with Mooch whining at the door to alert them to the intruder's presence. She stared down at her hands in her lap, not sure how much to tell Gage about how things had played out in the dining room. When she'd gotten as far as telling him how she came to be downstairs instead of waiting up in the bedroom with the door locked, Nick suddenly took over.

"I caught him loading up a grocery sack with the silverware. He probably didn't realize we were even in the house."

For the first time, he met Callie's gaze head on. "We didn't bother to turn on any lights when we came back from town."

He leaned back in his chair and stretched his legs out, maybe trying to appear far more relaxed than he was. "Austin tried to make a break for it when he saw me, but he froze after he got a good look at my Beretta pointed right at his head."

Gage looked up from his notes. "Was it loaded?"

She wanted to punch Nick when he simply shrugged. "It wouldn't have done me much good if it wasn't."

The lawman didn't much like his attitude, either. "Damn it, Nick, I warned you before that catching this guy is our job."

Now Nick's dark eyes were flashing cold and hard as he jerked up straight and glared across at Gage. "And maybe if you'd actually done your job, that little prick wouldn't have broken in here again. The last time he almost put Leif in the hospital. What if Callie had been here alone?"

Gage shot her a look that was tinged with guilt.

All right, this was getting out of hand. "But I wasn't, and neither of us was hurt. Austin is in custody. Case closed."

She shivered even though the room was warm. "Right now I'd like to go home. I'm supposed to leave in the morning for Portland and still have a few things to do."

Both men frowned, but it was Gage who spoke. "How long will you be gone? I'll need you to come in to the office to make a formal report, and it would be better if you did it while everything is fresh in your mind."

And she wanted to put all of this behind her. "I'll stop by on my way out of town."

"Nick, will you be around in the morning in case I have any questions for you?"

"Yeah, I'll be here. Leif borrowed my truck. Until he gets back, I'm pretty much stuck here."

He made it sound like if he'd had wheels, he would be gone. The idea made her sick. It was one thing for her to leave town, but she suddenly realized how much she needed for Nick to be there when she got back. How would she ever stand to let him drive away for good?

The answer might be as simple as she couldn't.

Gage stood up. "Okay, then. I'll see you in the morning, Callie. You, too, Nick. But if you don't get your truck back by noon or so, I'll come out here. In fact, just plan on me showing up. I'll want to take another look around after I've had a chance to talk to Austin. I'll need to take pictures of everything, but that can wait until tomorrow. After that, you can get started cleaning up his mess. That's always the first step back toward normal."

Gage gave Callie a long, hard look before turning his attention to the third member of their little group. "I don't expect any more trouble tonight, but I'm guessing Callie will sleep better knowing she isn't alone. I will, too, for that matter."

Nick nodded. "I'll keep an eye on her."

Okay, Gage might be right about that, but that didn't give them the right to make this kind of decision for her. "But Austin is in custody! I'll be fine."

Maybe. Well, probably not. She decided arguing wasn't worth the energy, especially seeing the same stubborn determination in Gage as she did in Nick. "Having said that, I wouldn't want to be the cause of you losing sleep, Gage."

"Good decision, Callie. Officially, this a crime scene,

and I don't want either of you back in here until after I'm done going over everything in the morning. For now, I want to snap a few preliminary pictures. Nick, get whatever you need for the night, and then I'll drive both of you next door."

Had her reluctance to walk through the woods been that obvious? Probably so to an experienced lawman like Gage. "Sounds like a plan."

Right now she also needed a minute or two alone. Her world had just shifted on its axis, which left her with a whole new reality to face.

"I'm going upstairs to get my shoes."

With that, she simply walked away.

Chapter 28

❧ ❧

Nick sat in grim silence the entire way back to Callie's house. He rode behind her in Gage's car and stared at the back of her head. What was she thinking? How badly had he scared her? He didn't ever want to see that much fear in her eyes again, especially knowing that he was the one who had put most of it there.

Even so, he wouldn't lie to himself. He'd wanted to choke that little bastard to death for scaring Callie, for defiling Spence's home, and most of all, for spoiling what would likely be the last night Callie would share Nick's bed.

He flexed his fingers in the darkness as he remembered the flutter of Austin's pulse, the ragged sound of the man's words as he'd pleaded with Callie to rein in Nick, and the disgust he'd felt both for Austin and himself.

The interior of the car was suffocating. There wasn't enough room and not enough air. He winced as the dark shadows in the woods outside of the window crept too close to the car. Any second now Nick's control would shatter, and he could find himself back in the narrow streets of Afghanistan. Night patrols were always the worst. Only Mooch's presence next to him helped keep Nick grounded in the here and now. As soon as the car coasted to a stop, he was out and heading for the backyard with the worried dog right on his heels.

A quick circuit around the perimeter gave him the space and time he needed to regain control. By the time he reached the driveway again, Gage was gone. What the hell? Didn't the man have more sense than to abandon Callie like that?

Nick stopped twenty feet short of where she stood. "He left you alone?"

She started toward him, but he backed away, matching her step for step. "He didn't want to, but I convinced him I was perfectly safe. I said it was obvious Mooch needed to take care of business and that you'd both be right back."

At the moment, Nick wasn't sure who had made him angrier: Gage for leaving or Callie for covering for Nick. "He shouldn't have believed you."

Callie crossed her arms over her chest and gave him a hard look. "Why not? You're here, aren't you, so what I told him was nothing but the truth. We both know you would do whatever it takes to keep me safe, Nick."

But what if he was the danger? "I scared you earlier . . . you know, with Austin."

This time when she moved closer, he forced himself to stand his ground. Callie swallowed hard a couple of times before she finally spoke again. "Yes, Nick, you did, but the truth is I was more scared *for* you than I was *of* you."

It wasn't the first time she'd told him that exact same thing, and he wanted to believe her. By now, she was almost within touching distance. He had to stop her, but how? Maybe some cold, hard facts would work.

"If you hadn't been there, I might have killed him, Callie. God knows I wanted to."

"But you didn't."

"Listen to me, damn it." He thrust his hands out toward her. "Honest to God, for a minute there it was a toss-up between whether I shot him or choked him. Killing the enemy is all I'm good for anymore. It's all I've known for years now. There's nothing left of me at all. Hell, look at me! No wonder I've hijacked not only my best friend's hometown, but his house and even his woman."

The reality of that statement grated like broken glass on his conscience, and acid-hot tears burned their way down his cheeks. At least the darkness saved him from having to see the revulsion in her eyes.

"Go on in the house now. Mooch and I will stay out here and make sure you're safe until you leave in the morning."

Stubborn woman that she was, Callie reached out to take his hands in hers. "I'm not going anywhere, Nick."

God, he needed her touch more than he needed air to breathe. Selfish bastard that he was, he would stand there all damn night as long as she was willing to hold on to even some small part of him. When he tugged her forward, closing that last bit of space between them, it felt as if he were jumping off a cliff.

She slammed against him, her arms offering sanctuary. He breathed in her scent, drawing it deep inside himself. It was a soothing balm that took the heat out of his pain. For the longest time, they stood there in the darkness. Slowly the maelstrom of emotions writhing in his chest dissipated. Thanks to Callie, the negative ones were the first to go.

Breathing was easier now that his anger, fear, and self-loathing had faded into the background. All that was left were the good things: the comfort of her body against his, the soft warmth of Mooch pressed against the side of Nick's leg, and finally, his love for this woman.

And because he loved her, he had to let her go. "Callie, you need to get to bed. I wouldn't want you to fall asleep at the wheel on your way to Portland."

She snuggled closer. "Weren't you listening? I said I wasn't going anywhere, and I meant it."

What was she trying to tell him? Had she changed her mind? No, he slammed the door shut on that line of thought. Hope was too precious an emotion to risk recklessly. He tried again. "You can't stay out here all night."

"No, I can't, and neither should you."

When she tried to step back, he reluctantly let her go. But instead of walking away, she captured his hands again. The dim glow of the porch light bathed her pretty face in its light.

"Nick, there's clearly something I need to tell you. I'm asking you to let me get it all out before you say anything, because I honestly don't know if I'll ever find the courage to try again."

He nodded, that bit of hope still fluttering softly in his heart.

"First of all, yes, Snowberry Creek was Spence's hometown, but it's mine, too. You're not taking his place here; you're sharing mine. That house is also mine now, not his. But you knew Spence as well as I did. Do you really think he would have resented his best two buddies taking up residence there? You know there wasn't a selfish bone in that man's body."

When Nick slowly nodded, Callie went on. "I've

told you this before, but evidently I didn't make myself clear on the subject. Yes, I loved Spence, but like a brother. Nick, I wasn't *in* love with him. I'm telling you right now, if he ever felt anything other than friendship for me, he never ever said a word about it to me."

She gave his hands a soft squeeze. "Nick Jenkins, what I feel for you is so different and so much more than anything I ever felt for him. He and I were best friends, but that's where it ended."

Then she turned Nick's palms over and studied them. "These hands have fought for our country. I can't imagine what it was like for you over there, but I'm so very proud of your service, Nick. Everything you did, you did to save lives, not take them."

Contrary to her request that he remain quiet, he just couldn't. Even though his throat was so tight it was hard to talk at all, he had to say something. "I didn't save Spence."

"No, but you did save Leif, and I'm betting there are a lot of others who owe their lives to you, just like you owe yours to them."

Instantly, all the ghosts of his friends who didn't make it back paraded through his head. But thanks to Callie's healing words, those who had survived marched right in step with them.

She was talking again. "These same hands built that beautiful gazebo for me and in memory of Spence. They also helped save Mooch and drove him here so I could give him a permanent home for the first time in his life."

She lifted his hands up to her face and pressed a soft kiss on each palm. "They'll remember how to do so much more, Nick. It will take time, but you'll find your way back to normal again. I just hope that you let me walk that road with you, because I love these hands."

Slowly she raised her eyes to meet his. "I realized earlier that I couldn't stand the thought of going to Portland, not if it meant coming back here to find you packed up and ready to leave. I don't want to live anywhere where you're not."

He frowned as he tried to decipher that last part. "Good, I think."

Callie laughed and shook her head. "I guess I'm not making much sense here, am I?"

When she didn't go on, he prodded her a bit. "I thought you were really hoping they'd offer you that job."

"So did I, but there's Mooch to consider." She knelt down to pet the dog. "It wouldn't be fair to take him away from you. He likes me, Nick, but he loves you. That all-important comrades-in-arms thing is unbreakable. Besides, he's been uprooted enough for one doggy lifetime."

She stared up at Nick with her arms wrapped around Mooch, holding the dog close. "I'm asking if you'd consider a package deal, one that includes fixing up Spence's house and turning it into a home for the three of us: you, me, and Mooch."

After giving the dog one last squeeze, she stood up again. "The bottom line is that as much as I love Mooch, Nick, I love you even more."

God, he'd felt calmer in the heat of an ambush, but he'd learned long ago how to act decisively when lives depended on it. Right now, it was his life that was on the line.

He caught her up in his arms and swung her around and around with Mooch barking as he joined in the strange human game.

"And I love you, Callie Redding. I'd be a fool to turn down an offer like that."

When he finally set her down, they were both breathless. "I may have to serve out the rest of my enlistment, Callie. I don't have any choice about that, but I won't be signing up for another tour. Not if you'll be waiting for me here in Snowberry Creek."

"Mooch and I will be here for you, Nick, no matter how long it takes."

It was time to seal the deal with a kiss. He meant to keep it short and sweet, but his Callie had different ideas on the subject. They went from zero to sixty in two seconds. If they didn't slow things down and quickly, they'd end up naked back down on the grass again.

It took a hell of a lot of effort, but he managed to pull back. "Let's take this show inside. I'm afraid of what one of Gage's deputies might see if I don't get you behind closed doors right now. He mentioned they'd be swinging by several times during the night to keep an eye on things. The poor guy has already had to tiptoe around a couple of delicate situations involving the two of us in his reports."

"That he has." Callie laughed and buried her face against his chest. "Sounds like you might have some interesting plans in mind for the rest of the night, Sergeant Jenkins."

"I do." Determined to keep his eye on the objective, he tugged her along toward the front door as he talked. "Not just for tonight, though. I'm thinking of signing on for a much longer tour of duty, like the one with the 'until death do us part' option."

Callie stumbled a bit, but he kept her from falling. "Sorry, was that too much too soon?"

Her answering smile was everything he could have hoped for. "Not at all, soldier. And for signing on for an extended tour, I'm prepared to offer you a very inter-

esting enlistment bonus package. Want to come upstairs to my bedroom where we can discuss a few of
your options in greater detail?"

"There's nothing I'd like better, Callie."

And as Nick waited for her to unlock the door,
Mooch stopped to stare up at the stars and whined.
What was he seeing up there? The answer seemed obvious, so Nick sent a silent prayer flying upward into
the night sky.

"Spence, I promise to do everything in my power to
make her happy."

The darkness surrounding them was deep and silent, but Nick could have sworn a hand touched his
shoulder. Maybe it was only the night breeze, but then
again, maybe not.

He wasn't in uniform, but he offered up a quick salute and whispered, "Thanks, buddy."

And feeling more at peace than he had in years, he
followed his lady inside.

Epilogue

❧❧

"You three look so handsome. Now, hold still so I can take the picture."

Callie held up the camera and waited for Nick, Leif, and Mooch to get situated. Both men were in uniform, and Mooch wore his dog tags with a camouflage scarf tied around his neck. All three looked solemn, and she knew better than to try to make them smile. She knew what this moment meant to the two men, and Mooch's mood was a reflection of theirs.

They'd decided to have a few friends over for an official dedication of the gazebo. She'd made sure Nick knew how much it meant to her that he and Leif had built it both for her and in memory of their friend. Although both men were showing definite signs of coming to terms with Spence's death, it was still hard at times for all three of them. That was why she'd made sure to call this event a celebration rather than a memorial.

After she snapped several pictures in rapid succession, Nick called out, "Hey, Gage. Come take the camera so Callie can be in the next shot."

Nick and Leif made room for her between them, and Mooch sat right in front of her. She felt dwarfed by her two companions, but she couldn't imagine anywhere else she wanted to be.

Leif leaned in close enough to whisper, "You know it's not too late to realize I'm a better catch than Sarge is."

Nick immediately smacked his friend on the back of the head. "Yes, it is too late, Corporal. Now, shut up and smile."

Leif ducked back out of reach. "But we both know it's true!"

The man she loved shot his friend a nasty look. "Yeah, maybe we do, but she doesn't. Don't screw this up for me."

It was time to put an end to their sniping. "Come on, guys, get serious. People are waiting on us."

Her two soldiers immediately resumed their positions, both smiling down at her before turning their attention toward Gage. He winked at Callie before snapping the picture. "Okay, now, pick up the paintbrush and get busy. Syd's getting impatient to dive into the food."

The little girl rolled her eyes. "Dad, I'm not the one who got caught sneaking cookies."

The lawman laughed. "Okay, guilty as charged."

Nick led the way into the gazebo. Inside, he picked up a small paintbrush and a jar of paint and held it out to Callie. "Ladies first."

"No, I think it should be one of you two who signs first."

He offered the brush to Leif, who also shook his head. "Nope, it was your idea. Besides, you outrank me."

Nick drew a deep breath and dipped the brush into

the paint. Earlier in the day, he'd stenciled the dedication on the back wall of the gazebo. The wording the three of them had agreed on read, "In celebration and remembrance of the life of Corporal Spencer Lang. Wheelman, we miss you."

Using the paintbrush, Nick signed his name. Leif went next, and finally Callie wrote hers. It was hard to see how legible her writing was through the sheen of tears that filled her eyes, but she managed to get the job done.

When she was finished, she handed Nick the brush and kissed both him and Leif on the cheek. "Thank you both for this. It means so much to me. I feel like it's the first real step toward making the bed-and-breakfast real."

Their silence worried her. Was the moment too much for them? Nick had told her he was having fewer episodes where he got trapped in the past, but still.

"What's wrong, Nick?"

He made eye contact with Leif. "Corporal, stand guard."

Leif immediately positioned himself in the doorway, his back to Nick and Callie. What in the world was going on?

Nick finally smiled down at her and dropped to one knee. He held up a small box.

"Callie Redding, I know we've already talked about this, but I want to make it official. Will you do me the great honor of marrying me?"

As he spoke, he lifted the lid of the small box to reveal a beautiful ring. "I hope you don't mind, but this belonged to my grandmother. She gave it to me years ago in the hope I would find someone who made me as happy as my grandfather made her. I had my mom ship it out to me from Ohio."

Callie's hand was trembling as she reached out to pick up the ring. "Sergeant Nick Jenkins, I would be honored to marry you and wear her ring."

He grinned as she slipped the sparkling diamond onto her finger. Then he crushed her in his arms for a big hug and a quick kiss.

Leif claimed first honors in congratulating them, although he once again questioned Callie's taste in men. Word spread through the crowd, resulting in a barrage of hugs, handshakes, and best wishes.

Despite all the happy chaos, somehow Callie found herself alone and staring up at the words written in black on the back wall of the gazebo. Her smile faded just a little as she silently read them again. "God, Spence, I wish like heck you were here to help us celebrate this moment."

He would have been happy for her, and for Nick, too. No doubt he would have given them some kind of grief over her taste in men, as Leif had, but that would have been for show.

"You know, somehow I think he is here, Callie."

A familiar pair of strong arms wrapped her in their comforting embrace. Holding her close, Nick whispered near her ear, "Wheels would be happy for us, Callie. I know that for a fact."

"I was just thinking that very same thing." Her smile returned full strength. "He wouldn't want his memory to make us sad, especially today. So, soldier, what do you say we go be happy enough for all three of us?"

Nick grinned and gave her a kiss that held the heated promise of a more private celebration later. "I say that's an order I'll be glad to carry out every day for the rest of our lives."

Don't miss the next book in the Snowberry
Creek series—turn the page for a preview!

More Than a Touch

Coming from Signet Eclipse in January 2014

L eif made it out of the clinic in one piece. Barely.
Right now his leg ached, his head throbbed, and his
pride was shredded.

Yeah, on one level he appreciated Zoe Phillips' efforts to make things easier for him by moving him to
the room with the lower table. But damn, did she really
think he wouldn't notice the room was decorated for
kids? It was hard to miss all those cutesy zoo animals
painted on the walls and the box of toys in the corner.

He hoped he hadn't been too much of a jerk. It was
hardly Zoe's fault that he was in pain. Hiking his ass all
over the cemetery earlier when he was scheduled to see
her and that huge guy who was going to be his physical therapist hadn't been smart. The long-overdue talk
with Spence had left him emotionally drained and
hurting before he even got to the clinic. Then having
the two of them twist and turn his ankle like it was a
fucking pretzel hadn't helped much, either.

He was supposed to come back in two days to see
both Zoe and Isaac again. Between now and then,
they'd promised to come up with a plan of attack to

start rebuilding the strength in his leg. Good luck with that. He wasn't holding out much hope that anyone could put his Humpty Dumpty leg back together again.

It was time to kick it into gear and head back to the house. Nick had loaned Leif his truck for the day, but he didn't want to abuse the privilege. He checked the time. Maybe he could squeeze in one more stop along the way. Now that it looked as if he'd be stuck here in Snowberry Creek for a while, he needed to buy his own set of wheels.

As soon as he pulled into the parking lot of the small dealership on the outskirts of town, he knew he'd made a tactical error. He needed something practical, not flashy. The smart thing to do would be to drive straight back out of the parking lot, but evidently he was stuck in dumb mode. Before he could stop himself, he was out of Nick's pickup and headed straight for temptation itself.

The truck wasn't new, but somebody had taken damn good care of it. The finish was a bright, shiny red, polished to a fault. The interior was absolutely pristine. He slowly walked around the truck with the hope he'd find something that turned him off. No such luck. Right now he knew what a fish felt like nibbling at the worm while doing its best to ignore the danger.

Approaching footsteps warned him the local angler had noticed Leif's interest in the truck. The salesman came trolling by hoping to set the hook good and proper.

"Good afternoon, Corporal. I see you picked out the best vehicle on the lot."

Leif wouldn't know. He hadn't bothered to look at any of the others. He peeled his eyes away from the truck long enough to glance around. The salesman wasn't exaggerating. Everything else looked faded and shopworn by comparison. That was probably an unfair assessment, but then, he'd always been a sucker for red trucks and cars.

"How much?"

If it was way out of his price range, there wasn't any reason to even take the truck out for a quick spin. That didn't keep him from opening the door to the cab to take a better look at the interior. Meanwhile, the salesman prattled on about everything but the price: one owner, well-maintained, blah, blah, blah.

Finally, Leif pegged the man with a hard stare. "I repeat: How much?"

The price the salesman quoted didn't exactly send Leif into sticker shock, but it was a close call. He immediately stepped away from the truck and headed back toward Nick's.

"Thanks—that's all I needed to hear. No use in wasting any more of my time or yours. I'll be going now."

He hid a smile as the salesman trotted after him sputtering. "Look, Corporal, I should have made it clear that was the price before we apply the military discount. Why don't you come inside and have a seat? I'll get us each a cup of coffee and then see what other discounts we can offer you."

Leif made a point of looking at the time. "I suppose I have a few minutes. But I've got to tell you"—he leaned closer to read the man's name tag—"Chuck, you'd have to come way off that price for me to even consider buying that truck. Way off."

Chuck looked relieved. Maybe sales hadn't been so good lately, which could work in Leif's favor. As he followed the salesman into his office, Leif couldn't help but wonder which one of them was about to hook a big one.

*   *   *

An hour later, Leif walked out of the dealership twirling the keys to the truck on his finger. He'd already called Nick to tell him why he was late getting back. His friend had immediately offered to come get his own truck so Leif could drive his new purchase home. Evidently, Callie had errands in town and could drop Nick off at the dealership.

They should be pulling into the parking lot at any second. While he waited, Leif circled the truck with a big grin on his face. If he'd had any doubts about the wisdom of buying the first truck he'd looked at, they'd been vanquished by the test drive. The truck hummed with power and handled like a dream.

He'd just finished his second lap admiring all its attributes when Callie pulled into the parking lot. She and Nick joined him in staring at the truck. Why weren't either of them saying anything?

"Well?"

Nick let out a low whistle. "Hot damn, Corporal, she's a beauty. I can see why you bought her. Hell, I'd have been tempted myself."

Callie joined in. "You know, I'm pretty sure I know who used to own this truck. If I'm right about that, you can rest assured it was well maintained. Mr. Wolfe takes good care of everything he owns."

"That's the name the salesman told me. He was surprised I wasn't familiar with it, but I told him I was new to the area. Sounds like the previous owner is one of the big fish in this little pond."

"That's true. His family actually founded the town. His company employs a fair number of people in the area." Callie trailed her fingers along the fender. "Well, congrats on the truck, Leif, but I'd better get going. See you both at dinner."

She paused to give the sergeant a quick kiss before

heading back to her car. Both men watched in silence until she was gone. Leif was getting used to the idea of Nick and Callie hooking up, but it had been slow going. Even so, it was nice to see his friend smiling more often.

Meanwhile, he handed Nick his keys. "Thanks both for the loan and for coming so I could drive this baby home."

"No problem."

Nick kept his eyes firmly on the truck, but he definitely had something on his mind. Leif figured it was one of two things. Either he wanted to know what was up with Leif's leg or whether buying the truck meant Leif was going to stick around Snowberry Creek for a while.

He bet it was the prognosis for his leg that had the man tied up in knots. "Sarge, I wouldn't want you to choke on whatever it is you're trying to hold back, so just ask me. Either it'll piss me off or it won't. Besides, the suspense is killing me."

"Okay, fine." Nick released the breath he'd been holding. "So, how did it go at the clinic today?"

Score one for Leif. "I go back in two days to find out what specific form of torture the therapist has in mind for me. He and Zoe, the nurse practitioner in charge of my case, are going to work up the plan together."

Nick knelt down to study the front tire on Leif's truck, staring at it as if the tread depth were the most fascinating thing he'd ever seen. "Are you going to do what they say?"

What choice did he have? None, not if he didn't want to be tied to this fucking cane the rest of his life. "I'd be scared not to, considering the size of the guy in charge of my PT. I don't know what Isaac did in the navy, but he could bench-press a submarine."

"How about Zoe? What is she like?"

"Nice enough. Former army. She said she'd had experience working with injuries like mine."

Looking back, he bet she'd seen far worse, too. Something about the expression in her eyes had hinted that she'd had her fill of mangled limbs and bodies.

"Was she pretty?"

Not exactly. Her features were a little too strong to be merely pretty. The word "striking" came to mind, especially with the contrast between her nearly black hair and bright blue eyes. He had to say something, though, if he didn't want to give Nick the idea he'd been attracted to Zoe.

"I didn't really notice. I was too busy trying not to punch somebody while they screwed around with my leg."

Nick had moved on to poking around under the hood. "So, does this mean you're going to hang around long enough to help me rehab Spence's house for Callie?"

"Yeah, I guess it does, at least for now."

It wasn't as if Leif had anywhere else he needed to be. Unlike Nick, he wasn't close to his family, something he'd had in common with Spence. Part of the reason he'd enlisted in the first place was to get away from his folks. They weren't bad people, but they'd separated about the time he'd started high school. Overnight everything he'd ever known was gone, sort of like the way the beautiful symmetry of a spiderweb could be destroyed by the touch of a careless hand.

They had each remarried shortly after the divorce was finalized and started second families. That had left Leif bouncing back and forth between two households, neither one of which ever really felt like home.

Oh, he knew his folks had loved him and still did. He'd never doubted that much about them, but that didn't mean he fit in with their new lives. Everyone, him included, was more comfortable with the occasional short visit between deployments. They wouldn't know what to do with him if he showed up on their doorstep needing a long-term place to crash.

He could get his own crib, of course, but living in his hometown held no appeal. It had been years since he'd had any contact with the crowd he'd hung out with in high school. Sitting on his ass by himself night after night? No, he didn't think so.

"I'm glad to hear it, Leif. There'll be enough to keep both of us busy for a long time to come." Leif put the hood down. "I have to report back long enough to get processed out. I shouldn't be gone all that long, but I'll sleep easier knowing you're here to keep an eye on Mooch and the house. Callie will appreciate the company, too."

Nick's announcement didn't really come as a surprise. The man had already been waffling about reenlisting when he'd arrived in Snowberry Creek looking for a home for Mooch, the dog their unit had adopted in Afghanistan. Soon afterward, he'd sent for Leif, hoping to use him as a buffer between himself and Callie. Yeah, like that had worked.

It had been obvious from the get-go the man was fighting some pretty strong feelings for her. Well, that battle had been waged or maybe won. It all depended on how you looked at it. Now it would take a crowbar and dynamite to pry Nick out of Snowberry Creek.

Leif didn't blame the man. Nick had served his time and his country. God knows the man deserved a little happiness in his life. Leif hoped his decision also meant that Nick had shed the shitload of guilt he'd been carrying ever since an IED had changed both of their lives forever.

"I'll feed the mutt and keep the lawn mowed." He started to take a step, but as soon as he shifted his weight, his bum leg almost gave out on him. It was definitely time to get back to the house and take one of his pills. Maybe two.

He ignored Nick's look of concern and opened the door of the truck. As he climbed up, gritting his teeth against the pain, he cautioned his friend, "But all bets are off if Callie starts sending all the cookies she bakes to you."

Nick laughed. "I'll make sure she holds a few back for you."

"A few, my ass, Sarge. I'd better get my fair share, especially if you want me to talk you up to Callie's parents when they get back. After all, you managed to get engaged to their daughter without their ever having met you."

His friend swallowed hard. "It's a deal."

Leif laughed at the sick expression on his friend's face. Callie's parents were coming back from their summer in the sun in another two weeks. They'd wanted to come sooner, but their departure had been delayed when Callie's father threw his back out golfing. Now Nick would be gone before they returned.

Leif turned the key in the ignition, once again taking pleasure from the smooth rumble of the engine. "See you back at the house."

And if he burned a little rubber driving out of the parking lot, who could blame him? A man was entitled to have a little fun with a new toy.

ALSO AVAILABLE FROM

Alexis Morgan

A SOLDIER'S HEART
A Snowberry Creek novella

AN ORIGINAL NOVELLA AVAILABLE ONLY AS A DOWNLOADABLE PENGUIN SPECIAL

Before they can return home, Nick, Spence, and Leif must finish out the last days of their third deployment in the US Army and their first in Afghanistan. But they are all in danger when an ambush situation leaves them in deadly peril—until a stray dog saves the day. And when they rescue the pooch from the firefight, each of the friends finds a little piece of himself he thought he lost.

Available wherever books are sold or at
penguin.com

facebook.com/LoveAlwaysBooks

ALEXIS MORGAN

MY LADY MAGE

A Warriors of the Mist Novel

Oppressed by a cruel guardian whose dark magic threatens to destroy her people, the beautiful and courageous Merewen calls upon the legendary warriors of the mist—those cursed by the gods and summoned only when a champion is needed and the cause is just. In Gideon she finds more than a champion, and in his arms, more than protection. However, their enemies are fighting with a power darker than anything they imagined, and should Gideon fail, she will lose everything she holds dear—including her heart.

"Plenty of mystery, action, and passion to keep you flipping pages well into the night."
—Fresh Fiction

Available wherever books are sold or at
penguin.com

facebook.com/ProjectParanormalBooks

S0452

LOVE

ROMANCE

NOVELS?

For news on all your favorite romance authors,
sneak peeks into the newest releases, book
giveaways, and much more—

"Like" Love Always on Facebook!

 LoveAlwaysBooks

Penguin Group (USA) Online

What will you be reading tomorrow?

Tom Clancy, Patricia Cornwell, W.E.B. Griffin,
Nora Roberts, William Gibson, Catherine Coulter,
Stephen King, Dean Koontz, Ken Follett, Nick Hornby,
Khaled Hosseini, Kathryn Stockett, Clive Cussler,
John Sandford, Terry McMillan, Sue Monk Kidd,
Amy Tan, J. R. Ward, Laurell K. Hamilton,
Charlaine Harris, Christine Feehan...

You'll find them all at
penguin.com
facebook.com/PenguinGroupUSA
twitter.com/PenguinUSA

Read excerpts and
and reading grou

Subscribe to Peng
and get an
at exciting new ti
long befor

PENGUI
us.pe